A GIFT
of the
EMPEROR

Therese Park

D1510281

"Through Soon-ah, the novel's heroine, an innocent high school girl of seventeen, Therese Park passionately and movingly tells the story of comfort women's incredible survival in the face of unbelievable suffering and inhuman abuses."

—Bonnie Oh, Distinguished Professor of Korean Studies,
Georgetown University

". . . at long last, with [Therese Park's] help, the truth about her former countrywomen has started to surface, and the world is listening."

—*The Kansas City Star*

"*A Gift of the Emperor* is a compelling narrative of human survival in the face of unspeakable horror. Soon-ah's story is one that bears witness to the endurance of one woman's spirit in the midst of sheer violence."

—Christine Choy, Associate Professor, Tisch School of the Arts/
Institute of Film and Television–Graduate Division,
New York University

". . . an allegorical novel of epic ambitions and proportions, in the guise of a narrative about one woman's sufferings as a military sex slave. Through the voice of Soon-ah, called "Keiko" by her Japanese "masters," Therese Park tells the story of identities lost and then recovered, of possession by others and self-possession—a story that is as much about the whole Korean nation in the first half of the twentieth century as about a particular comfort woman's struggle to return home to her family."

—Margaret Stetz, Associate Professor,
English and Women's Studies, Georgetown University

A GIFT
of the
EMPEROR

Therese Park

Spinsters Ink
Duluth

First edition, October, 1997
10-9-8-7-6-5-4-3-2

Spinsters Ink
32 E. First St., #330
Duluth, MN 55802-2002, USA

Cover Photos Courtesy of National Archives

Production: Liz Brissett   Lou Ann Matossian
              Helen Dooley   Ryan Petersen
              Joan Drury   Kim Riordan
              Emily Gould   Erika Thorne
              Marian Hunstiger   Liz Tufte
              Kelly Kager   Nancy Walker
              Claire Kirch

Library of Congress Cataloging-in-Publication Data
Park, Therese, 1941–
    A gift of the emperor / Therese Park. — 1st ed.
    p.   cm.
    ISBN 1-883523-21-4 (alk. paper)
    1. Comfort women—Korea—Fiction.
    2. World War, 1939–1945—Women—Korea—Fiction.
    I. Title.
    PS3566.A674718G54   1997
813'.54—dc21   97-25489
                                                    CIP

Printed in Canada on recycled paper

Acknowledgments

I am grateful to you, Spinsters Ink, for publishing this fictionalized story of real-life atrocities inflicted on women half a century ago.

Thank you, Kelly Kager, for your careful guidance during revision of this book.

Thank you, Bruce, for your encouragement and unlimited patience.

Thank you, Susanne, Irene, Christine, for challenging me, loving me, and reshaping me into an almost American mom. I needed it.

Dedication

I dedicate this work to all victims of forced sex-slavery in the Japanese military brothels during World War II.

On the front wall of our high school classroom hung a huge portrait of Emperor Hirohito. Sitting on his dazzling white horse, looking at a distant mountain, he seemed divine, as though he could rise into the sky like a real crane. He considered himself a crane, the symbolic bird of divine grace. We bowed to him every morning with devotion and sang "Kami-gayo," the Japanese national anthem, as loudly as we could.

When the bowing and singing were over, we felt sanctified. We feared Emperor Hirohito, our Imperial Majesty, as much as we feared God. For him, we girls in Dong Myung Girls' High School in Sariwon would be glad to sing, dance or perform a play at any time of the day or night, just as we had on his son's last birthday. That day coincided with Japan's triumphant victory in the rubber-producing countries in Southeast Asia, and we received a gift from the Imperial Majesty himself—a rubber ball. Afterward, Miss Lee, our only Korean teacher, joked that if Japan had conquered Arabian countries, we would each have gotten a bucket of oil instead.

Japan became our fatherland in 1910 when it abolished the Yi dynasty, forcing King Kojong to retire, and annexing our country as its colony. Although my father taught me and my brother Wook that the Japanese had murdered Queen Min, poisoned King Kojong, took the crowned prince and princess to Japan as hostages, and robbed the Korean people of everything, at school we learned to worship Emperor Hirohito and his gods. We had to. Otherwise, life was too dangerous.

One day, soon after I turned seventeen, I discovered who Emperor Hirohito really was: he was neither a deity nor a lord but a man deranged by power, a man who believed he could give life to his soldiers by giving us, the girls in his colonized country, death. Like the Korean timbers, which the Japanese chopped from our mountains and hauled to Japan to build warships, we were taken from our homes under the pretense of being trained as nurses and factory workers and sent to the military brothels surrounded by barbed-wire fences.

On a brilliant spring morning in 1942, I walked to school, as I always did, watching our neighbor's cattle grazing on our soybean field, where grass and weeds grew taller every time it rained. Since my brother Wook had been conscripted as a Japanese soldier a year ago and my father murdered by Japanese policemen four months later, our soybean field lay without soybeans, attracting neighborhood cattle that methodically cropped the grasses and weeds. Soon it would be auctioned off and the Japanese farmer who had acquired most of the soybean fields in our area recently would buy it at a ridiculously low price.

During the past two years, the Japanese had taken most of our property except for the house we owned. When my father couldn't pay the harvest tax because the price of soybeans had plummeted under new Colonial Policy, the Japanese soldiers took away our cattle. After my father died, my mother sold our last two pigs to keep me and my younger brother Chin Soo in school. The only things left with us were about two dozen hens.

In spite of the gloom in my head, my feet carried me along the narrow road and across the bridge. I walked into the two-story building that had a vertical sign "Dong Myong Girls' High School."

Miss Yamakawa, our homeroom teacher, greeted me and my classmates with an uncharacteristically broad smile. I became suspicious. She never liked any of the Korean students. She was especially strict with us about speaking Korean. Whenever one of us accidentally said something in Korean, she picked up her thin bamboo stick and lashed our palms until red marks appeared and tears welled up in our eyes. When a student spoke Korean more than three times in a month, she sent her to the principal. In a severe case, the parents were labeled "thought criminals" and turned over to the police. We spoke only Japanese.

"I have good news for all of you today," Miss Yamakawa announced when we had finished bowing and singing to our Imperial Majesty. "Two special delegates are visiting our school to deliver an important message from our Imperial Majesty. Isn't it exciting? Be extremely courteous to them, girls! Show your loyalty to your fatherland!"

Delegates from the Emperor! My heart fluttered with fear and excitement. "Another gift, maybe?" we whispered to one another. "What would it be this time?" I wanted a pair of socks or a towel, but my friend Kyung Hwa wanted a cosmetic box with a mirror inside.

Socks and towels were rare. Our town of Sariwon in the northwest region of Korea became poorer and poorer as the

Japanese recruited all working men to the battlefields and stole our grain and livestock. More and more farmers gave up their farmland when they couldn't pay the harvest tax, and more and more Japanese became our landlords. Necessary items such as rice, towels, socks, sugar, flour, canvas shoes, and underwear were rationed according to the number of people in a household, but we never got enough. Many young daughters of farmers left for big cities to look for wage-paying jobs, but such jobs were impossible to find, and they settled for room and board.

The thud of boots halted my thoughts. Two soldiers with many decorations on their chests walked in and bowed their heads to the picture of the Emperor, then bowed to Miss Yamakawa. One of them, a slightly built, pale-looking man, took the podium, locking his hands behind him.

"My beloved Korean sisters! Today I have a very special message from our divine Emperor," he said in Japanese. "Our Imperial Majesty needs your help. He has been worried about our soldiers fighting all over Asia and in the Pacific. Every wounded soldier breaks our Emperor's heart. That's the reason he sent us to talk to you, my sisters. As the divine nation, our fate is to help other Asian countries discover their strength and resources and liberate them from the Westerners, don't you agree?"

"Yes!" we chorused.

"But the Westerners are killing our soldiers with their deadly weapons. We can't lose our brave soldiers, can we? That's why our Imperial Majesty wants you to join his mission to tend the soldiers' wounds, talk to them, and entertain them with your talents. You will be the Emperor's special gifts to the soldiers! He promises that you'll be treated with respect. You will have clean rooms, three meals a day, and wages. He will send you home for New Year's Day and the August Full Moon Day. Do our Imperial Majesty a favor, and he'll return the favor to you. Thank you for listening, my sisters. Now I want you to welcome my comrade." The soldier saluted the Emperor's portrait again and stepped down.

Miss Yamakawa clapped. We all clapped.

A short, broad-shouldered man took the podium. "My beloved sisters!" he said in Korean. We were stunned. He was Korean, not Japanese! We looked at each other, then at Miss Yamakawa. But Miss Yamakawa was smiling as if she hadn't noticed anything unusual. How curious, I thought.

"Whenever I look up at our Emperor's portrait, a lump rises in my throat and tears gather in my eyes. Our beloved Imperial Majesty, a gentle and noble man, is grieving for our deceased soldiers and worrying about the injured ones. He feels pain and anguish because he loves every one of them just as he loves each one of you. After all, my sisters, we are a big family! We must fight together for the world's reunification. Think about our young and brave soldiers fighting at this very moment!" The soldier's voice suddenly got louder. "Can we merely sit by and watch them? Can we let those barbaric Westerners ruin the world? No, my beloved sisters! We must fight them! The time has come and we Asians must unite to drive those barbarians out of our territory. Let us join the Emperor to save our own people!"

Miss Yamakawa abruptly stood up, throwing her arms into the air and shouting, "Long live the Emperor! Long live Japan! Banzai! Banzai! Banzai!"

We all stood up too and yelled at the top of our voices, "Long live the Emperor! Long live Japan! Banzai! Banzai! Banzai!"

The soldiers shouted too, "Banzai! Banzai! Banzai!"

Miss Yamakawa sat down and we all sat down.

The soldier smiled broadly, showing his bright teeth. "I am truly moved by your love and devotion to your fatherland, my beloved sisters! I know you all want to help our Emperor. Those who want to help the Emperor, raise your hands!"

All hands went up.

"Very well! I am proud of you. Because you are so kind and caring, our Emperor wants each of you to have a very special gift. Come forward and receive his gifts!" He lifted a large box from the floor and set it on Miss Yamakawa's desk.

Immediately we formed a line, chattering excitedly. When my turn came, I looked in and saw the box was filled with white handkerchiefs with a red sun painted on them. I picked one out and put it in my pocket.

Two weeks later, four solemn soldiers with stethoscopes on their chests and black leather bags in their hands walked into the classroom. Four folding-screens were brought in for each corner of the room and all of the windows were covered with curtains.

Miss Yamakawa announced, "Girls, the military medical crew is here to give you physical exams. Take your clothes off and stand in line."

We were terrified. We had never had a physical exam at school before and didn't know why we needed one now. When we asked this, Miss Yamakawa replied, "Because you're going to join our Majesty's brigade. Hurry, girls! Our soldiers don't have all day!"

Soon I stood naked before one of the soldiers who was only a little older than my brother Wook. He pressed his stethoscope against my breasts and my rib cage, listening intently. Then he looked at my navel and my abdomen and ordered me to turn around and touch the floor. While scribbling something on his writing pad, he asked, "Do you know if anyone in your family has syphilis or gonorrhea?"

"What do you mean, sir?" I asked.

"That's all," he said.

When I got home, I told my mother for the first time about the Emperor's delegates and the physical exam I had had that day. I hadn't told her about the delegates for fear that she would scold me for wanting to leave home.

She became hysterical. "You know what you're doing?" she yelled. "They're going to take you to a brothel, you stupid girl!"

"It's not the same thing, Omma," I said apologetically. "I'm only going to be a helper for the Emperor. I will be tending the soldiers' wounds or entertaining them, you know, singing and dancing."

"You don't know anything!" she yelled again. "How can you volunteer to go away without asking me? I heard at the Food Distribution Center that the Japanese want virgins to join the Women's Army of Great Japan. Don't you know what that means? To hell with the Emperor! How dare he use schoolgirls as whores! Damn the Emperor! Damn the Japanese!" My mother turned around and spat.

I didn't say anything. I thought she was losing her mind talking like that. She could be taken to the police station and tortured or imprisoned or both. But my mother continued cursing, "Every Japanese in this country deserves to be shot and buried in a pile of feces! But even pigs wouldn't go near them. Know why? Because they stink worse than pigs, much worse!"

"Omma, someone might hear you," I cautioned.

But she didn't hear me. "Remember Auntie Shim's second daughter, the girl with a wart on her neck? She died in a brothel in Manchuria. It's true. Her cousin came back and told her mother that the soldiers cut her belly open because she got pregnant. And you know the barber's daughter who came back with a baby? She killed herself. You don't believe me? Her parents kicked her out when the baby wasn't yet a month old, and later they found her body floating in the lake, face down. No one knows what happened to her baby. I think she killed it and buried it somewhere in the woods."

Omma threw herself on the mat and cried bitterly, her chest heaving. Between her sobs, she said, "I wouldn't let you go even if my eyes were covered with dirt! Aigo, Soon-ah ya, don't leave me, you hear? You and Chin Soo are all I've got.

How can I live without you? The Japanese are taking every-thing from me, my husband, my oldest child, and now you...."

I cried too. I was afraid of becoming a gift of the Emperor after all.

Later that afternoon, my mother put my long, sleek hair up into a bundle and fastened it on my crown with a chopstick. This was how married women wore their hair, and it indicated that I was a married woman, not a virgin. Then she locked me in the underground shelter my father had dug a year earlier. It was covered with a large board with many holes punched through it. I was glad to see small patches of sky through the holes.

Sitting in the dark shelter hiding from the Japanese, I was puzzled: who was my enemy? We had dug the shelter last year when the Japanese ordered us to, saying that the Americans were going to bomb the entire country. Several nights a week a siren went off, and we moved into the shelter, shivering in the dark. But not a single bomb had been dropped on our village as long as I could remember. My mother stored sacks of grain and bushels of potatoes in the shelter because it was cool in summer and warm in winter.

But instead of hiding from Western barbarians, I was now hiding from Japanese. *What does this mean?* Then I remembered General MacArthur's promise.

A month ago, an airplane had appeared in the sky, dropped a large dust-ball, then flew over the mountain, its silvery wings glittering like knife blades. As we watched, the dust became thousands of white flyers. All the neighborhood kids chased them. I too chased and grabbed one on the hill behind our house and rushed home to read it to my illiterate mother. To my surprise, it was written in Korean. It said: "Dear Koreans: I, General Douglas MacArthur, the Supreme Commander of American Forces in Asia, solemnly declare that the Korean people are not our enemies and that America will not bomb Korean towns and villages. We will make every effort to deliver freedom to you as well as to other countries in Asia. I urge you to trust us and cooperate with us in any way you can." It was signed by both General MacArthur and Mr. Syngman Rhee: the one in English and the other in Korean.

My mother wept when I finished reading. Although she didn't say anything, I knew why she was crying. My father would have been happy reading such a flyer.

My father had been a Presbyterian minister. Our house was next to the church, and I used to hear a carriage stopping in our courtyard in the middle of the night and footsteps running toward the church. I heard my father slipping out the back door like a shadow to meet them. One early morning, seven armed Japanese policemen marched into our courtyard and ransacked our house. This was after Liberation Army members killed a Japanese policeman who had tortured and killed many Korean activists.

When they couldn't find anything, the policemen bound my father's hands with a rope and made him kneel on the bare dirt. A policeman with a mustache yelled at my father, asking where the Liberation Army people were hiding, but my father didn't respond. It seemed he had been expecting this, for he was wearing his white silk Korean outfit which made him appear radiant in the morning sunlight.

The soldier barked at him, "Speak, Chōsenjin!" Korea was called Chōsen then. "Where are the traitors?"

My father didn't answer.

The soldier struck him with the butt of his rifle, barking, "You want to die, you stubborn mule?"

Still my father didn't respond.

The soldier hit him again and again. With each blow, my father sank further into the dirt, spitting blood and swallowing dust. I bit my own thumb. I couldn't watch him, and yet I couldn't close my eyes, for fear that he might die when my eyes were closed. My mother cried, sobbed, howled, tearing her hair out.

Suddenly, my father lifted his blood-stained face to the sky. "Dear Heavenly Father," he said solemnly in Korean, "if Thou art ready to receive this worthless servant, let Thy will be done! In Thy mercy we live and die. Come, Lord Jesus, speak to these men to open their eyes and see Thy powerful presence. . . ."

I heard a sharp, metallic thud, and he fell forward, struggling to breathe. I remember blood soaking the dirt and the saber next to him glinting in the sun. I was numb. I don't remember much after that except a dozen neighbors mourning at the burial.

❧

Hiding like a mole in the shelter, I ate whatever my mother brought me, sometimes a boiled potato and other times a small portion of cooked barley, and slept during the day. Once in a while she brought me a large bowl of uncooked rice, and I sorted out the tiny pieces of gravel from the grains of rice under the dim light coming through the holes. Every bag of rice we got at the Food Distribution Center contained gravel. This was a common practice of Japanese businessmen who came to our country hoping to get rich quick. It never affected the Japanese in Korea since they shopped at markets specifically designated for the divine people of Japan. Sorting out tiny pieces of gravel from rice was time-consuming work, but we had to do it in order to stay alive.

My exile in the shelter lasted only six days. I had fallen asleep and was dreaming of wolves when I heard a truck rolling into our courtyard, a man's voice shouting at my mother in Japanese, asking where Keiko Omura was, using my Japanese name. I could hear everything, even the soldier's loud breathing. My mother replied nervously in her broken Japanese that she had sent me to my aunt's house in Seoul.

"You stupid liar!" the voice yelled, and I heard Omma crying, "Dōzo! Dōzo!" More noises—maybe a soldier's hand striking her and Omma falling. Then the boots marched away toward the house.

Cowering in the shelter with my nose touching the dirt, I thought my last day on earth had come. I held onto a bushel of potatoes next to me and cried as I heard the boots returning. It was too late to think about why the Emperor would send armed soldiers to get his helpers. It was too late for crying, too.

The boots pounded on the board above my head. "Here, open this!" a soldier ordered, and the board was removed. Sunlight poured down on me. I pretended to hear nothing and embraced the bushel even more tightly as if it would save my life.

Several hands grabbed me and pulled me up. I saw four pairs of dark eyes looking at me hatefully. One heavily decorated soldier stepped forward and slapped me repeatedly until I tasted blood in my mouth. Dazed, I hoped this man was the same man who had slapped my mother a few minutes earlier and tried to feel her warmth coming through his hand. If she felt this pain, I knew I could sense it.

Two soldiers savagely dragged me to the courtyard as if I were a wild hog, then to the truck. My mother yelled, "Salyo-juseh-yo! Let her alone!"

One soldier pushed her. She fell backward, hitting the ground with her hips. Getting up, she begged, "Dōzo! Dōzo!" but the soldier butted her with his rifle. She fell again, this time hitting the ground with her right elbow. She struggled for a moment to get on her feet. I noticed her mouth bleeding. She begged him more, bowing frantically.

Suddenly, the soldier with the decorations on his chest turned towards the chicken coop and lifted his rifle. The shells burst and the chickens flew out one by one. The chickens fell to the ground as the soldier shot them. Feathers danced artfully in the air and then slowly sank down onto the lifeless bodies.

My mother collapsed onto the ground, weeping helplessly.

The soldier pushed me up onto the truck. A dozen girls in the back of the truck looked at me with panic in their eyes. I recognized at least three classmates, but we couldn't speak: no sounds could escape our lips. The truck moved with a loud *brrrrm* and began rolling toward the main road, leaving behind our courtyard where a heap of dead chickens and Omma lay still.

I saw Omma getting up, wild-eyed. I was worried that she would follow the truck, screaming her head off, and the soldiers might shoot her. Instead, she ran in the opposite direction, toward the church. *What is she doing?* I wondered.

As the truck sped down the dirt road, I looked back at the neighborhood through tear-filled eyes. The church steeple, the windmills, and the hills seemed to be flowing on a river. Then everything froze. Our church bell was tolling! It must be Omma who was pulling the rope with all her might, desperately trying to halt the horrific crime she had just witnessed.

Several neighbors, mostly women and older men, rushed out of their homes barefoot and stood, paralyzed. A woman burst into tears, crying, "Aigo! Aigo! Someone, please stop them!" but no one stepped forward: they only stood there, wringing their hands.

A thought struck me hard: *I might never see Omma again! I might never see those ginkgo trees and weeping willows, either.*

Cupping my hands, I shouted, "Omma, take care of yourself, you hear?" My voice cracked and I cried like a dog howling at the moon. Soon others joined the howling match: "*Ommaaaa! Ommaaaaa! Take care!*" The cries echoed through the neighborhood and soybean fields before merging with the mournful sound of the church bell.

The truck wound through hills and villages, finally stopping at a shabby-looking inn surrounded by trees and bushes. It was dark. No house was nearby. As I looked around the silhouettes of the distant hills and mountains, fear numbed me.

A soldier went to the door and knocked. An old woman in her sixties appeared, bowed at him, and received a white envelope, secretively glancing at us. Then the soldier signaled us to climb down the truck. We followed the old woman into a large room with straw mats on the floor. After we each ate a rice ball the size of my fist, covered with salt and seaweed, we slept on the floor without a cover.

The next day five more girls arrived and seven the next, and we were twenty-four by the end of the third day. Most of the girls were about my age, except for four older women about twenty-five or six and three younger ones whose chests were flat. We didn't say much but stared at one another, trying to read each other's minds. Only one woman cried loudly, covering her face. We all looked at her. Between her sobs, I overheard her saying that she was going to be a nun and that she would rather die than become a whore for Japanese soldiers.

Then another woman, a woman with heavy make-up on her face, yelled at her, "Please shut up!" We all looked at her. "Don't act as if you're immaculate," she said in a southern accent. "It's the war that's making us whores, nothing else. Do you really care about who you are and what you're going to do when so many people are dying? Just think about whether or not you'll come back alive!"

With that, the room became quiet. Everyone seemed to be wondering whether or not they'd come back alive. A skinny kid with braided hair jabbered innocently, "I know we'll come back alive. If not, my father wouldn't send me to that factory in Yokohama where my sister is. He said anything is better than dying from starvation. We were surviving on the bark of trees and . . ."

"Shut up, you too!" the woman with the painted face yelled again. "I'm not interested in such a depressing story. I'd much rather be a whore and eat like a human being than eat the bark of trees like a caterpillar."

No one said a word.

The next morning the soldiers made us exercise. When finished, they lectured us on what to do when we boarded ship. "Chew on a rope when you have seasickness," the soldier said. "If the ship is torpedoed, wait for the whistles, then jump into the water. Don't hesitate! Always keep a piece of white cloth in hand to signal *SOS* to passing ships."

Jump into the water? I looked around to see if others were as frightened as I, and they were, although no one said anything.

At the end of the fourth day we were loaded again onto a truck. We drove to the port of Haeju while watching the magnificent sunset which stained the sky orange-red. An hour later we boarded a military ship flying a huge Japanese flag on the deck. We walked down a long flight of steps and entered a large room with straw mats on the floor. The smell, similar to rotten eggs, nauseated me. The soldiers brought us blankets and turned the lights off, saying, "You have a long journey ahead of you, Chōsenjin! See you in the morning."

With a loud whistle, the ship moved. The sound of waves hitting the side of the ship frightened me. Several girls cried, calling out "Omma! Omma!" I buried my face in my hands and wept. After a while the room was quiet, except for the noises of the waves rising and falling. On my right was my friend Kyung Hwa, who had once been our class leader, on my left was the older woman who wanted to be a nun, and next to her against the wall was the young skinny girl whose name was unknown to me.

"Onni," the young girl whispered to me when I brought her a blanket, calling me "Sister."

"Yes."

"I'm scared."

"I'm scared too. We're all scared." I patted her thin shoulder, trying to smile in the dark.

"Do you think the Japanese will kill us?"

"No, I don't think so. They'll make us work like dogs, but they will not kill us."

"Do you really think they'll send us home for the Full Moon Day?"

"I don't know, but I hope so. Don't you think it'd be nice?"

"Yes, Onni. It'd be really nice."

"Try to get some sleep now. Worrying doesn't help anything."

"Thank you, Onni."

I came back to my mat, but I couldn't fall asleep. I kept worrying about Omma. Now she had no one to look after her and Chin Soo, who was only seven. She had depended on my father for everything. She worshiped and adored him. Since he had died, my mother's only joy was tending the balsam plants that she had planted on the same spot where his blood had been spilled. The balsams were my father's favorite flowers. The red blossoms reminded us how our father had died.

Suddenly, loud footsteps in the corridor startled me. I sprang up. Screams erupted from the next room. I pulled the blanket tightly to my neck, noticing my rapid heartbeat. Then our door jerked open and a mob of dark figures rushed into the room. Before I could think about what to do, a huge black shadow knocked me down. I smelled alcohol on his breath. He pushed his hand into my chogori, the Korean tunic, and grabbed my breast. I screamed. The dark figure struck my face repeatedly. Hot liquid gathered in my mouth and rushed out of my nostrils.

His hands tore my skirt and underwear. "God, help me!" I

couldn't tell if the scream I heard was mine or that of other girls in the room. A huge bolt struck between my legs and drilled into my flesh. It was so painful I couldn't breathe.

Struggling for air, I fought with the dark figure, kicking and screaming.

I pushed the soldier with all my strength, but like a tombstone, he didn't budge. I bit his arm. He slapped me hard with his free hand. I wasn't about to let go of him: I bit him harder. He struck me repeatedly and I passed out.

I couldn't tell how long I had been lying there. The room was filled with anguished cries and moaning. This was what awaited me and the other girls! We were bones to dogs. The soldiers would devour us piece by piece until nothing was left. This was what the Emperor had in mind, so his soldiers would conquer more countries, kill more innocent people, and become the most feared species on earth. The wind whispered to me to run to the deck and plunge into the sea. Yes, that was what I must do. End everything here and don't go another step. Yet my body disobeyed me and I couldn't move. My mother's voice rang in my ears, "Soon-ah ya! You must come home. I can't live without you!" Hot tears gathered in my eyes and I sobbed. I noticed a faint light peeking into the room through a mist-covered window. I closed my eyes: I couldn't face the light.

$\mathcal{A}$bruptly, the door opened and two soldiers came in blowing whistles. "You lazy Chōsenjin!" they barked, poking us with their rifles. "Get up! Time for exercise!"

I wasn't asleep, but I wasn't wide awake either. I tried to get on my feet but fell over as if the floor had suddenly moved. There was a huge blood stain on my mat. I didn't know I was bleeding. The mat next to me also had a large blood stain, but the occupant of the mat, the woman who wanted to be a nun, wasn't there any more.

A soldier slapped my face. "Gono bakayaro! Stupid! I told you to get up!" he barked. He looked even younger than me. I wanted to spit at him, but I only stared angrily. Many girls in torn clothes got up and obediently walked up the staircase like well-trained circus dogs. Several others were still struggling to get on their feet.

"Get up!" he yelled again, kicking me.

I wanted to grab him by the throat and strangle him, but I didn't even have the strength to stand. I tried to push myself up, but my legs felt so weak. I cried.

Another whistle shrilled. Two more soldiers came down. "Take them to the deck!" the younger of the two ordered.

A heavy-set soldier approached me with a disgusting grin on his face. "Aha! I know what this one wants," he said. "She wants to be carried." He pulled me up from behind, his cheek almost touching mine. I tried to elbow him, but he grabbed my waist so tightly that my effort was useless. He moved toward the corridor. To my horror, he had the same breath as that of the man who had raped me. It wasn't as strong as the night before, but it was unmistakably the same stench. My heart began to race.

"Oh, you're getting excited, aren't you?" the soldier said, moving his hand to my breast.

I quickly wrapped my arms tightly around my chest, pushing his arm away. Then I shivered with anger: I saw my own teeth marks on his arm! The red and purple circle, too visible not to notice, was the size of a Japanese silver coin. I was burning with a revengeful desire. But what could I do? Helplessness suddenly drained my will to live.

The soldier dropped me in the middle of the deck with the other girls. The sun was warm and plentiful. Ripples of sparkling blue water glittered in the golden sunlight, and seagulls leisurely glided through the air like silvery specks in the wind. How could everything be so beautiful after what had happened? How could life go on after such a nightmare? I couldn't understand. I envied the birds. If I had wings I would fly home, squealing joyfully.

"Attention!" a soldier suddenly barked.

We became alert.

"Line up!" he ordered.

We reluctantly lined up in three rows.

A heavily decorated officer wearing knee-high black boots appeared and walked toward us. In the fervent sun, his black eyes glowed with malicious authority. He had a sharp-looking face, like a well-varnished wooden sculpture.

"Count off!" a soldier yelled, glancing at the girl at the end of the front line.

"Ichi, ni, san, shi, go, roku, shichi, hachi, kyū . . . twenty-three!"

"Twenty-three?" the soldier barked.

Twenty-four had left Haeju. I remembered the empty mat next to mine, the woman who wanted to be a nun, who hadn't been there when I woke up.

"Count off again!" the soldier barked.

"Ichi, ni, san, shi, go, roku . . . twenty-three."

The soldier turned around and reported to the officer.

"Twenty-three?" the officer exclaimed, twitching his eyebrows. "I thought there were twenty-four Chōsenjin and sixteen Chinese."

"Yes, sir, one Chōsenjin is missing, sir!"

"What do you mean, one is missing?"

"I don't know, sir!"

"Don't tell me you don't know! You must know. Go find her. Look everywhere. Don't report back until you find her!"

Soldiers scattered in all directions, leaving a thundering vibration under my feet.

We looked at one another. Where was she hiding? Did something happen to her? I couldn't think of any place she could hide. There were no bathrooms. The soldiers had brought two chamber pots for the twenty-four of us and told us to empty them and wash them as needed. I could almost hear the woman's long and agonizing sobs. Now that she was missing, I wished I had known her.

The soldiers came back one by one. "She's nowhere, sir!" one soldier said.

The officer walked toward us, his slanted eyes eager to find something we didn't have. "Does any one of you know where she is hiding?" he asked.

We said nothing.

Just then a soldier rushed back with a bundle in his hands. "Sir," he said, saluting the back of the officer's head, "I found this next to the emergency exit!" His voice quivered as he handed the bundle to the officer.

The officer unfolded the bundle. A chima, the Korean skirt, flapped furiously in the wind. In the middle, I saw a huge darkened blood stain, as large as the Rising Sun in the center of the Japanese flag on the mast.

"Well? What is this?" the officer yelled.

"I don't know, sir!"

"I told you not to say 'I don't know.' Tell me why this dirty skirt was next to the emergency exit! Was there anything else?"

The soldier handed him a blue rubber shoe. "This was with the clothes. I believe she jumped in the water, sir!"

"She jumped into the sea!" a girl behind me shrieked. It was my classmate Kyung Hwa's voice. "She killed herself! She chose to die rather than go with them!"

Her voice unleashed my anger, and I, too, shouted, pointing at the chima, "Look! That's the Japanese flag he's holding! It's painted with her blood!"

The officer walked over and slapped my face, zap, zap, zap! I saw lights flashing in my eyes. I crouched down, covering my face. He paused and I stood up again. "Kill me!" I yelled. "Kill me now! You are going to kill us anyway! It's better to die now than to be used as your sex slaves!" I was totally unaware of what I was doing. It felt as if a fearless stranger had suddenly stepped into me.

Immediately, a soldier grabbed his bayoneted rifle and rushed over.

The officer raised his palm toward him, looking me over from head to toe, then front to back. "No! I can't kill you now," he said, his tone dropping a notch and the corners of his mouth curling slightly. His eyes met mine with annoying tenderness. "I don't want to be blamed for another useless death, not that your life is important to me. We are going through much expense hauling you to the Pacific Islands. You can be very useful to our fighting soldiers."

"Kill me now," I repeated in a calm voice.

Ignoring my request, he turned to the chubby soldier and ordered, "Lock these two up," pointing at me and Kyung Hwa, "and watch them. Don't let them jump into the sea. We can't let sharks and killer-whales have them instead of our soldiers." Stiffly, he moved away toward the captain's cabin.

The chubby soldier pushed me and Kyung Hwa toward the staircase. As we walked downstairs, we heard the soldiers shouting, "Ichi, ni, san, shi. Ichi, ni, san, shi . . ." The soldiers were forcing the girls to exercise. I envisioned the girls reluctantly moving their arms and legs up and down at the soldiers' command, while their minds wandered away with the girl who had jumped into the sea. I knew they all envied the dead girl. She had nothing to worry about. How wonderful to be an invisible ghost and glide through the air without fear of being tortured or killed by the Japanese!

After passing through a long corridor, we entered a small room with two army cots facing one another. The walls were dirty with words written on them in black ink: "Hail Emperor Hirohito!" "Die for the glory and honor of Nippon!" The floor was filthy with rat droppings, candy and cigarette wrappers, and pictures of naked women in all different positions.

As if he sensed our disgust, the soldier mocked: "Don't be confused, Chōsenjin. You're not our honored guests. You're here for us, remember? Have sweet dreams, darlings!" Laughing, he kicked the door shut behind him and left.

I looked at Kyung Hwa's frightened face. She looked at me, too, but she didn't seem to notice me. I sat on the cot, afraid of my own words. I tried to see what lay ahead of us, but I couldn't think. "Kyung Hwa ya, I don't know if Omma is okay,"

I said, as if the only person I feared for was my mother. "I think the soldiers went back and did something to her now that she's all alone."

"I don't know," Kyung Hwa said automatically. "My Omma moved in with my grandma after the soldiers raped her twice."

I didn't tell her I too had watched a soldier rape my mother while my father was still alive. He had been taken to the police station early that morning, and my mother was alone in the house. That afternoon we had a teachers' meeting at school and were let go early. Coming home, I noticed a pair of black boots with gold buckles on our front step. Only Japanese policemen wore such boots and I felt all my hair rising.

I heard a voice murmuring. "Stop! It's time for my children to come home from school." It was my mother's voice.

"You stupid woman!" a man's voice said in Japanese. "Would you rather die?" I heard the clicking noise of a pistol.

"No!" My mother's voice pleaded, followed by the zapping noise of a hand striking human flesh. Motionless, I listened to her soft moan, a rustling noise of clothes, her muffled cry.

I stood there shaking. *Should I rush into the room yelling and screaming? Then the soldier would certainly shoot both Omma and me.* I tiptoed and hid behind the kitchen door.

After what seemed like an eternity, my mother sobbed loudly. *At least she isn't dead,* I thought, noticing sweat on my forehead and the tears running down my face. *At least we still have a mother.*

Soon I heard the rice-papered door sliding open. I pressed my face against a tiny hole in the door and looked out. The soldier leaving the room was the stout man who had come and shouted at my father for the unpaid tax early that morning. He quickly looked in all directions before walking across the courtyard, briefly touching the front of his pants. His brisk walk made the chickens jump and rush to their coop.

My legs shook so much I sat and wept. I couldn't tell

whether I was angry or sad. I kept repeating to myself, *Omma was raped by a Japanese!*

Suddenly the kitchen door creaked and Omma asked me, "When did you come home?"

"I just got here," I lied.

"What are you doing here? Why didn't you come into the room?"

I didn't know what to say. I didn't want her to know I was there when she was raped. She didn't have to know. It would be better for me, for her, and for Father if I didn't know what went on in the room.

I quickly made up a story. "Omma," I said, acting childish, "I flunked my math test today and Miss Yamakawa was angry. She sent me to the principal. Sorry, Omma, I'll do better next time."

"Oh?" she said, but I knew she wasn't listening. Her cheeks were red. She opened the pantry door with her trembling hand. She took out a gourdful of rice, but the gourd slipped out of her hand, spilling rice everywhere. She stared at it vacantly.

I frantically got down on my knees and scooped up rice, anger bursting. "Look what you did, Omma! What are we going to eat tonight? You always said I was clumsy, but look!" I yelled, crying.

That Sunday my father gave a long, moving sermon on God's unconditional love. It was only one of my father's many good sermons, but to my mother it was a rod. She bent her head and cried for the entire duration of his sermon.

I felt compassion for her, and yet strangely, I couldn't look at her face. I thought somehow she was dishonest, unclean, and had fallen out of God's grace. My father didn't know she had been raped. This thought tortured me. *Didn't he have to know? Wasn't it up to him to forgive her or divorce her?*

I had adored my father and argued with my mother. She wasn't intellectual like my father was: she couldn't read, couldn't talk intelligently, and she was fiercely protective of me and my little brother since my older brother had been taken by the Japanese. Although she never scolded me for my attitudes, she knew that I didn't respect her as I respected my father. Now, the thought that I might never see her again stabbed through me. What was she doing? Was she shedding tears, looking up at the Southern sky, as she often did for my older brother Wook? Or was she kneeling in my father's church, praying? I wanted to run to her and ask her to forgive my bad attitudes. My heart ached with such intense longing that I leaned my forehead on the cot and wept. *If God loved me, He could have prevented this from happening,* I thought. What was He doing when He saw me being taken away from home, loaded onto the ship and raped? Where was He when the girl carefully took her skirt and shoes off, mumbled a prayer or two, and leaped into the roaring sea?

Kyung Hwa suddenly drew a long, pathetic sigh, declaring, "I'm so hungry!"

How disgusting, I thought. I looked at her as if she were a worm. How could she think of food at a time like this? To my amazement, my stomach grumbled loudly. I was hungry too. I was shocked. When my bottom was still bleeding and my chima and underwear were all torn, showing streaks of bare skin here and there, how could my tummy feel hunger? How was it possible that my stomach craved food when I was in pain? I was disgusted. Still, I was terribly hungry.

But all morning no food came to our prison. I couldn't shake off the thought of food, any food, and I remembered my father's last birthday when all our relatives had gathered around our black lacquer table, eating and praising my mother's excellent bulgoghi, grilled beef seasoned with soy sauce, sugar, and garlic. That day Father had decided I was too skinny. "Soon-ah, you don't eat enough! You must gain some weight. Here, eat more bulgoghi!" Using his chopsticks, he lifted a large piece of grilled meat from his plate and dropped it into my rice bowl.

My throat ached as I tried not to cry. Soon a sense of lethargy came over me.

I dreamed I was walking on a narrow trail. A thick layer of fog surrounded me, and I couldn't see an inch ahead. I heard bombs exploding nearby, but I didn't know where I was going. Suddenly, the sky opened and bright sunlight, brighter than a thousand suns, was shining in my eyes. Somewhere I heard my father calling me, "Soon-ah ya! Come this way!"

"Yes, Father, I'm coming." I ran toward his voice. I could see him standing on the shore next to a white ship, waving his hand toward me. The ship gleamed and music delighted my ears. I ran as fast as I could. Finally I arrived at the shore, but my father was nowhere! Startled, I called, "Father! Where are you?"

The door to the ship opened and Miss Yamakawa came out. She had a sarcastic smile on her face. "Look at you, Chōsenjin! You are nothing but a whore!" she yelled.

Trembling, I looked at myself. I was stark naked! Not a single stitch of clothing was hanging on me. Panicking, I covered my bare breasts with my hands, but Miss Yamakawa pushed my hands off. She took a piece of chalk from her pocket and wrote "Conquered!" on my chest. Her chalk dug into my flesh like a knife, and I saw blood trickling down. I screamed. She slapped me again and again and I woke up.

The chubby soldier was slapping my face. "Get up, Chōsenjin! Do you think you are in Tokyo Plaza Hotel?" he demanded.

I only stared at him.

"Come with me!"

I got up, noticing that Kyung Hwa was gone. "Where is my friend?" I asked.

"How am I supposed to know?" he said, walking ahead of me. I had enough strength to walk without stumbling. We passed along the corridor again and came to a room at the far end of the boat.

The soldier opened the door and told me to go in.

I walked in, feeling as if I had just stepped into a tiger's cave. *Stay alert*, I told myself.

The officer who had slapped me on deck in the morning was sitting alone next to a bed, wearing a blue silk kimono with a huge crane embroidered on the front. "How are you feeling?" he asked.

I stared at the floor. I hated his fake kindness. *He's playing a game*, I thought. All divine people loved to play games, even Miss Yamakawa. She always gave us a sugar-coated lecture before punishing us with a bamboo stick, saying how much our Majesty in Tokyo loved Koreans and why we shouldn't speak Korean, but Japanese.

"I thought you might be hungry. Here's some food." He lifted a tray from his desk and put it on the bed. I saw a bowl of steaming rice with meat and vegetables! My mouth watered helplessly, but I clenched my teeth. "I'm not hungry, sir."

"Not hungry? Are you sure?"

"Yes."

"All right. When you change your mind, let me know. I'm keeping it here on my desk." Smiling, he put it back on his desk.

I dropped my gaze to the floor again, wishing my ordeal wouldn't be too long and too painful.

"There's something I want you to understand," he said, lifting himself from the chair and pacing in the narrow space between his bed and chair. "In this world, there are only two kinds of people, the powerful and the powerless. The world is ruled by the powerful and the powerless must comply. Our nation, Imperial Japan, is on the verge of conquering the entire world, and people must accept this new reality. The powerful should guide the powerless and the wise should teach the foolish. It's a simple rule. Does it make sense?"

No, I wanted to say. *This is not an animal kingdom but a human world where people live, loving one another and pondering what's beautiful and meaningful in life. But if I tell you this, you'll beat me.*

The captain continued as if he thought I agreed with him. "By understanding this wisdom, your life in the Pacific Islands will be easier and more acceptable. Sometimes it's better not to fight so much." He paused, then said, "You know, I always thought Chōsenjin were ignorant, dirty, and lazy, but you make me think differently about your race. We were told that your people's intelligence level is little higher than that of guinea pigs, but I'm finding out that isn't true. For a Chōsenjin, you seem intelligent and quite attractive. How unfortunate that you were born a Korean!"

I bowed to him deeply, acting innocent and simple-minded. "Thank you, sir. I'm genuinely grateful that I'm in your hands rather than another Japanese soldier's."

"Oh? Why do you say that?"

"Last night, sir, an unknown number of soldiers came into our cabin and did unspeakable things to us. I'm sure you wouldn't have allowed this to happen if you knew about it, sir."

"What unspeakable things?" he asked, while avoiding my eyes.

"The unspeakable things, sir . . . the same things that the Imperial soldiers did to Chinese women when they invaded Nanking."

The officer suddenly roared with laughter. He laughed until tears appeared in his eyes. "Ah, unspeakable things! Have you seen rows and rows of dead bodies lying on the streets of Nanking?"

"Only in the pictures, sir."

"Have you seen a river that is covered with floating corpses, dead animals, children's toys, and women's lingerie?"

"No, sir."

He abruptly opened the cabinet above his desk where rows

of liquor bottles stood. He grabbed a bottle, pulled out the cork with his teeth, and tilted the bottle into his mouth. The liquor gurgled in his throat, making music. He wiped his lips with the back of his hand and turned around, wearing a sickly smile.

"For a soldier, having sex before battle is like drinking a magic potion. It liberates you from the fear of dying, and afterwards you feel as if you've just kissed an immortal chalice. That was the reason why so many women were raped and killed in China. Some soldiers . . ." he laughed again, "had sex with dying women because there were no live ones around."

My legs felt weak and my teeth began chattering. His face began to look familiar. I knew what could be expected.

"When I first joined the army," he continued, belching loudly, "everything bothered me. I gagged and vomited when I killed a civilian. My superior officer saw what I was doing and lectured me. He said killing a hundred people a day is a lot easier than killing just one. Soon I mastered the art of killing. The more I killed, the faster I was promoted, and by the time we were done with the Nanking civilians, I was a captain. In war, killing is the only sensible thing, don't you think?"

His gaze met mine and I turned to the portrait of the Emperor Hirohito on the wall as if he would save me. The officer came closer and began walking around me, breathing heavily on my face, my neck, and my shoulders. The smell of alcohol sickened me. I kept looking at Hirohito's portrait.

The captain stopped walking in front of me. "In the end, we'll all die! Nothing matters after you're dead, isn't it true? The dead bodies, yours or mine, will attract the maggots and will decay eventually!"

He tore my tunic with both hands and pushed me on the bed. I didn't fight. I lay there. He was the conqueror, I the conquered. My fate had been decided thirty-three years ago, even before I was born, when the Japanese took over our Yi dynasty, pushing away Russians, Americans, British, and Chinese who had drooled over our tiny peninsula, so tiny it was almost invisible on the map. Maybe this tragedy had been expected since the Creation.

The captain jumped on top of me, spreading the smell of alcohol all over me. I tried to listen to the sound of the waves. It seemed the sea was shouting in protest. The wind cried sharply, scratching the window. Was that the ghost of the dead girl? I believed it was: she seemed to be telling me that Kyung Hwa was in the next room, going through what I was going through now, and all the girls in the large room were being raped again.

Finally I heard a huge splash on the side of the ship and wished a hurricane would come.

$\mathcal{A}$s if God were granting my wish, a torrential storm hit the sea late that night and the ship nearly sank. Most of us became violently ill. My stomach had been empty all day and I threw up only yellowish liquid. I lay gagging and heaving for a long time in absolute helplessness. The thought that I had not lived long enough to know what life was all about tormented me. And what about Omma and Chin Soo? How could I die, leaving them behind? Also, I wanted to be a mother someday and raise my own children. The *Life* magazine which my father had received from an American preacher was full of advertisements. I often flipped through the pages, dreaming that someday I could live in a tiny white house with a green lawn and red roof, just like the homes in the magazine.

As the wind worsened, it hissed against the side of the ship and I was scared. It reminded me of the ghost stories I had heard when I was younger. *The ghosts always come with the sound of wind,* my friend Min Ja used to say. She had tried to convince me that she had seen a woman ghost, but I didn't believe her. Now things were different. A girl had died in the sea only hours ago and the sharp wind sounded like her spirit howling at the soldiers. As if confirming this, the door to the corridor swung open with a loud clatter and water rushed into our cabin. We screamed.

The soldiers kicked open the emergency exit on the wall and threw down several ropes. We climbed the ropes, pushing one another. While waiting their turns, some girls prayed aloud "Amitaba, Amitaba," some pleaded "Jesus, help us," and the men yelled, "Hurry up, you fucking whores!"

On deck the wind was so strong that we clung to the rail. Lightning flashed in the middle of the sky, showing thick, angry black clouds twisting, rolling, and squirming furiously. Monumental waves rose, almost touching the sky, then fell into the dark abyss. I knew Death was near me, yet I was thrilled. God finally lifted His powerful rod to punish these Japanese soldiers. They deserved punishment, to say the least. I secretly told God, *If it is impossible for You to save me from dying with these devils, Thy will be done!*

A soldier threw rafts into the sea and shouted, "Listen to me, *Chōsenjin!* When you hear the sound of three whistles, jump into the water! Don't hesitate."

Jump into the water? As I looked down at the expanse of black water under my feet, goosebumps rose on my arms. I'd rather gradually sink with the ship than jump into that darkness, I thought. We waited on the deck for three whistles, while my thoughts tangled and untangled, but they never came. The wind died at the first sign of light on the horizon, and soon the rain stopped. The black clouds slowly moved north, and by mid-morning the sea regained its splendid beauty under the multi-colored sky. The sun spread its golden beams across the ocean surface, blinding us, as if everything had been a joke.

Still, we were glad to be alive. For a while we forgot that we were heading to some unknown island and busied ourselves scooping water.

Everything around us was wet and sullen. Splashing around with a bucket in my hand, I wondered which was worse, dying in a storm or living with fear. It seemed I was nothing but a stone thrown on the street. The passing feet that kicked me and stepped on me had no concern for me because I was only a stone lying in their path. Was dying better than being kicked and stepped on? Did I have the courage to die?

No. I couldn't think of dying, at least not yet. *So be it!* I said to myself. *I choose to live because I can't die. When I have no power to change the present situation, what point is there to lament? Tomorrow might never come.*

Later that afternoon we arrived at Formosa to refuel and repair the damage caused by the storm. The ship was anchored about a hundred yards offshore and the captain and a few crewmen rode a small motor boat to the mainland. A few Chinese comfort women also moved onto the island in another small boat. I watched their expressionless faces with sympathy. I had known they were on the ship but had never seen them because they had been locked in a cabin just as we had been. *So long, friends,* I whispered. *Be courageous! There must be a meaning behind all this, although we can't understand it now.*

When the ship cast its long, broad shadow onto the sea, a repair crew arrived and began drilling and hammering. Four young soldiers watched us with bayoneted rifles as we mopped the corridor and the deck. When we finished, we sat on the deck to watch the sunset. The red sun was about to plunge into the ocean, clothing every cloud in pink and orange and turning the layers of the mountains into a long purple wall. One patch of pink cloud above the mountains was the shape of a huge bird with its wings wide open. While we watched, the sun slowly dipped into the water and the sky changed to lavender and gray. We could see the evening stars twinkling at the edges of the sky. When I was a child I used to make wishes to those early stars. Omma might be watching them now, I thought. Those stars could see Omma all the while she washed rice to make dinner and took in the laundry from the clothesline in the courtyard. I could almost see Omma again, pulling my abductor's sleeve, crying and begging him not to take her only daughter. I could hear the gunshots, the clucking chickens, and Omma's hysterical sobs.

Just then one particularly bright star caught my attention: it blinked at me as if signaling something. I sat erect. The star turned, making spirals. Then all of the stars, a dozen of them, turned, dragging their bright silvery tails. I blinked. I didn't know what was happening. I saw my father standing before me in his radiant white Korean outfit.

"Father! How did you know I was here?" I exclaimed.

"My child!" he said, his voice full of compassion. "I can see everything from where I am. I'm with you."

"How are Omma and Chin Soo?"

"They're well, Soon-ah. Omma misses you and wants you to know she loves you very, very much."

I began weeping. "Father, I want to go home. I miss Omma and you and Chin Soo so much. Let me go home, Father, please...." I heard my voice coming from far away.

"Soon-ah ya, I'm afraid that's not possible," said his gentle voice. "It pains me to say this, but you'll have to die many deaths before you can truly live. Unless you're willing to die, you'll never know what life is all about. Be strong and pray. Your Heavenly Father will protect you. Be strong.... Be strong...." His voice faded away.

"Father! Don't leave me! Come back!" I cried.

"Who are you talking to?" Kyung Hwa said, nudging me with her elbow. At once, everything disappeared, Father's voice and the circling stars. Even the colorful clouds vanished from the darkening sky. I quickly wiped my tears.

"Let's sing!" Kyung Hwa said, trying to be cheerful.

"Sing?" I said, reluctantly.

"Yes, Soon-ah. Come on, you have a beautiful voice. Let's sing 'My Hometown.'"

She began singing, and one by one, we joined in:

> My hometown is a little village in deep mountains.
> Azaleas and cherry blossoms adorn the hills.
> Weeping willows dance on the edges of the pond.
> My hometown, the little village in deep mountains.
>
> My hometown is a little village near the ocean.
> Ships bring fortunes from faraway lands.
> Children run barefoot on the silvery sand.
> My hometown, the little village near the ocean.

Hearing us sing in Korean, the soldiers tensed up and lifted their bayonets but relaxed again when they realized that we weren't creating any problems. Mostly, I thought, they didn't want anything to happen while their commander was absent.

Encouraged, Kyung Hwa started another song.

> Cuckoo, cuckoo, cries a cuckoo-bird in the woods.
> Pukook, pukook, cries a crane over the rice paddy.
> No words from my brother in the battlefront.
> Only the ginkgo leaves fall in the gusty wind.
>
> Guidool, guidool, cries a cricket on the porch.
> Sirp, sirp, cries a locust on a treetop.
> Where's my brother who had promised me silk shoes?
> Only the cold moon glares at me without a word.

We sang every Korean song we could remember and hummed some American songs. All my classmates knew "Danny Boy" in English, although we couldn't pronounce it correctly: we hummed, over and over, fearing that the Japanese soldiers might kill us for singing American songs.

Late that night the captain and other soldiers returned and our journey continued. The soldiers handed each of us a small bag containing a pair of socks, underwear, a towel, and a white hairband that said "Women's Army of Great Japan."

Every night I was called to the captain's cabin. I did everything the way the captain told me to do it. He seemed to be pleased with the way I kowtowed to him, massaged his arms and legs and front and back. I also shone his boots until they glowed like gems and lay on his bed at his command without any air of resistance. I separated my mind from what was happening to me so that the physical abuse I received every day wouldn't destroy me completely. Father used to say that the Japanese could destroy our bodies but never our spirits. Even the day he died, I knew his spirit was fully alive. Otherwise, how could he have prayed in Korean, knowing that the Japanese would kill him?

On the sixth night, our last night on the ship, the captain rose from his bed and sat at his desk after my duty was finished. "Keiko," he said with a tinge of tenderness in his voice, "I have decided to recommend you to an officer's House of Relaxation. I'm sure you'd be happier there."

I didn't say anything.

He scribbled several lines vertically on a white sheet of paper, stamped his seal next to his name, then handed it to me.

"Give this to the manager of the Comfort Station, whoever it might be, and he'll arrange it with the military officials. You can fool many Japanese people with your flawless Japanese and your physical beauty. You are too good for common soldiers." He smiled.

I looked at him mutely.

"Although you are a Korean, we Japanese men know how to distinguish a daffodil from patches of dandelions. Of course, it's not my decision and it depends on the officers at the House of Relaxation, but there's a good chance that they might want you to work for the officers instead of the common soldiers."

I had no grateful heart for his generosity. *What difference would it make? Biting dogs are all dangerous. Would I feel better when mauled by a German shepherd instead of a mutt?* I bowed to him.

The captain nodded, smiling. Obviously he was proud of himself: he thought I was grateful. Leaving his cabin, I sneaked out on deck and dropped the note into the sea. The wind caught it, tossed it into the air, and played with it for a while. The white paper turned and turned, drawing several mysterious lines in the dark sky, before disappearing into the intense darkness.

As the ship pulled into port the next day, whistling, we saw a large Japanese flag flapping on the rooftop of a modern building and two dozen armed soldiers standing immobile on the dock, facing the ship. Dark, native people walked back and forth around them. The unfamiliar palm trees, the brown native huts along the seashore, and the strips of white sand bordering the island confirmed the distance between where I had come from and where I now stood, although I had no idea where I was. Against the clear sapphire-blue water, the volcanic rocks, the huts, and the green mountains looked unreal as though I was looking at a hand-painted landscape.

Finally, our feet touched earth, marking the end of our seven-day journey. Soon an army truck flying a Japanese flag appeared at the far end of the road, raising dust.

Ten minutes later we arrived at a compound surrounded by stockades and a barbed-wire fence. On the gate was a sign written in Chinese letters: "Imperial Japanese Military of Palau Island—35th Army."

Some girls began crying. One girl muttered, "Why would they want to keep us inside a barbed-wire fence? Are we pigs or chickens?"

Our barrack had a long corridor in the middle and rooms on each side. On the left wall at the entrance, the rules of the House were posted in black ink:

The following rules must be strictly observed by all employees:

*This house is limited strictly to the
Imperial soldiers of Japan.*

Patrons must procure health certificates and condoms.

*No acts of violence or drunkenness are permitted on
the premises, nor should any unreasonable demands
be made of the house employees at any time.*

Never kiss the employees on the mouth.

*Necessary antiseptic measures with the prescribed
solution must be used after each intercourse.*

*Anyone violating the above rules will thereafter be
denied entrance to the house.*

I was angry, scared, and disgusted. At the same time, I didn't care any more. This was my destiny.

A dark-skinned, scrawny man assigned each of us to a room. Mine was the last room on the right. It was the size of the underground shelter back home. Holding a small wooden chest in one corner and a bucketful of water with a dipper in another, there was barely enough room for a sleeping mat against the wall.

Who was the previous occupant of this room? A girl like me? What kind of pain did she endure? Is she still alive?

Looking out the narrow window, I had a view of the endlessly stretching barbed wire fence and a creek flowing alongside. Beyond the fence was a jungle full of tangled vines and thick bushes and to the left stood a row of small huts where some western clothes flapped on a clothesline and colorful toys were scattered on the ground. The occupants of those huts could be European or American missionaries, I thought. I had heard that many Westerners became prisoners when Japan invaded the Pacific Islands last December.

Then I thought I heard singing. Listening closely, I recognized the voice. Kyung Hwa was singing "My Hometown" again, as if a spell had been put on her lips and she couldn't help but sing. I hummed along with her, my gaze lifted to the sky. It comforted me to think that somewhere under that sky, Omma was anxiously waiting for me to come home. I wished I could dream of home.

⁂

The next morning at seven a shrill whistle woke me and a soldier ordered us to gather in the courtyard. We bowed to the flag, sang "Kamigayo" toward the horizon where the sun came up, pushing away the grey mist, and exercised, shouting, "Ichi, ni, san, shi! Ichi, ni, san, shi!" The flagpole accompanied us, rattling loudly against the wind.

At eight our breakfast, a large steamy pot of gruel, arrived, dangling dangerously on a pole two soldiers carried, one at each end. It gave off a suspicious smell, like burning rubber. Some girls wrinkled their noses, but no one complained.

As we ate, we saw a long line of soldiers forming in front of the building, shouting, giggling, and exchanging obscenities. We looked at one another. I felt weak. I dropped my spoon.

The manager, Mr. Nakamura, the scrawny man, appeared at the door.

"Girls, you must look pretty for our Imperial soldiers!" he said, showing his protruding front teeth. "As soon as you're finished eating, go back to your room and powder your faces. That'll make them feel very special!" Then he walked over to me.

"Keiko, you must be our first hostess for today!"

"Hostess?" I asked.

"Yes. Sergeant Saigo ordered me to make a list earlier but I didn't have time to do it. You must come with me at once!"

I followed him.

In front of the barrack stood a table. A soldier wearing glasses and a white armband was busily collecting money and giving out a yellow ticket to each soldier who paid him. In front of him, a pile of Japanese money peeked out of a tin box painted with a samurai face.

By listening to the murmuring conversations, I gathered that thirty minutes of our ordeal cost a soldier one yen and an officer two. However, due to the large number of soldiers, they must not take more than ten minutes.

The manager pushed me toward the soldier at the table. "Sergeant Saigo, this is our hostess for the morning. Isn't she very pretty? She's like a lotus just bloomed for our imperial soldiers!"

The soldier, a young man, looked me up and down, grinning. "Hmm, not a bad looking hostess," he said and handed me a white sash that said "Women's Army of Great Japan" written in red ink. He told me to wear it.

I did.

"Your job is to greet the soldiers," Sergeant Saigo lectured, "Stand right here and say, 'Welcome to the Comfort House! We are delighted to serve you,' and bow. Do you understand?"

My gut twitched in protest but I had no choice. The tragic show had already begun. Soldiers began walking in. I bowed to them until my neck felt stiff. Some soldiers touched me as if I were a cheap whore and whispered, "I will see you in bed soon," as they passed by. I tried to numb all my senses so that my brain wouldn't think about why I was there or what I was doing. *You're a mannequin!* I told myself. *You can't hear or feel or think!*

Still, tears welled up in my eyes. I pictured Father, standing in front of a congregation. A Bible passage popped in my head. "Love and compassion for sinners and evil doers. Blest are those who are persecuted, for the reign of God will be theirs."

I began to see that these men were as powerless as I was. I felt better. They didn't want to be here. They had been fighting for too long and were sick of being the Emperor's malicious puppets. And they didn't know when the war would end! Given a choice, they'd run home immediately, abandoning their weapons and positions. They too were the victims of Hirohito's reunification policy. With this new awareness, I continued the bowing and greeting.

After a half-hour lunch break, I was sent to my room, and another girl, Yong Ja, took my place. I received soldiers until eight that night. Each soldier hurt me. Some of them slapped me when I screamed. I hated them. But more than anything, I hated my existence. By the end of the day, I didn't know who I was: I couldn't be the same girl whom my parents loved dearly and tried to protect with all their might. I was nothing more than an outhouse in a field where any Japanese soldier could release his bodily fluid.

Several different types of soldiers had passed through my room that day. Some rushed into the room with extreme urgency, but weren't anxious to leave when the time was up. These were young boys who didn't know why they were away from home and fighting, endangering their lives. Some cried, holding me tightly as if I were their beloved mother. They seemed to think that visiting the Comfort House was the greatest reward for being the Emperor's soldiers.

Some acted as if they were the scions of the most noble families in Japan, and we Korean girls were the filthy pigs they couldn't even look at. But oddly enough, they didn't mind disposing of their seminal fluid in us.

Only one soldier was different. He was polite. He asked me questions. He said he was a war correspondent for some newspaper in Kyoto.

"Do you mind if I ask you a few questions?" he began.

"Yes!"

But he asked me anyway. "How is the war shaping your life?" His manner was pleasant, as if he were interviewing a Hollywood star.

How is the war shaping my life? "Very well, thank you," I said tartly. "How about yours?"

I thought he smiled. "We're told that you Korean girls volunteered for the Women's Army, but is it true? If it is, what made you join the brigade? Money or devotion to your father-land?"

I clenched my teeth. Money? Devotion to my fatherland? I wanted to slap him. "There isn't anything to say." I tried hard to control my anger.

"Please, don't take it personally, Miss. I'm here doing my job. Your cooperation can be an eye-opener for some inland people. It's wartime. We are all in the same boat, struggling to survive."

"Curiosity can hurt people," I snapped. "I'm surprised you don't seem to know that! I'm not a monkey at the zoo, you know."

He was quiet for a moment. "Sorry if I hurt your feelings," he said.

His apology angered me even more. "Please leave me alone!" I said. He left.

The last soldier was evil. He gave me a purple bruise on my face and turned my room upside down. He was slightly older than the others and walked into my room rigidly and hatefully. He had two huge red scars on his face, one on his forehead and another on his left cheek, both about two inches long.

As soon as he got in bed he began kissing me, violently and disgustingly. I gently pushed him away, saying, "Sir, you aren't supposed to kiss me on the mouth. You're violating the rules set by the military."

To my horror, he got up, stripped naked, and reached for his saber. Twitching his facial muscles, he lifted the saber above my head and looked at me through fierce dark eyes.

I closed my eyes. I thought he was going to kill me. My eyelids fluttered and my teeth chattered against my will.

"Yyyyaaaht!" he shouted. The lamp next to my bed burst and the glass-chips fell on my face. My cheeks burned. I tried to remember a Bible passage: Blest are those who . . . who . . . but I couldn't remember the rest of the passage. I was shaking violently.

With another "Yyyyaaat," the saber hit my pillow. I thought I lost my left earlobe, but I didn't feel blood rushing out of it. Only the rice hulls jumped on my face. I pretended I was already dead.

Then I heard the manager's voice asking him what was wrong.

The soldier yelled, "This Chōsenjin is disrespectful of all imperial soldiers! I'll kill her if she doesn't apologize!"

"Keiko!" the manager called me sternly. "You know better than that. Apologize to him at once! Tell him it won't happen again."

I sat up, covering myself. I bowed to the soldier, shaking. "I am sorry, sir! I was only concerned about your own safety. The rules on the wall say the soldiers must never kiss the employees on the mouth. Please, sir, you must read it again if . . ."

A burning sensation numbed my left cheek. I saw the soldier's fist striking me again and again. I saw thousands of bright stars twinkling in my eyes. Before I could gather what was happening, he pulled my hair with startling force, dragging me to the floor. I hit the floor hard. He kept hitting me as if determined to beat a demon out of me. Each blow contorted my body, like the limb of a tree in a violent wind.

"So you can read, is that it?" The soldier shouted, heaving. "Are you saying you're educated but I'm not?"

"No, she's not saying that," the manager said, pleadingly. "You must not be violent. I'll call the MP at once if you don't stop this!"

"Violent?" The soldier turned toward the manager. "I'll show you what violence really is," he said. With another "Yyyyaaat!" he rose straight into the ceiling like a huge featherless bird, and his left foot struck the manager's chin.

The manager hit his head against the wall and sprawled on the floor.

Two sentries rushed into the room, blowing whistles.

Before they handcuffed him, the soldier calmly dressed as if nothing had happened, gathered his hat and saber, and walked out, leaving behind the huge mass of broken glass, a roomful of rice hulls, and an angry manager.

Embarrassed at his own pitiful look, the manager yelled at me, "Chōsenjin must know how to behave like a Chōsenjin!" Then he got up, shaking dust from his pants.

A memory flickered through my mind as I sat on the floor. My neighbors killed a rabid dog a couple years ago. No one knew where it came from. The dog's eyes were bloodshot and didn't seem to see accurately. Its mouth was full of a foamy substance, and its hair was matted with burrs and what seemed to be its own waste. It walked zigzag as if the road was curvy, growling at the men approaching it with hatchets, shovels, and brooms. Finally, a hatchet struck its head, and with a loud cry, the dog sprawled in the middle of the road. I could never forget its long and tragic tongue that licked the dirt.

The face of that evil soldier kept me awake that night while the smell of my own blood turned sour. I had no energy left in me. Have I had twenty-three soldiers or twenty-five? I had lost count.

Somewhere far away a bird was crying ever so mournfully. A rhythmic pattern repeated itself in its cry—three short chirps, pause, then two longer ones. It was music. What kind of bird was this? A handsome tropical bird or a tiny bird with an injured wing, separated from its own flock? It must be an injured one, chirping helplessly, attempting to fly again, dreaming of its own warm nest. All my pain melted into hot liquid, and finally, a sob escaped my lips.

Once a week we enjoyed the luxury of tasting freedom under the blue sky. Every Thursday morning, two soldiers brought huge bundles of green uniforms, dumped them on the wide rock next to the creek, and ordered us to wash them. Most of the uniforms had dark blood-stains. We scrubbed them with soap as large as a brick until the blood stains dissolved in the water. Then we hung them on the barbed wire to dry.

Occasionally, we watched a flock of American airplanes flying south, wings glittering against the sun like silver birds. We were told the Americans were fighting to recapture all the Japanese islands in the Pacific Ocean. Every day we saw a battalion of soldiers marching and running in the field, singing Japanese military songs. There was a rumor that soon we would be moving to another island.

Washing the bloody uniforms in the creek was a welcome

labor. Some girls thought the uniforms were from the dead soldiers and others said they belonged to the injured. In either case, we loved the freedom of being outside the barbed wire fence all day, breathing clean air under a brilliant sun while the clear water caressed our hands.

In the jungle next to the creek stood wild rubber plants and bushes and trees loaded with berries and fragrant flowers. The thought of berries melting on our tongues made us restless. We had been hungry ever since we left home. Most of the time, we had some gruel with green leaves and small chunks of tofu, but as the days went by the gruel became more and more watery. Now we couldn't grab anything with our chopsticks. We tasted rice only on special occasions as if it were sacred food. The last time we each had a bowl of rice was the day the Japanese captured ten thousand American soldiers on some island in the Philippines.

While washing the uniforms, we carefully measured the chance of being caught by the sentries who patrolled around the fenced area against the degree of our temptation for berries.

Kyung Hwa and Ayako were the brave souls of the bunch. They counted the soldiers' footsteps between the spots where they faced us and where their backs were turned to us, reassuring everyone that there was enough time for one of us to sneak into the woods, pick some berries, and come back before the guard turned around again. We unanimously agreed it was a worthwhile adventure since we must live first before worrying about dying.

We took turns sneaking into the jungle four times that afternoon and returned with berries, papaya, bananas, and the long green stems with sweet flesh. We sang "My Hometown" as a signal that the soldiers were away and stopped singing when the soldiers were about to turn toward us. We munched on the fruits and berries and chewed on the sweet, tender stems acquired with our own hands.

"It tasted better than anything I ever ate," Kyung Hwa said proudly when we gathered on the porch that night.

"Manna from heaven can't be better than that!" I agreed.

"If the apple Eve gave to Adam in the Garden of Eden was as good as those berries," Ayako said, smiling mischievously, "I can't blame Eve for luring Adam into sin."

"Aigo, stop talking that Bible stuff," Hae Sook yelled, frowning. "This is not a Sunday School!"

In any case, our new adventure into the jungle elevated our spirits as well as our metabolism.

The following week, I was the first to go into the woods. It was beautiful. The sun filtered through thick green leaves, and red and purple berries glowed on every branch like jewels. The moisture in the woods created a transparent fog, and the air moving upward in the slanting sun made the jungle a mysterious sanctuary.

I gathered at least two bowlfuls of berries, a few bananas and mangoes fallen from the trees, and some yellowish fruits that had a sour fragrance. When my skirt couldn't hold any more, I turned around.

I saw something squirming under a bush. I stepped back; I thought it was an animal. As I approached the bush, slowly and carefully, I saw a tiny foot with five little toes. I bent down and pushed the branches back to get a better view of the child. It was a boy about five or six years old with golden hair and ivory white skin. His dirty clothes told me that he had been lost for some time.

I gently shook him, afraid he might scream at me. He only squirmed. He will die here, I thought. But what could I do? The only thought I had was that the child might belong to one of the huts next to the jungle.

Then I heard the girls singing. I quickly got up, dropped a handful of berries next to the child, and hurried toward the creek. As I returned to my spot, I dumped everything on the rock next to me and began washing the uniforms. My appetite for berries had vanished. I was worried about the child now.

"What took you so long?" Kyung Hwa came over and whispered, grabbing a handful of red berries and stuffing her mouth. Kyung Hwa and I had no secrets between us.

I told her about the child.

Her eyes widened. "Maybe we can save him, Soon-ah," she said.

"No, it's too dangerous," I said. "We must leave him alone."

She stared at me as if she had never seen such a heartless person, muttering, "You've changed."

"Have I? Maybe I have. But what's the point of saving him? So that the Japanese can kill him in samurai fashion?" I said defensively.

She wasn't listening. "That's it!" she said, looking into the creek. "That's who they were looking for last night! Soon-ah, do you remember seeing the lights flashing in the woods?" she asked.

The previous night several of us had been sitting on the front steps watching the stars and chattering. Some special training had been going on in the camp all day and we hadn't received any soldiers. Someone said, "Look, something's going on in the woods," and we all looked toward the woods. Some lights were blinking in the dark.

"That's the Japanese ghosts trying to find their way to hell," I said, but no one laughed. Someone else said they were the military policemen trying to capture a runaway soldier.

There had been many runaway soldiers since we arrived, creating commotions in the wood. Often we had heard sharp whistles, shrieking voices, and barking dogs shattering the stillness of the night. Several soldiers had been beheaded in the woods, I had heard.

"They might have been the boy's parents looking for him," Kyung Hwa said excitedly. "We must find his parents. We must!"

"But how?" I said, incredulously. "If the soldiers find out, they will kill him, don't you know it? When you yourself don't know how long you will last here, why worry about others?"

"No, we must do something!"

"Leave him alone!"

But Kyung Hwa ran into the jungle as soon as her chance arrived. We waited until the soldiers turned their backs to us and began singing. We sang louder and louder as the time passed. We were all aware of the danger we were facing now and couldn't tolerate the thought that something terrible would happen: they would soon discover Kyung Hwa's absence. We sang the entire first verse but no sign of Kyung Hwa anywhere. In the middle of the second verse, the soldiers began walking toward us. We stopped singing. I felt a chill on my back. I tried to pray but words tangled in my mouth.

As the sentries approached, looking directly at us, an idea flickered into my head. I abruptly stood and moved around a little, acting as if I were in need of emptying my bladder. I held the front of my skirt and rushed to a bush, sensing the soldiers' eyes were following me. I sat behind the bush and emptied myself.

As I returned, the soldiers were looking at me, laughing and pointing. I covered my face with one elbow as if I were embarrassed, fiercely glancing back at the woods trying to see any movement there. When I lowered my elbow, the soldiers were stiffly walking away.

I was relieved, but Kyung Hwa still wasn't back. We began singing again. We sang faster and faster, trying to indicate to Kyung Hwa that she should hurry. We sang the entire second verse. Stopping for breath, I heard a sound like a puppy whining. It became louder. It was a child's cry. Luckily the sound of the creek muffled the noise somewhat, but it was clearly audible from where I was. I couldn't breathe.

Then Kyung Hwa returned. Her face was red from running.

"He's alive," she panted.

I didn't say anything. Obviously, she didn't know that the child was somewhere closer and was crying.

"He's not dead!" she said louder, as if she thought I couldn't hear her clearly enough.

"The soldiers will be walking this way any minute," I said quickly, turning around to see if the child was visible. My heart dropped. The little boy, his hair shining like gold threads, was standing behind the bush where I had urinated only minutes ago. *He must have squeezed himself through dense trees and vines to get here so quickly,* I thought.

"Hey!" he yelled as soon as his eyes met mine.

I quickly turned my back on him. My hands shook. The soldiers were walking in our direction again. I abruptly began beating the uniform I was washing against the surface of the creek, splashing. I hoped to block the view and the sound of the child from the soldiers.

The soldiers drew closer. It seemed every step they took pushed us into a deeper panic. I thought I would faint any minute.

The child yelled louder, "Hey!"

The soldiers stopped walking. They cocked their rifles and looked in our direction. My knees trembled violently. I heard the swishing noise of the branches behind me and another "Hey!" still louder.

The soldiers began running toward us.

My knees buckled and I sat down against my will.

With loud popping noises bullets hit the water, shooting columns of water everywhere. Kyung Hwa leaped into the bush where the child stood. I had no time to stop her as the rocks around me sparked bluish lights and an invisible hand pushed me, making me fall backward. I thought I heard Kyung Hwa shriek.

The shooting stopped as suddenly as it began. The soldiers

rushed to us swinging their rifles. "Get up!" one soldier shouted at me, poking my leg with the tip of his rifle.

I got up, shaking. I was surprised I wasn't hurt. *Was Kyung Hwa hit?*

The soldiers ordered us to return to the comfort station and they ran to the bushes. They pulled Kyung Hwa's limp body, and dragged her to the House as if she was a bundle of laundry. I saw her blood marking two straight lines on the dirt.

Dazed, I began to follow the soldiers. I stopped. I wanted to see the boy; he might be still alive. I walked fast to where he had stood, yelling at the top of his voice.

His tiny body lay still behind the bush as if peacefully resting. The massive blood stain under him told me he was dead. I wanted to shake him and scold him: *Why were you lost in the woods, you naughty little boy? Why didn't you listen to your mother?* But instead I bent my head and cried. To me, he was another Chin Soo, my little brother back home whose voice I often heard at night.

I gently closed his eyes and covered him with large rubber plant leaves. Whistles shrieked from the compound, and I got up.

Until late that night, I sat by Kyung Hwa's bed as she struggled to breathe. She was spitting blood and making a gurgling noise through her throat. My attempt to get a doctor for her had been denied. According to the nurse who gave Kyung Hwa some white powder for pain, the medical crew had left Palau Island to treat the injured soldiers in the south and had not returned yet. I couldn't bear the thought that my only friend was dying, and I yelled at the nurse, accusing her of lying. It was a waste of energy and I returned to watch my friend die.

We had known each other as long as I could remember. Now she was leaving me for good, and the distance between home and Palau Island seemed intolerable.

I kept wiping her forehead as the beads of sweat formed

rapidly. Between laborious breaths, Kyung Hwa told me that the child was sitting up when she found him in the woods. She picked some berries and fed him. He kept jabbering to her, maybe in English or French, but she couldn't understand a word he was saying. She carried him on her back and ran to the huts in an attempt to look for his parents, but there was no one, only the doors swinging back and forth in the wind.

Then she heard us singing and tried to tell him to stay in the woods until she came back later, but he clung to her desperately. She couldn't stay with him, nor could she leave him behind. As our singing got louder and faster, she finally pushed him to get away.

Her tears rolled down the side of her face when she finished. "You were right, Soon-ah, I should have listened to you," she said.

"No, you did the right thing. At least you showed him you cared for him."

A faint smile appeared on her lips. "Soon-ah ya, would you do me a favor?"

"Yes, of course."

"When you go back home, please go see my Omma for me, will you?"

"I will," I said with a tight throat.

"Tell Omma that . . . I loved her until the end. Also, tell her that I tried to save a child, too. She, she'd like to hear that." She struggled to push words through pale lips but stopped.

I grabbed her hand and squeezed. "Yes, Kyung Hwa ya, I'll tell her everything about you. I'll say, 'Mrs. Lee, your daughter wanted to save a little boy who was lost in the woods. That's how she was killed. She could have saved him if the Japanese didn't shoot, but . . . I was very lucky to have a friend like Kyung Hwa. She helped me so much.' That's what I'll tell her. Your Omma will be pleased."

Suddenly her hand slipped out of mine and hit the side of her mat.

"Kyung Hwa? No!" I screamed.

Her eyes fixed on my face, she was still as if she were forcing herself not to breathe. Her lips parted, forming a smile.

I fell on her, sobbing. "I hate you, Kyung Hwa! How can you leave me alone in this awful place? I thought we were friends. You're so selfish!" I cried aloud.

She responded to me with a deadly silence. When my tears finally dried, I looked at her serene face for the last time. Indeed, she was a lotus, the magical flower that has its root in the mud but arises from it in dazzling beauty.

The next morning, they wrapped Kyung Hwa's lifeless body in a white sheet, dropped it into a straw bag, loaded it onto a wagon, then pushed the wagon over the hill behind the compound. Sergeant Saigo pulled and the manager pushed, cursing and swearing in Japanese. The lonely funeral procession disappeared while we stood on the front steps and wept. Kyung Hwa was the second person to die since we left Korea. We wondered who would be next. Shortly, black smoke rose from behind the hill. They had burned many dead soldiers there before and the sickening scent of burning squid would hang in the air all day long. I couldn't understand why such a terrible smell rose from a burning body.

One day of survival was never a victory: it only brought another long day to hate, then another. Attempting to keep myself from crumbling seemed useless, and I missed my friend.

Every time I looked at the hill where Kyung Hwa had disappeared, I wanted to run there and bring her back.

One evening after dinner when the soldiers stopped coming in, and the manager fell asleep in his chair at the entrance, his head resting on the desk, I sneaked out of the back door and ran to the graveyard over the hill. In the middle of a gently sloping field was a huge rock, as large as Emperor Hirohito's portrait in our classroom in Sariwon. I felt my hair rising and goose bumps crawling on my arms when I saw a large soot-covered metal drum sitting in front of the rock, surrounded by a mess of half burned firewood and a heap of dark ashes. *That's where Kyung Hwa was burned!* I quickly turned my eyes to the left where about thirty wooden sticks were pointing at the sun-setting sky. I walked through the sticks and weeds, looking for the most recent grave, sensing my heart beating fast. Then I stood before a stick marked "Comfort Woman–1" protruding from a square meter of red dirt.

This was what's left of Kyung Hwa! I squatted down and touched the dirt. Unlike the look of it, it was hard like a large rock.

"Kyung Hwa ya," I whispered to her, sensing a lump in my throat. "I hope you're happy where you are. I can't stand not having you around. I miss you so much, Kyung Hwa ya. You took everything with you—your laughs, your revengeful thoughts and plots against the Japanese, and your encouraging words. We all miss you. Manager lectured me today for not smiling at the soldiers. I guess one of them complained. . . ."

Swallowing the lump in my throat, I heard footsteps. I turned, trembling. "Ayako!" I cried. "You scared me."

Ayako looked as scared as I was. "I'm sorry, Soon-ah, I didn't mean to scare you. I saw you sneaking out the door and decided to follow you." She lifted a bouquet of withering flowers from her skirt pocket. "Look! They're already dying. I picked them today. . . . " she said, touching the red petals.

"They're beautiful!" I said, taking the bouquet from her.

"Kyung Hwa will appreciate your thoughtfulness." I laid the flowers next to the stick that said "Comfort Woman–1." The flowers added much color to her resting place. "Look, I can see Kyung Hwa smiling," I said.

"Damn Japanese!" Muttering angrily, Ayako bent her head and cried. I cried too, looking down at the red flowers.

Ayako and I became friends after that. She was only a year older than me but looked much older and more mature than her eighteen years. She reminded me of Kyung Hwa because she too was outgoing and had many wild thoughts in her head. Unlike most of us, Ayako didn't have a Korean name because her father didn't think it was necessary since we had no country of our own and Ayako was only a girl, not a boy.

But Ayako had something none of us had—a dream. She wanted to be a landowner someday and support her parents in their old age. Since she was the oldest of five girls, she was determined to perform a son's duty. She greedily kept all of the yellow tickets she received from the soldiers: her drawer was full of them. Occasionally, she might exchange some for needle and thread or paper, but she never exchanged them for a jar of lotion or a pair of socks or shoes like the other girls did. Every night she emptied her drawer and counted them over and over again, like a usurer counting money. Once I asked her, "What are you going to do with those tickets when a bomb drops and kills us all?"

"*Aigo!* Why such a gruesome thought?" she reproached me, rolling her eyes. "Didn't Mencius say, 'Plant a persimmon tree today even if you know you'll die tomorrow?' Soon-ah, these tickets will bring me a thousand pieces of gold someday," she said, shaking a handful of them in the air.

Ayako loved to say, "Mencius said this" or "Confucius said that" but we really couldn't argue with her because none of us were experts about those Chinese thinkers who died long before Jesus was born. We envied her, however, because she wasn't sorry for herself. She was one of the rare Korean girls who had "volunteered" to be a member of the Women's Army of Japan. Japanese officers had visited her parents and courteously offered three hundred yen if they'd allow one of their daughters to join the Women's Army of Japan. And she did.

"My father, lying on his mat, only mumbled unintelligibly, his dark eyes wandering aimlessly about the ceiling," Ayako told me as I sat on her mat and listened. Sitting on the floor like Buddha, her back against the wall, Ayako's mind was with her father ten thousand li away.

"Once he was a well-to-do farmer with many tenants farming for him. But after the Japanese took over the country and drafted all of his workers to Manchuria, his situation changed rapidly. He lost everything. Soon he couldn't pay the harvest tax and couldn't even feed us—Omma and his five daughters. To make the situation worse, the Japanese tortured him when he refused to give up the land that had been in his family for centuries. While the unpaid tax increased, his health declined. Finally one morning, all of his land was auctioned, and a Japanese farmer bought it at a hideously low price. That night, my father tried to hang himself. It was awful, Soon-ah!" She stopped and covered her face with her trembling hands.

I felt tears gathering in my own eyes as I remembered my father being murdered by the Japanese. One thing we Koreans had in common were unlimited tears.

She wiped her eyes and continued, "Our neighbors came and lowered his limp body from our old persimmon tree in the backyard. Watching him struggling to come back to life, I swore to God I'd do anything for Him if He'd let Father live. As if God had heard me, two Japanese officers walked into our courtyard a few days later and told Father that if he would allow one of his daughters to join the Emperor's brigade, he would receive three hundred yen from the Japanese government. I immediately handed them Father's seal without thinking twice about it. Omma cried bitterly and tried to take the seal away from me, saying, 'We'd rather die than sell you,

Ayako!' but I won. Three hundred yen! Think about it, Soon-ah. Who would turn down an offer like that?" Her face glowed like a heaven-bound soul.

I told her my family's tragedy that night, too: that my brother was conscripted in the army, my father was murdered, and Omma was raped by a policeman in broad daylight.

When we didn't have to receive soldiers or when we were at the creek, we talked endlessly, recycling our memories of home and beating our heads, trying to see what lay ahead of us. One day while the image of the jungle shimmered at the bottom of the creek, Ayako confessed that she was in love with a Korean conscript. My mouth fell open. This was a big scandal! No Koreans or Chinese were allowed into the Comfort Houses: we were strictly for the Japanese Imperial soldiers. How could she do this?

"Are you out of your mind? What if they find out?" I hissed at her. Such information could easily leak to the manager. Then what?

"He never touches me, Soon-ah. He only wants to talk," she said, defensively. It was obvious that she wasn't too comfortable with the idea either.

"It doesn't matter what he does or doesn't do. He isn't supposed to be in the compound. How did he arrange the visit?"

"He told me he bought a ticket from a Japanese soldier who makes money by selling tickets at a higher price to Korean and Chinese conscripts. Can you believe it? He paid three yen to come see me." Ayako's face bloomed as if she had suddenly discovered she was worth three yen.

"He's crazy!" I said.

"Well, if he isn't worried about being caught, why should I be? I'm sure he knows what he's doing. Anyway, I like him a lot, Soon-ah. His name is Moon Ho," Ayako chattered away.

I acted as if I wasn't listening. I couldn't believe she was that stupid. Wasn't she sick of the smell of her own blood draining out of her? Didn't she have enough pain when the Japanese men forced themselves on her?

Obviously unconcerned with my disgust, she kept on talking, "Moon Ho is a sensitive man. When he first came to see me, he stood in the middle of the room and wept as if he thought my room were a funeral parlor. I had received soldiers from ten that morning and I couldn't keep my eyes open. I glanced at him once, but I had no strength to argue or tell him to stop crying. I drifted to sleep while he was still standing there. Some hospitality, huh?"

I ignored her glance penetrating into the side of my face.

"He came back the following week, and his eyes were teary again the moment he saw me. It really bothered me. 'I'm not dying, you know,' I snapped. 'Why are you crying whenever you see me?' You know what he said? 'Forgive me. I didn't mean to upset you.' His voice was congested from crying. He walked over to me and held me in his arms, crying louder. 'I'm sorry! I'm very sorry that you women have to go through this! We men are responsible for your agony!'"

"Why did he say that?" I asked.

"I don't know, but I had tears in my eyes too. I was sad for him as well as for myself. He was my age, a boy forced to fight for Japan. Surely, somebody must be responsible for this, I thought."

"But who?" I said angrily. "Emperor Hirohito?"

"I don't know who," Ayako's voice was subdued. "It doesn't matter, really. What matters is that it might be our fate, the fate of all Koreans, to shed tears like this, holding onto one another. Our feelings are all we own, Soon-ah!"

I didn't say anything. I vigorously scrubbed the uniform on the rock, looking at my reflection in the water trembling like a mirage.

"After our tears dried, we talked: he was a law student at Tokyo University before he was conscripted, and I told him I was a high school girl before I volunteered for the Women's Army. His eyes got red again. He has a sister back home a year younger than me and he hopes that she is all right. Watching him closely, I thought, *He's handsome!* He wears glasses, has ink-black hair and smooth, gentle facial lines. I thought to myself, *I wouldn't mind if he touches me.* But we only talked until his time ran out."

"I can't believe you. You're too crazy!"

"He comes to see me regularly now," Ayako went on, ignoring me. "Once in a while, I wonder what it'd be like if we became lovers. Do you know what I mean?"

"What do you expect me to say? Do you want me to jump up and down?" I snorted. I didn't know why I felt so angry.

"But Soon-ah," she said, rising to her feet, stretching her back, and looking over to where some colorful birds circled around a nipa tree, "at night I'm full of crazy thoughts. I see myself in a wedding ceremony, wearing colorful bridal garments and bowing at Moon Ho, his parents, and his ancestors in the framed-pictures. People throw rice at us, shouting good wishes and longevity. When I wake up, I want to scream. I hate what I see around me. I'm too angry to realize it's only a dream."

"How can you think about a man and marriage after all this torture? Aren't you sick of men?"

"No, I'm not," Ayako said decisively, and squatted next to me. "Soon-ah, you don't know everything about men, okay? What you see is not everything. There are good men too." She looked at me as if I were a child ignorant of life and romance.

I snorted. "You'll regret it, Ayako, acting so stupid. Men are men, Koreans or Japanese! They want only one thing from women, and that's all they want. Please don't tell me about your sickening romance any more. I can't take it!" I rose and changed my place.

I avoided her after that. I knew something was coming. I was angry too and I missed Kyung Hwa. What would she say if she knew Ayako were seeing a Korean conscript in the compound? Certainly she'd agree with me that Ayako was crazy.

But Ayako still made an effort to talk to me. She left a note on my door one morning: "Soon-ah, you are my best friend forever. Please don't be angry with me. It hurts!"

I never responded to her note.

One evening at dinner, she came over and whispered in my ear that she had something important to tell me. I waited until the table was wiped and all the dishes were washed and put away before following her to her room. Beaming with a strange smile, she said, "Promise not to tell anyone, okay?"

"Okay."

"Moon Ho and I made love last night."

"What?" I actually felt my mouth dropping.

"It's true. We planned it and did it!"

"You'll both get killed, Ayako!"

"They'll never find out. We are in love, Soon-ah. He told me I'm his first love. He was a virgin, you know."

I felt sick. What kind of ignorant behavior was this? Who cared whether he was virgin or not! "Ayako, I can't stand the thought that I might lose another friend. The soldiers will have a field day when they discover this. Are you not afraid? Do you think the Japanese are going to forget about their rules? If you care enough for Moon Ho, you must stop seeing him immediately. You only have one life to live."

Ayako smiled: I knew she wasn't afraid of being caught. She looked at me as if she worried about me instead of herself. Maybe she thought I was jealous of her because she had something I might never have?

"Nothing can change the way we feel," she said. "We crossed a bridge last night, a bridge of love. We took an irreversible step toward the unknown, holding hands. Soon-ah, it's so wonderful to be in love," she said and looked at the darkening window, her eyes glowing.

"I wish you my best," I said sarcastically and turned around. "Bye, Ayako!"

"Look!" She suddenly rose, opened her drawer, and pulled out a black nightgown, scattering yellow tickets carelessly. It was as transparent as the wings of a dragonfly. "Moon Ho told me he bought this at a shop near the Officers' club. He went through so much trouble to get this for me for our honeymoon."

"Honeymoon? How romantic!"

"Yes!" she said, blushing a little. "Last night was the beginning of our new life together. We're inseparable now, Soon-ah. Look, he gave me this ring, too." She extended her left hand toward me. "It's pure silver. He said if we survive the war, he'd buy me a diamond ring. Isn't he so beautiful? He had tears in his eyes and thanked me for accepting his ring. Soon-ah, I don't envy any woman, not even Empress Nagako."

I said nothing and walked out the squeaking door. My heart was heavy: I knew nothing could change the situation. It was only a matter of time before the Japanese would find out about them. I could almost see Moon Ho being beheaded by an executioner. As soon as I came to my room, I wrote her a note:

> My dearest Ayako:
>
> I feel so helpless. It seems there's nothing I can do to prevent you from seeing Moon Ho. You don't seem to see the danger around you and Moon Ho. I'm happy that you are in love but I'm terrified at the possibility that you might get caught. Please be careful, okay? I sincerely hope that everything will be okay and you'll be happy with Moon Ho forever.
>
> Lovingly,
> Soon-ah

A few days later, I met Moon Ho. That morning we heard an ear-shattering siren, indicating that a special training session was beginning in the field. Once in a while a siren would go off, and the soldiers fought with invisible foes, running, kicking, shooting, and shouting. It was entertaining when we had nothing else to do, but a nuisance when we tried to rest. Ayako had awakened with a cold that morning and was in bed, so I went out alone to join the idle girls watching the soldiers.

A long, thick line of soldiers appeared at the far end of the road, singing a familiar military hymn:

> *Under the Rising Sun I pledge my allegiance,*
> *Without glory and honor I shall not return.*
> *Till the trumpet blares our victory,*
> *I'll fight, courageously and steadfastly.*
>
> *To Imperial Majesty I pledge my allegiance,*
> *I, the descendant of samurais, fear no death.*
> *Even mountains and rocks obey my command.*
> *I'd rather die than shame Imperial Majesty.*

They marched rigidly, looking ahead and moving their legs and arms mechanically. Only one soldier wearing glasses in the middle row turned his head and looked searchingly at us.

I knew it was Moon Ho: his face was too Korean not to recognize it. I didn't know how to signal him that Ayako wasn't feeling good and was in bed.

As the soldiers marched away the military hymn drifted along with the words of devotion. I was anxious to tell Ayako about Moon Ho and turned around. Then I heard a panting voice behind me. "Please, ma'am. Is Ayako all right?"

Standing against the fence and sweating profusely, Moon Ho was slightly trembling. I looked around to see if the manager was nearby before I quickly whispered, "She's fine. She has a cold. Nothing to worry about."

Moon Ho dug in his pocket, took out a small bag of candy, and pushed it through the chain link fence. "Please, give this to her. Tell her I'll be back as soon as the drill is over."

I hurried to Ayako. She lay in her bed with her eyes closed. She looked feverish.

"Somebody asked me to give this to you." I dropped the bag of candy on her comforter.

"Who?" Ayako jumped up and opened the bag. "How sweet!" she cried, her eyes sparkling. She dumped the bag. A dozen colorful jawbreakers fell out.

There was something nauseating about watching my best friend madly in love when I had no one. I almost wanted to smother her with her pillow. Instead, I said acidly, "That lover of yours might get killed if he's not careful. He abandoned his line while his commander was watching. Tell him to behave like a normal soldier if he doesn't want to die."

"I'll tell him," Ayako said, playing with her jawbreakers, but she showed no signs of anxiety. She picked up a red candy and gave it to me. I shook my head. I didn't want to eat candy from her lover.

"Come on, take it!" she insisted, pushing it into my palm. "You're my best friend, Soon-ah. Never think I don't love you anymore because of Moon Ho. I do! Friends and lovers are different. But your heart has space for both. A friend is someone you appreciate and trust for the rest of your life, but a lover is someone you want to die for. Believe me, you'll understand when you have a lover."

I reluctantly took it. I peeled the clear wrapper off and popped it into my mouth. The cinnamon taste soothed my hurt somewhat and I said, "I love cinnamon candies. Omma used to buy them at the Japanese market for our birthdays."

Ayako dropped one into her mouth too. We sat and quietly sucked the candies, listening to another military hymn approaching us.

> *Run, samurais, run!*
> *through thickets, rivers, and fields.*
> *victory is your only aim.*
> *Run, samurais, run. . . .*

"Soon-ah, the parade is coming back, isn't it?" Ayako asked, lifting her comforter. Her legs under her cotton nightgown looked thinner than I remembered.

"But you're sick!"

"I want to see Moon Ho," she said, standing, trying to find her shoes.

"You have a fever, Ayako. You'd better stay in bed."

Stubbornly, she wrapped herself with a white shawl, and hurried outside.

I followed her. A different group of soldiers was passing by now. We waited for Moon Ho's group to appear. After a long wait we caught a glimpse of him. But alas! I wish I hadn't told Ayako about him. He now was at the end of the line, separated from his own group. Behind him was Sergeant Kimura, whose nickname was "Shark." Moon Ho was jogging, hollering some unintelligible words and holding his rifle across his head. A large sandbag was attached to his back where sweat made a huge dark spot. His steps faltered as if he would collapse at any minute, his sweat-covered face glistening against the blazing sun.

Ayako moaned, "Moon Ho!"

I didn't know how to comfort her. "He'll be all right, Ayako!" I said, pulling her away from the fence, trying to take her back to her bed.

She shook her head, her fingers clung to the wire fence like the claws of a caged bird. "They're going to kill him, Soon-ah!" she blurted. "If I had a gun, I'd shoot that Sergeant Kimura!" She leaned her forehead against the fence and cried.

Sadness struck me and I looked up at the sky. Two white birds with bushy heads were flying over our heads toward the sea, innocently crooning to one another. Where were they moving to? I wondered. To build a new nest somewhere? I understood Ayako's pain. They couldn't fly away like those birds. In this doomed place, they couldn't even tend their dreams. My heart twisted.

But Moon Ho survived. He came back the following week with sunken cheeks and smiled broadly, showing his broken front tooth, when he saw Ayako running toward him.

I was in the hallway greeting soldiers and Manager was near me, collecting money. I knew he saw everything—Moon Ho's smile and Ayako's excitement. As Moon Ho and Ayako walked to her room, holding hands, Manager's gaze followed Moon Ho, unwilling to let go of him. I knew what he was thinking: no comfort woman would show so much excitement at seeing a Japanese soldier.

"Isn't it a beautiful day, Mr. Nakamura?" I said, trying to shift his mind from Moon Ho.

"That boy who's with Ayako . . . ," he said, without looking at me, "Isn't he a Chōsenjin?"

"Chōsenjin?" I acted shocked. "Mr. Nakamura! Do you think they'd be brave enough to come here, knowing they'd be punished? Most of them are too scared even to be alive. I've never seen a Chōsenjin or a Chinese yet since I've been in Palau."

But Manager wasn't too convinced. "He doesn't look like one of our boys," he said. "He's too tall for a Japanese. I'm going to investigate this!" He moved toward Ayako's room.

I didn't follow him: I didn't want to show that I was overly concerned about a Chōsenjin, a worthless conscript.

The manager came out a few minutes later with a strange smile. "Keiko, I was wrong!" he said, rather softly, making me suspicious. "He not only speaks like a Japanese but is intelligent too. He gave me this!" He lifted a silver pipe covered with intricate flower designs. "This is made in a little village called Yui where many artistic people lived a long time ago. This is worth at least a hundred yen!" Muttering, he disappeared into his room.

That night I warned Ayako. "How can you act so innocent when Manager was watching you? You're so thoughtless sometimes." Ayako laughed. "Aigo, you worry too much, Soon-ah. I wish you could've seen Moon Ho when Manager walked in here. He tricked him, telling him that he had been born in Tokyo and that his ancestor was Mochizuki, a samurai retainer to Shingen, who moved to Okitsu near Yui and founded Managuchi-ya, a well known hotel on the coast. He's something else! Manager only said, 'Ah so! Ah so!' smiling like a puppy."

"I hope you're right, Ayako."

Soon, the rumor reached us that Division 35 from Palau, a total of 6,000 soldiers, would be moving to Guadalcanal to build an airstrip there. Ayako burst into tears when Manager announced at breakfast that the rumor was true and the division was indeed leaving in five days. "It's much worse than you think, girls," he said in a low voice. "Our soldiers are dying from diseases like malaria, dysentery, and beriberi. The island produces basically nothing and often the merchant ships don't reach it because those Yankees sink them," he said, spitting into his grayed handkerchief that had once been white.

Five days weren't long for lovers. What could they do in five days? How could they properly say all the things they wanted to say? No soldiers came to the comfort station after the manager announced the news.

Ayako grieved as if Moon Ho were dead. While crying and sighing, she cut her Korean dress, made a red silk pouch, and embroidered on it, "To Moon Ho with love." She asked me to cut off a lock of her long hair and put it in. I did. She also severed a small portion of her transparent black nightgown in the shape of a heart and enclosed it in the same pouch. Then she waited for Moon Ho, night and day, sniffling and crying.

On the night before their departure, I woke up to a soft tapping noise on the door and knew it was Moon Ho. Ayako's door quietly opened and I heard her footsteps. The back door opened and closed. The manager had a telephone connected to the military police, and I worried the noise might wake him up. After Ayako and Moon Ho safely walked into Ayako's room without disturbing the manager, I was relieved and tried to go back to sleep.

But I was wrong. A few minutes later, I heard Sergeant Kimura walking in with an MP, shouting at Manager, and rushing toward Ayako's room. There was no way Sergeant Kimura could've found out about Moon Ho and Ayako unless Manager phoned him.

All of us rushed out and huddled together in the hallway, crying and shivering. Sergeant Kimura was yelling: "You worthless Chōsenjin! You disobeyed me again." The thud of boots followed. Moon Ho was screaming. Then Ayako's sharp cry, "Stop hurting him!" rang in the air again and again. Her voice made us cry even harder.

Gunfire startled us into silence, ending Ayako's scream. I couldn't move nor think, imagining her falling on the floor, spurting blood everywhere. I pulled my hair to halt my ominous thought. As if confirming my fear, Moon Ho growled in Korean, "You dwarf, I'll kill you!"

Sergeant Kimura roared, too. "You lazy Chōsenjin! You hate to obey me, don't you? I'll grant your wish!" I imagined the two men rolling in blood, Ayako's blood. The MP blew the whistle again, but it sounded frail and meaningless.

Another gunshot ended all noises. We were too afraid to find out who killed who. If Moon Ho killed the Sergeant, the Japanese army would certainly behead him. If Sergeant Kimura. . . . I couldn't think any more.

After a few minutes, I saw Sergeant Kimura walk out of the room, his skin as pale as a ginger-root, sweating heavily. Blood stains on his uniform confirmed all my fear. The MPs followed him and they disappeared into the darkness.

The manager went back to his own room, clicking his tongue and muttering, "Damn Chōsenjin! They left me more bodies to get rid of!" I ran to Ayako's room to have a last look at her and Moon Ho. It was horrid: Moon Ho was still alive, elbowing inch-by-inch toward Ayako, bleeding profusely and breathing laboriously. It seemed he was determined to touch Ayako's lifeless hand two feet away. I pushed her toward him. She was still warm and covered with blood. Moon Ho grabbed her hand and dropped his face on it. Then he let out his last breath of air, *Uhhhhhh!* like a punctured tire.

Looking at them holding hands together in the puddle of blood, I was more angry than sad. Hysterically, I opened Ayako's drawer, took out all of the yellow tickets, and threw them in the air. Watching the yellow papers flying in all directions and landing slowly on their bodies, I laughed coldly, "I'm happy for you, Ayako, I really am! Where's your persimmon tree?"

$\mathcal{M}$onsoon arrived. The sky turned black in the middle of the day and the wind shouted, racing down the dusty road, snatching bundles of dried leaves from the rooftops and skirts and blouses from our clotheslines. Trees and bushes convulsed violently, throwing leaves and limbs into the air. Thunder roared and the rain, as hard as bamboo sticks, beat down the earth as if the bottom of the sky had given in.

The sulky weather brought mildew and dysentery. Several girls became feverish, passing bloody stools. I too was sick: I bled and endured nausea. A fourteen-year-old girl became the first victim of dysentery, dying alone in her room. She too rode the wagon and disappeared over the hill.

On the same day, a soldier in yellow overalls came with a truck and sprayed the entire building with a milk-white liquid that gave off the same strong scent of the antiseptic solution we had in the bathroom. When finished, the soldier told us to gather in the kitchen and handed each of us a packet of tiny white pills, as tiny as mung beans. "This is medicine. You must take one in the morning and one at night before bedtime," he lectured us. "Dysentery is a serious illness: it can kill you. Once contracted, you might experience high fever, painful diarrhea, and bloody stools. I advise you to eat only boiled food and get plenty of rest."

"Get plenty of rest? How can we do that?" a voice muttered softly, but no one responded.

"Now, girls," Manager clapped his hands twice, appearing from the hallway. "Sergeant Sasaki suggested that a trip to the clinic might be a good idea at this point," he said, turning to look at the soldier. When the soldier nodded approvingly, he asked us, "Can you be ready in five minutes? He can drop you off on his way there."

The Women's Diseases Unit in the two-story military hospital was filled with comfort women from all over Palau. The smell of sweat and alcohol was so strong that I sat next to a window where the salty breeze soothed my nausea. Every woman in the room was fanning herself with something— bamboo fans or paper fans or magazines or bare hands. Nurses, all Japanese, were busily moving about the room, occasionally glancing officiously in our direction.

Some girls flipped through the magazines such as *Big Boys and Pretty Girls,* and *Dolls and Samurais,* which contained explicit pictures of naked men and women, and giggled secretively, whispering to one another. Others talked about sexual diseases:

"Never contract syphilis, girls. Once you get it, you can never get rid of it, never!" a woman warned.

"*Aigo,* do we have a choice? When a soldier gives it to me, should I say, "No, thank you, sir!" and give it back to him?" one woman asked in a sarcastic tone.

They laughed.

"You know what you should do?" another asked.

"What?"

"Japanese are polite people, you know. You should bow to the man giving you the germs and say 'Arigato!' Why not be polite about it?"

They laughed again.

"That's not funny! Syphilis is not something you can laugh about. I have been the victim of syphilis as well as Fluid 606. *Uggghh!* Whenever I swallow that medicine, all my intestines start squirming in my belly. Listen, just be careful, okay? Use the antiseptic solution regularly."

I covered my ears. I had already heard too much about syphilis, the incurable disease that affected your eyesight as well as your brain activity, and I didn't want to think about it. I let my eyes wander about the ceiling where two wooden beams joined together, and remembered Omma's birthday was approaching. This was the first birthday she'd celebrate without Father. She and Chin Soo would sit before Father's dome-like grave and she'd talk to him, her voice quivering. "Yubo! This is my first birthday I celebrate without you," she'd say. "Last year we were four, remember? But now only you, me and Chin Soo. The Japanese took our daughter to a brothel somewhere in the Pacific. Are you able to see her from where you are, Yubo? Please let her know we're all right and tell her to take care of herself. Send Wook our love, too. I try not to worry too much. . . ."

"Omura Keiko!" a woman's voice startled me. A nurse stood in the middle of the room with a chart in her hand. I quickly stood, saying, "I'm she."

She motioned me to follow her and walked ahead of me, her hips swaying. We passed a long corridor, turned a corner and walked into a large room where four beds lay in each corner. Despite the folding screens standing next to each bed, I could see half naked women lying on the beds with their legs wide open.

Up close, the nurse didn't look older than twenty-three or twenty-four. She ordered me to undress from the waist down, and climb onto the empty bed.

I did.

"Bend your knees and open them wide."

I did that too.

She picked up a funnel-like instrument from the table at the foot of the bed and pushed it into me. A shock of cold tingled my spine and I shivered. By the way she looked at me, I knew she disliked all Koreans.

Then she squeezed some cold fluid into me and poked my organs with a long instrument until they hurt. I wanted to mention my ongoing bleeding but my tongue was stiff.

"Are you using the antiseptic solutions after each intercourse?" she asked in a harsh tone.

"Yes."

"Are you insisting that the soldiers use saku, the hygienic condom?"

"Yes, but some soldiers refuse to use them."

"You must insist! It's up to you whether or not. . . ."

"I do insist," I cut her short. *How stupid*, I thought. "Why do you think I don't insist? Because I'm dying to conceive a Japanese baby?"

The nurse lifted her face and looked at me as if I had insulted the entire Japanese race. Her dark eyes pierced into mine like arrows and I stared at them. I disliked her, but more than anything, I disliked myself lying in this ridiculous position, needing her service.

"You have a bad attitude, Chōsenjin!" she declared coldly. "I'll not tolerate this!" She dropped the funnel-like device noisily on the table and took off her gloves.

She can get me in trouble, I thought. She could order a guard to drag me out of the hospital or she could slap me in the face or kick me until she was satisfied. I imagined myself laughing my head off as she struck me and kicked me repeatedly.

Instead, she picked up a silver bell and rang it loudly. A doctor with a mustache rushed in. "What's the matter?" he asked.

The nurse turned her chin toward me. "Doctor Kuwana, tell her that it's her responsibility to insist our soldiers use saku. Tell her what her stupidity might cost her and us." She stomped out of the room.

The doctor looked at me sympathetically. "Do you realize how important it is to use saku, young lady?" he asked.

"Yes."

"Then why aren't you following the rules?" He didn't seem contemptuous like the nurse.

"Some soldiers hate to use it. When we insist, they get angry and beat us. We can't control them."

The doctor winced. He then put his gloves on and picked up the instruments from the table.

What fate was this lying here, letting these Japanese touch me? I felt bitter. *I'm only seventeen.* My hands tightened and my nails dug into my palms.

The doctor took off his gloves.

I tried to read his mind. The wrinkles between his eyebrows deepened and his jaw clamped tightly as if he would never open his mouth again.

Is this bad news? Did I contract syphillis? My heart raced.

But the doctor's next words shocked me even more. "Your uterus is swollen. I think you're pregnant."

"Pregnant? Are you sure?"

He walked out of the room. The wooden cafe-door swung back and forth behind him indifferently.

The same nurse came in, drew blood from a vein, and gave me a clear cup for a urine sample.

I was scared. What if I was pregnant? I didn't want to have a Japanese baby, but what about the mortal sin I might commit by destroying it?

Half an hour later, I was gritting my teeth fighting pain while the doctor scraped my womb. I knew they might be destroying a life, but what could I do? Would God punish me for this? I overheard the nurse whispering, "Doctor Kuwana, if more Chōsenjin become pregnant, we will soon run out of medical supplies. Why don't you teach them once and for all that they *must* use *saku* whether they like it or not?"

Doctor Kuwana didn't say anything for a moment, then said, "We must educate our soldiers first! They're the ones who must know about human sexuality and conception."

Hot tears flowed down the side of my face and the pain left me. I could tolerate any pain or any hardship as long as there was an understanding heart, any heart, I promised myself.

When he was finished, the doctor scribbled something on a white sheet of paper and handed it to me. "Give this to your manager. You must not receive soldiers until the bleeding stops."

Four girls from our House got injections for gonorrhea and syphilis and were ordered not to receive soldiers. Two girls received some white powder for the lice that attacked the sexual organs.

When we came back to the House, Manager wasn't too happy. The fact that seven out of twenty girls couldn't receive one single soldier for an unlimited time was a hard blow, especially when a new shipment of soldiers had just arrived.

That evening, Manager cut seven squares of cardboard out of a brown box and wrote "Avoid!" with red ink on each. These signs were for all the incompetent women at the compound.

With the "Avoid!" on my door I was able to rest in my room for almost an entire week. I felt so weak and slept so much that I didn't even know the monsoon had moved away. On the fifth day, I slipped out the back door for the first time and sat on the porch, lost in the wilderness of beauty. In the shimmering heat, the bushes were full of red and yellow blossoms flirting with the sun. The creek murmured meditatively, glinting in the golden light. I was grateful that I still had some useful senses left in me to see this dazzling beauty. When I had been taken from home, the hills and mountains had been aflame with the blooming red azaleas, but I had been so paralyzed with fear that I hadn't had any time to admire them.

My vacation came to an end on the seventh day. The manager came into my room after breakfast and said that Sergeant Saigo had just arrived with a truck. "He came to get you and the other freeloaders," he said.

"But I'm still bleeding. Doctor Kuwana ordered me not to receive any soldiers." I protested.

"Doctor Kuwana? What does he care?" he said cynically. "Anyway, get ready. You're not going to receive soldiers, I promise you. You must wear mompei, your work pants! He's waiting outside."

How could I argue? I dressed and went outside. Six other girls stood on the front steps with long faces. They all had orders from the doctor not to do any work. We bowed toward the flag, then listened to Sergeant Saigo.

"Today we are going to build a war memorial in Babeldaop, the largest island of Palau. The Yankees sank a Japanese ship last night and about thirty officers and two hundred soldiers died near Yap Island. You will be given specific instructions when you get there."

He handed each of us a headband that said "Women's Army of Great Japan," a white mask made of gauze, and a shovel. I felt dizzy in the violent sunlight, but climbed onto the truck anyway. We made five stops to pick up more women before we arrived at Babeldaop. We were altogether about thirty.

The hill where the Japanese War memorial was being built overlooked thick and somber jungle on the left and blue ocean on the right. A dozen islands crouched in the water like a family of green hippopotamuses playing hide and seek. On the slope, some dark people were digging graves. Men wore loincloths made of wide brown leaves; the women's palm-leaf skirts exposed their dark, pear-shaped breasts. Several rows of dead bodies lay on one side, and next to the bodies sat crates waiting for their silent occupants. Between the bodies and crates lay a pile of fresh rice plants, still wet and glossy in the sunlight.

Armed soldiers walked back and forth. One soldier divided us into two groups, ordering one group to put bodies into crates with a handful of rice plants and the other to dig graves. I knew that Japanese people enclosed rice plants in the coffin as a symbol of prosperity.

I stood next to a pile of bodies and began to dig. The stench nauseated me. I had the mask on but the smell was still offensive. The truth was that I was more scared than sick: what if these dead Japanese men suddenly leaped on top of me like the live ones did? I moved a few steps away from the corpses.

The stench became more intolerable as the sun heated the earth. Beads of sweat dripped from my face. It was sweltering and I grew even weaker. I stopped briefly to regain my breath, but a soldier immediately came over, pointing his bayonet at me. "Don't stop! Keep digging!" he ordered.

I kept digging. I was thirsty and dizzy. And the stench!

Suddenly, Ok Ja, who was working nearby, moaned. She had been suffering nausea since she started her daily injection for gonorrhea. "I'm going to throw up!" she announced, then bent over and did it too.

As if intrigued by her vomit, my stomach suddenly leaped toward my throat. My shovel slipped out of my hand. All my energy vanished. I was lightheaded. I clenched my teeth not to vomit, but it was no use. I crouched over and did it.

A sharp whistle numbed my ears. "Get up!" a soldier shouted. I managed to stand up. The hill began to turn slowly, then hot fluid gushed from between my legs. The hill turned faster. The whole universe seemed to be swirling at a startling speed. My knees gave out, and I slumped to the ground as though all the bones in my body had melted in the heat. I saw blood soaking into the dirt. My own blood! The ear-shattering noise of an airplane deafened my ears, and I wished it would drop a bomb on the soldiers.

The soldier poked my side with the tip of his rifle and yelled, "Get up!" but I couldn't move. Everything was black as if the sky had turned dark. Sudden fear overpowered me.

"Soon-ah," I heard Ok Ja's voice. "Are you all right?" I couldn't answer her nor could I see her. Another blow landed on my back, then another, and another. Vague images appeared in my eyes then disappeared. *Your Omma's birthday is coming*, a voice said. *I must get up*, I thought, but I couldn't budge. Everything was quiet and I felt no pain.

It seemed I was floating in white vagueness. *Where am I?* I wondered, waking up. I felt as if I had slipped into an eternity. Where was everybody? I forced my eyes open. I could see the ceiling, bright and white. Why was the ceiling squirming? I was dizzy looking at the ceiling. Then it split open, and a white bundle came down from the gap, slowly and persistently. I knew what was in that bundle. It was Kyung Hwa's body. She was dead and came back to haunt me because I didn't visit her grave. "Go away!" I screamed as loud as I could.

A hand shook my arm. A blurry figure was looking down at me. It looked familiar and unfamiliar at the same time.

"Are you all right?" he asked. Then I recognized him: the correspondent.

"The white bundle! Look!" I said, pointing at the ceiling with my trembling hand.

"What white bundle?"

"There, there! It's coming down, can't you see it? It's going to fall on me! I don't want her to take me with her to her grave. Please stop her!" My voice grew louder and louder and I was screaming, covering my head with my arms.

"You must be having a nightmare," he said, shaking me harder. "Look at the ceiling and tell me what you see!"

I looked up, only to see a perfect square of white joined by four surrounding walls. *Was it a dream? No, it can't be. I saw it. But what happened to it?* I tried hard to focus my eyes on the correspondent but he was still a blurry mass.

"Where am I?" I asked.

"In the military hospital."

"Why am I here?"

"The nurses told me you've lost much blood. They've been feeding you intravenously for three days."

I saw a tube connecting my arm to a large bottle hooked to a pole. Clear fluid greedily dripped back down into my arm.

"Why are you here? Do you live here?" I asked.

"No, I come here every day to make reports on who was injured and how."

"Oh," I said. I had no particular thought or emotion. I had a splitting headache and was very tired. My eyelids came down without any warning.

He pulled a chair from the corner and sat next to my bed.

"I'm Sadamu Izumi. We met once."

"I'm . . . Keiko," I barely whispered.

"I overheard a nurse saying that you almost died. They debated whether you would be worth saving or not. They don't have enough beds."

I remembered the blinding sun, the corpses, rice plants, dizzy spell, and the sweltering heat. How was Ok Ja? I wanted to ask but I couldn't form words with my stiff tongue. Why didn't they leave me there to die? I couldn't understand. I wasn't a bit excited about being saved. Except . . . *Omma would be sad.*

The next morning Izumi San came back. "I've just heard that they are going to release you today. Are you well enough to go back?" he said, looking inquiringly into my eyes.

I remembered my Father's eyes, the same gentle eyes. "I don't want to go back," I said, crying. "I wish they'd keep me here for a long time or take me back to that memorial place to let me die. They'll somehow make me work again, either receiving soldiers or digging graves. I'd much rather die than . . ." I couldn't finish, for I sobbed uncontrollably now.

Sadamu shook his head sympathetically, then took a tiny notebook out of his pocket and wrote on it furiously.

"What are you writing?" I asked, wiping my tears. I was afraid he might get me in trouble. I knew nothing about him except that he hadn't touched me when he came to the comfort house. Any Japanese soldier had the power of giving me life or death.

Sadamu put his pen and notebook back into his pocket. "I'm writing an article on Korean women in the Pacific war. That's why I went to the comfort house. I don't know if the newspaper will publish it or not, but I'm going to try anyway. Most of the inland people don't know what's going on in the Pacific, but someday they will have to deal with this madness!"

This shocked me. How could he talk like this about his own divine race? Is he trying to trick me, I wondered, so I'd accidentally say something against his people? I felt goose-bumps on my arms.

"There's nothing to worry about," he said and smiled when his eyes met mine. "Have you thought of moving to another place? There are several comfort houses on this island, you know."

"I don't think it's my choice," I said in a tiny voice.

"Why not? Your Japanese is better than that of many Japanese soldiers. Your diction is clear and your sentence structure admirable. Why not try to find a better place?"

When I just looked at him, still trying to figure him out, he rose from his chair and walked out.

Five minutes later, he came back. "On the other side of the Koror Island there's a place called House of Serenity. It's a high-ranking officers' vacation place. The whole area is developed for officers: there're bath-houses, restaurants, groceries, a theater, barbershop, even a jewelry shop. I've been there many times to interview officers. It's much more luxurious than where you are, Keiko. The manager is a Korean man, Mr. Kim. I just asked him if he could use a well-speaking, beautiful Korean young lady. Guess what he said!" Sadamu smiled.

It seemed too simple, I thought, and made a long face. I didn't particularly like Korean men working for the Japanese. My father had warned me never to trust them. He said, "Those who work for the Japanese are dogs who wag their tails at thieves. They are useless."

"Well? Do you want to go back to the same comfort house or move to the Officer's House of Serenity?" he asked.

What choice did a comfort woman have? "Thank you, Izumi San. You have been most kind. I hope I can do something for you someday."

He blushed and dashed out the door, his earlobes reddening. Obviously, he thought I was hinting at my services as a comfort woman. *How stupid,* I thought. That's all they think about. I felt a sly satisfaction thinking that all Japanese must be ashamed of themselves for letting their country use Koreans as slaves. I knew I could never make them feel bad enough for what they did to us, so why should I feel bad for what I said?

Later that afternoon, Dr. Kuwana released me from the hospital, and I moved into the House of Serenity. Sadamu came with a jeep and took me to the comfort house to pick up my belongings before we headed to the new place. Mr. Nakamura didn't say a word when Sadamu told him everything was arranged by the military although he looked angry.

Ok Ja and the other girls were with soldiers, and I asked Manager to please tell them goodbye for me, but he said nothing.

Mr. Kim, the manager of the House of Serenity, greeted Sadamu with a strong handshake and a broad smile, showing his gold teeth. Then he took us to a room facing the gigantic pool of blue water. "Keiko, this is your room," he said, flashing his gold teeth. "I hope you like it. I'm giving you the room with the best view of the ocean. I know women like a good view, among other things."

"Yes, I like it a lot."

"Good! I like smiling women. We'll do all right together!"

We toured the house, while Mr. Kim explained: the House of Serenity was owned by a Tokyo businessman who valued authentic Yi Dynasty-style Korean entertainment. This was a high class Kiseng House, a whorehouse, and they had two Korean musicians—both women—who could sing old-time music and play ancient Korean musical instruments such as kayagum and kumoongho. Besides the musicians, there were eight Korean girls, four Japanese, and six Chinese—all comfort women.

The three-story European-style home reminded me of a small theater. The first floor was an elegant restaurant with a stage in one corner and a bar in another. The ceiling was open to the second floor and people downstairs could see the officers and women walking along the long balcony laced with rails. The third floor was a luxurious apartment, Mr. Kim said, but was sealed. The owner and his wife lived there when they were on the island.

After the tour I walked Sadamu to his jeep. "I have a favor to ask you," I said.

"A favor? Oh, dear!" he said, his face lit with a mischievous smile.

"My brother is on one of these Pacific Islands, but I don't know where. His Japanese name is Yoshio Omura, and he's twenty years old. He was conscripted while he was a student at Seoul University. Would you be able to find out where he is stationed?"

Sadamu's expression changed to the solemn face of a preacher. He wrote down my brother's name, birthday, and date of recruitment. "I'll try. I can't promise you anything, but I'll certainly try." Coughing, the jeep left, carrying Sadamu in it.

Deep anguish surrounded me when I was alone in my room. The thought that my brother might not want to see me after all tortured me. Would it be better if I didn't see him? I didn't think so. This was my life even though I was ashamed of it. There was nowhere I could hide.

From my second-floor bedroom window the sunrise was magnificent. A tint of grey appeared at the center of the horizon like a soft feather, then the sky bloomed with pinkish light on the edges and mauve in the middle. Within minutes the red balloon-like sun rose, pushing away the gray mist from the earth and throwing a sheet of gold on the surface of the ocean. The mountains, the jungle, and the palm trees changed into sparkling green robes. Watching this, I prayed "Our Father, who art in heaven . . ." Now that I had a desperate hope of hearing from my brother, everything spoke to me with meaning. The dense forest murmured in a new language and the tropical birds sang cheerful songs. "Lord, I'll do anything, if you let me see my brother again," I pleaded.

Since moving to the House of Serenity, I had more time to think about my situation and why we were treated the way we were and what caused the Japanese to hate Koreans so much.

Once my father had lectured me about my bad behavior and how important it was to honor the integrity of others. It was on one of those days Omma had been impossible and I accidentally said something to her that I wasn't supposed to. All morning she had yelled at me while I was trying to help her in the kitchen. "Don't rattle the dishes," she said, so I stopped rattling. A minute later it was, "Don't spill water all over the floor, for God's sake!" so I was careful not to spill water. Less than two minutes later, she yelled again. "Good heavens! Why are you making so much noise, dropping everything? You're the most careless girl in the entire neighborhood! What kind of man would take you as wife?"

I was so angry I snapped, "Omma, if you're so perfect, why can't you even read?" I regretted it immediately, but it was too late. Omma burst into tears and Father called, solemnly, "Soon-ah!" from the front room. I came out with my head lowered.

"Sit down!" he ordered me.

I sat down.

"Have you forgotten about your filial duty to your mother?"

I shook my head.

"What is the most important thing for human beings to remember all their lives?"

"To respect their elders and honor the integrity of others," I said. This was a short version of his favorite lecture which I had heard over and over.

"*Grreh!* If you can't honor the integrity of your mother, you can't honor your own integrity. Then you're no better than a piglet in a pigsty!"

The truth of the matter was that one's integrity had nothing to do with the way people treated one another, I now discovered. I was forced into sexual labor by the Japanese army for no reason other than that my country was Japan's colony. I wasn't being punished by the Japanese for my lack of integrity but for my country's inability to defend itself. Being poor and powerless was a crime in the real world, and I hated being a Korean for precisely that reason. For centuries, our ancestors did nothing but fight amongst themselves in political wrangling instead of worrying about the country's economy, defense system, and its people's intellectual growth. They created the Yangban Society, an ideal society for scholars and politicians, and spent too much time reciting poems and admiring rice-wine and women. They didn't even know that many countries existed on the other side of the globe and that the rest of the world was making progress every day. That was how the Protectorate Treaty, which fated our country to become one of Japan's colonies, came about. Because of this shameful event, the Japanese killed my father, raped my mother, took my brother as their soldier, and dropped me in this Japanese military compound like a speck of dirt.

I didn't know much Korean history because we only learned Japanese history in school, but our father occasionally taught my brother and me Korean history after dinner. According to him, armed Japanese troops had raped the Yi Dynasty.

One morning in the fall of 1905, Ito Hirobumi—the foreign minister of Japan—and his troops marched into the Kyung-Bok palace to force King Kojong into accepting the Protectorate Treaty, which had been already prepared without our king's consent. When King Kojong refused, Hirobumi's soldiers dragged Korea's prime minister to the courtyard and beat him. But King Kojong again refused to affix his seal on the Protectorate Treaty. Hirobumi then ordered the Korean foreign minister to bring his own seal instead of the king's, threatening to kill him. The Korean foreign minister obeyed and Hirobumi affixed the seal of the minister of Foreign Affairs next to the King's name on the Treaty.

I often wondered if King Kojong displayed integrity as a noble king by not turning his palace into a slaughterhouse. What if he had ordered his Korean soldiers to capture every Japanese and savagely kill them like fleas? Certainly his soldiers could have turned the palace into a butchery. Perhaps then he could have avoided the Protectorate Treaty entirely, and my father would still be alive and I'd be in Korea, trying to remember my filial duty while I was in the kitchen with Omma.

Sometimes I saw ships fighting on the horizon and was afraid I might never go back to Korea. I couldn't tell whose ships they were, Japanese or American, but when large columns of orange flames leaped toward the sky and smoke darkened the horizon, pushing the ship into the water, all my hopes vanished and I feared death. Even if I somehow survived the war, I dreaded the thought of being left behind on this island, like the debris from the wrecked ships that wrestled with the waves. Whenever I overheard conversations from the officers that Japan was losing more men and merchandise than America, I secretly hoped the Japanese would lose the war, but that didn't guarantee that we would go home. We had no papers showing that we were Koreans. Americans might believe that we were Japanese and kill us all. Even if we had papers, who'd pay for the ship? The American government? Would we become an American colony when they won the war? Would American soldiers cut our noses and ears and rape us, like the Japanese said they would?

In spite of the gloom in my head, I tried to dwell on pleasant things and bowed my head to everyone who lived in the House of Serenity.

One of the musicians, Auntie Myung, who once had been famous in Pyongyang with Yi Dynasty songs, was fond of me. She bought me two Western dresses with floral patterns from the shop across the street and ordered me to wear them. When I did, she smiled broadly. "*Wah,* you look just like my daughter. Did I tell you? She died of tuberculosis when she was sixteen. Here, I have her picture!" She dug up her suitcase and pulled out a yellowed picture of a young girl my age, posing under a cherry tree loaded with white blossoms. She looked somewhat like me, only much prettier. When I told her this, she almost cried. "No, you and her are just the same. You're the incarnation of my daughter." From then on she told everyone that I was her "daughter."

Seven days after I arrived at the house, Manager ordered me at breakfast to come see him after I ate. "You have to begin receiving guests today, Keiko. I asked the doctor about your D&C and he said a week is enough for a woman to recover. In your case, it's been more than ten days."

"I'm still bleeding, Mr. Kim," I said pleadingly.

His wife appeared from the kitchen. "Use cotton. Roll it tightly and stick it in there. They don't mind." She opened her closet, took out a small box of cotton, and handed it to me, along with a paper sack.

"What are these?" I asked, looking into the sack. A pink kimono, a jar of cream, and a small tube that said, 'Gel for saku' were in it.

"You'll look so pretty in that kimono, Keiko. The soldiers will drool like dogs when they see you tonight. Here, take this mirror with you too." She grabbed a standing mirror in the corner and gave it to me. "A pretty girl like you must be able to groom yourself properly."

Some of the officers who came to the House of Serenity were more cruel than the common soldiers at the comfort house I had lived at earlier. It seemed they took pride in being heartless, and since the manager was Korean, they ignored the House Rules: many officers came into my room with their guns and daggers still attached to their belts.

One of the officers I received that day walked in with the smell of blood about him. I bowed deeply and greeted him, "Yoku Irasshaimashita. Welcome!"

"Where is your smile?" he said, inviting himself onto the

bed and unbuckling his knee-high black boots. I forced a smile on my face and bowed again. "Sorry, sir!"

"Are you mocking me?" he asked, looking at me through the corners of his fierce, dark eyes.

"No, sir. I have no reason to mock any Japanese man, sir."

"You Chōsenjin are all liars. I just killed two of your kind for disobeying my command. Do you know who I am?"

"No, sir," I said, dropping my gaze to the floor.

"Look at me, jorō—prostitute!"

"Yes, sir!" Instead of his eyes, I looked at his forehead covered with sweat.

"I'm the commander of thirty-six men. In my platoon, there are nine conscripts, six Chōsenjin and three Chugōkujin— Chinese. The Chōsenjin always try to run away, worthless Peninsulans! The two I just executed attempted to run away twice already. So, we killed them. I had them each dig their own grave and ordered soldiers to drill their swords into them."

I covered my ears, shivering.

"Do you want to hear the rest of the story?"

I didn't say anything, because if I said 'no,' he'd beat me.

"Answer me!" he shouted, getting on his feet. "Are you protesting my authority like those conscripts?"

"No, sir, I'm not protesting, sir. But I don't enjoy listening how you killed people, sir."

He walked up to me and slapped me. "You cheap jorō! Who said you have a choice?"

My face seemed to be on fire, but I endured it. *Obey him,* I ordered myself. "No one, sir!"

He yanked my arm, pushed me onto the bed, and ripped my skirt and underwear. For the next fifteen minutes, I bit my lips, fighting myself not to scream, not to cry, and not to feel anything.

When finished, he rose, wiping his sweat from his forehead. "Don't forget me, jorō. I'm coming back. Remember to smile whenever you see me."

After he left, leaving behind the thud of his boots, I had so much pain that I couldn't help but cry. Despite my desire to stay alive and all the strength I could muster, I felt utterly helpless. I staggered at the thought of seeing him again. But what choice did I have? This was how it would be as long as I was a comfort woman: always the pain of my flesh stretching, tearing, bleeding and receiving blows on my face more frequently than I ate meals everyday.

I moved to the mirror that Manager's wife had given me that morning and looked at my reflection. How thin and colorless I looked. I felt compassion oozing toward my reflection and I looked at it for a long time. It seemed the girl in the mirror was saying, "Rescue me, please!" But how could I? I hated my own helplessness as well as hers. Anger overpowered me and I picked up the jar of cream and smashed the mirror. With a loud clatter, the face disappeared. The mirror was covered with many lines crossing one another like a spiderweb. Surprisingly, no broken pieces had jumped from the frame. I could only see the vague outline of my face, cut in a thousand pieces, staring at me in chilling apathy through the cracks. I shivered. I wanted to shout at her to jump out and run away, but instead tears sprang to my eyes.

Angry? a voice said. *Remember, you are in a tiger's cave. Do you want to scream at the tiger and poke him? You fool! You must hide like a rabbit in a hole without even breathing.*

How true, I thought. I was in a bad dream. Soon I'd wake up and laugh, telling myself what a foolish dream I had had. Until then I must stay alive, no matter what kind of price I had to pay, hoping for the day all this would end. The Japanese could steal everything from me but not my secret hopes and dreams. All they could hurt was my flesh, nothing else.

Peace enveloped me and I moved closer to the mirror. I was amazed that the broken pieces of the mirror were still holding the obscure shape of my face, and I innocently touched the sharp edge. Immediately blood trickled from my fingertip. The moment I saw the red fluid flowing from my finger, I was awakened with certitude. Beyond these sharp edges of life, my heart was still pumping blood, vigorously and obediently, to keep me alive. I suddenly realized that what I had lost wasn't that much—a few kilograms of my flesh and my childish ideals. I still had my mind and my soul that kept telling me I must love myself in spite of the daily tortures I endured and never dwell on what I had lost. *You can only gain by eagerly living*, the same voice said. I wrote myself a poem:

> *Sifting through thoughts and feelings*
> *I found you, Spirit, crushed under heavy sighs.*
> *Picking up and holding you tenderly in my palms,*
> *I whispered softly:*
> *Never despair, Spirit!*
> *Flowers can bloom in a desert.*

I pinned it on the wall next to my sleeping mat.

"*I* can't help you. Sorry." Sadamu said one morning as he walked into the House and saw me sitting on a bench with the other girls, waiting for the guests to arrive. I had awaited good news. I had been reuniting with my brother in my mind, crying and laughing, and telling him bits and pieces of hometown news. All that disappeared with Sadamu's casual words.

Disappointed, I only looked at him.

Sadamu shrugged his shoulders. "Many Japanese ships are sinking in the ocean, either by torpedoes or mines. I sent letters to several correspondents I know in the Pacific to discover your brother's whereabouts, but only one from Guam Island responded. He said so many regiments are moving in and out of their divisions that it's impossible to know where anyone is stationed. It's the same everywhere, he said. There's nothing I can do except wait."

"I understand."

"Who knows, I might hear something tomorrow or the next day. Just be patient and sit tight, okay?" He walked to the door, saying, "I have to run. Many officers are leaving today to join General Hyakutake in Guadalcanal. I have to interview six of them before noon."

I patiently waited for him the next day and the next. He came back on the third day. The moment I saw him walking through the door, smiling, my heart raced. Finally, I thought, he had news about my brother.

I waited.

"How would you like to be my guest tonight?" he asked, his face lit with a boyish smile.

"Your guest? What are you talking about?" I said, my shoulders slumping.

"I'm invited to a Korean couple's home for dinner. They're pineapple growers and have two cute kids, a boy and a girl. I asked them if I could bring a friend along and they said I could. I've already told them about you, you know."

"You don't know anything about me other than . . ." I said bitterly, disappointed that he hadn't brought the news I'd been waiting for.

His smile faded and he looked uncomfortable.

"If you don't want to go, I understand, Keiko," he said, straightening his hat, as if he'd turn around and leave immediately. "But they're a nice couple, and I thought you'd enjoy meeting them. Why would I invite you if they're not a nice couple? Because I want to torture you?"

I laughed. He laughed too. I said, "Okay."

Around six that evening, Sadamu came back to pick me up. As we walked out the door, the manager said, "Have a good time, kids! Don't stay out too late."

Sadamu drove the jeep skillfully, and soon we were

moving off of Koror Island. The steel bridge hanging between Koror and Arabekesang blinded my eyes in the evening sun. Tall tropical trees approached and passed rapidly as the jeep sped along. A narrow creek appeared on the right and followed us for a while before it merged with a pond. On a large rock in the pond, two pelicans sat looking at their own reflections, and several dark, naked children stood at shore, throwing rocks at them.

"Look, the kids are throwing rocks at those pelicans," I said, breaking the silence.

"Kids? Where?" Sadamu said and turned his head toward the pond, but before he could see the kids or the pelicans, the road curved sharply left, and we faced a meadow dotted with goats and cows on the left and a forest on the right.

"I thought they might kill the pelicans," I said awkwardly.

"Pelicans are cleverer than kids," Sadamu said. "I'm sure they'd fly away if they thought the kids could hurt them."

I hope the pelicans flew away, I said to myself.

"Such a thick forest," Sadamu admired. "That forest reminds me of a folktale I heard about Palau Island. I always gather folktales wherever I go."

"What does it say?"

"'Legend has it that once a giant fell from the sky and his body parts scattered everywhere. One leg here and one arm there; his head in the north and his nose in the south. The local gods grieved and built forests and reefs to protect his body. Soon people emerged from his flesh.'"

"You mean, all these islands had been the giant's body parts?" I asked.

"Yes. Pretty interesting story, isn't it? The population grew with time, and when an American captain named Wilson and his crew members landed on the island in the late eighteenth century, 40,000 Palauans lived on the island. But the population quickly diminished as the natives contracted dysentery, influenza, and malaria, which the white folks brought with them. By the time the Germans occupied Palau in the early twentieth century, only about eight thousand lived on the island."

"Only eight thousand?"

"Yes. They were weak to those Western bacteria."

The scenery abruptly changed, and we were now looking at a green field where thousands of dark green plants lay on the ground, squirming and twisting in the wind.

"Look! We're almost there," Sadamu suddenly announced, stepping on his brake.

I saw a wooden gate with a picture of a smiling oriental man holding a pineapple in his hand. The paint was peeling on the board, but the man's face was well preserved.

I wanted to turn around and go back to the comfort house. I was terrified that these Koreans would know what I was doing in Palau and would look down on me as if I were scum between their toes.

"Wait!" I said.

"What is it?"

"I'm sorry, Sadamu, but . . . I don't think I should meet them. I'm not ready. I, I don't feel like meeting any Koreans."

"Why? They're expecting us," he said, wrinkling his forehead a little.

"I know, but . . . It's not a good idea, really. We wouldn't have anything in common. I don't know why I came in the first place."

Sadamu pulled the jeep to the side of the road and parked it. Dust rose in the air then descended on the windshield.

You're scared! a voice said. I was. I was ashamed to make Sadamu turn around too. "I'm sorry, Sadamu. I'm really sorry!" I moaned, wishing I could melt away like candle wax. Tears formed in my eyes.

Then I felt Sadamu's hand on my shoulder. "Keiko, listen to me!" he said gently. "It must be hard to trust people when so many men are taking advantage of you. But there's nothing you can do about it right now. I want you to know, though, there's another side of the fence. The Hyuns are good people. That's why I wanted you to meet them. But if you don't want to, we'll turn around and go back to Koror. That's no problem." He tightened his hand, and I felt his strong grip squeezing my shoulder. His touch suggested that I couldn't be scum: it even made me feel I could be important to him.

My head wandered and I realized the soldiers would be everywhere at the House of Serenity—in the restaurant, in the hallway, in every room, and on every bench in the courtyard. *Why do I want to go back there? Because I'm out of my mind?*

I wanted to bury my head in Sadamu's chest and stay there without thinking. But this was real life. Good things rarely happen in real life.

Shifting my tired eyes to the graying sky ahead of me, I asked Sadamu, "Why are you so kind to me? You're Japanese but you don't act like one. Why? Most of the Japanese I know wouldn't sit next to a Korean comfort woman, but you seem to like Koreans."

Sadamu's gaze rested on my face for a moment, then he said, "My nationality is a problem for you, isn't it?"

"Yes. I wish you weren't Japanese."

"What do you want me to be, then? Korean?"

"No, but not Japanese."

He laughed. "I think people should be able to choose their own nationality. Wouldn't it be wonderful to pick the country you like or dislike? It would be fun to research which country you wanted to belong to."

How silly, I thought. But at the same time, it made sense.

"Have you ever loved someone regardless of their origin?" Sadamu asked me.

"Everyone I know is Korean, Sadamu. I don't know anyone who isn't Korean."

"I know why you hate the Japanese, Keiko. You don't need to tell me. But still, don't look at the entire race through hateful eyes. There are many good people in Japan too, you know. People are people, not gods."

"How am I supposed to know the inland people? Are you saying that every Japanese person who comes to our country turns into a monster? All the Japanese I know have been horrible to us."

He sighed. "I wish I had an answer for you, Keiko, but I don't. I too hate some people in my platoon, but I can't condemn them. We all have problems. But we're all equal in the eyes of our Maker. He didn't create us to be perfect. Some behave like monsters but most people are decent, even Japanese."

"Do you really believe God made us equal?"

"Of course!"

"Then why do you keep calling me 'Keiko'? You never even asked what my Korean name is."

"I thought . . . You mean, you were forced to use the Japanese name?"

"Of course! Did you think we chose to adopt Japanese names because we envied the divine people? How ignorant!"

Sadamu sighed again, heavier than the earlier one. He reached and grabbed my hand. "I didn't know that. I had no idea. Why didn't you tell me that you have a Korean name?"

"Tell *you*, a Japanese man? We used to get in trouble in school for using our Korean names. We couldn't even talk in Korean."

Sadamu shook his head sympathetically. "Such cruelty! But I can't change other people. All I can do is recognize my stupidity and call you by the name your parents gave you at birth. What is your name?"

"'Soon-ah' is my name. 'Easy Child' in Chinese translation. My father told me I hardly cried when I was born."

"'Soon-ah!' I like it. 'An easy child to raise.' How practical!"

I smiled.

"Shall we continue to the Hyuns or go back to the House? You decide, Soon-ah."

"Who said I wanted to go back?" I asked him accusingly.

He laughed. "No one! I don't know where I got that idea!"

Sadamu drove on. By the time a small hut appeared at the far end of the road, it was dusk. A boy ran toward us, slamming a wooden door behind him and yelling in Japanese, "Sadamu's here! Sadamu's here!"

Sadamu jumped down from the jeep and patted the boy's head. "How're you, Buddy?" he asked. He turned to me. "Hoon, this is my friend, Soon-ah. Say hello!"

Mr. and Mrs. Hyun greeted us at the door. Mr. Hyun, short and round, reminded me of our neighbor who owned a poultry shop at the market. Mrs. Hyun looked more like a missionary woman. She not only prayed at the table with fervor but ate her dinner slowly and observingly as though it were her last supper.

The dinner was memorable. Kimchi, bulgoghi, steamed meat dumplings, seaweed soup, and seasoned fernbrakes were as delicious as my mother's. I ate heartily without saying a word.

Then I noticed Mrs. Hyun looking at me. Up close, she had a round, delicate face, the kind of face that could read your mind before you said anything. I was uncomfortable, realizing my huge appetite had been noticed by someone I'd just met. If Omma had been here, she would say, "Agha, why eat so fast? Always eat a small portion at a time and eat slowly. And never forget to thank the hostess."

But it was too late to worry about eating slowly now. "Everything is so delicious, Mrs. Hyun. You must teach me how to cook all these wonderful dishes."

"You are a very polite young lady," she said, smiling delicately. Her cautious words and gentle glance told me plainly that she knew why I was on Palau.

Determined to prove to her that I wasn't in need of her

merciful glance, I said, "I'm not trying to be polite. You're a wonderful cook, Mrs. Hyun. Really!"

Still, her eyes rested on mine. "Thank you. You seem like a girl from a good family. Your parents must have been heartbroken when they let you go, tss, tss, tss. . . . Are you able to write to them?" she asked earnestly.

I stopped eating. All at once, Omma's tear-stricken face sprang into my mind, and my father's final words rang in my ears. I swallowed.

"Yes, I'm able to write to them, of course!" I lied, looking straight into her eyes.

"That's good, I'm glad! Are you comfortable where you are? I hope I'm not asking too many personal questions."

"No, not at all," I said, fighting back tears. "It's really not that bad, thank you." What else was there to say? If I said I hated my life as a comfort woman, she'd ask me more questions and become more sympathetic, which I couldn't deal with. I never liked talking about my present situation to anyone, even to God. Why should I have to talk to someone I just met?

Just then the boy said in Korean to his sister sitting across the table, "Mia, look how messy you eat! Didn't Omma tell you to eat every grain of rice in your bowl?"

"Shut up!" Mia said, then turned to her mother and whined, "Hoon yi is bothering me again!"

I felt relieved when Mrs. Hyun shifted her attention to Hoon, but to my surprise, my eyes became misty.

"Hoon yi!" Mrs. Hyun flashed. "Can't you leave your sister alone? Shame on you, Hoon yi!"

"Yeah, shame on you, Hoon yi!" the little girl repeated and stuck her tongue out.

"I'm not doing anything, Omma," Hoon yi said defensively.

My brother Wook used to act like Hoon when he was that age. He used to embarrass and humiliate me in front of our guests. Now, twelve years later, I didn't even know whether he was alive or dead. We might never see one another again. Perhaps those memories were all I had of him. . . . Tears quickly gathered in my eyes and streamed down my face. In order to stop crying, I pinched my own leg under the table.

"Are you all right, dear?" Mrs. Hyun asked.

Now everybody looked at me, even the kids. I was so embarrassed that I wanted to crawl under the table and hide, as I used to do when I was Mia's age, but those wonderful days were gone too. This sent me a new stream of tears, and I frantically coughed to camouflage my sorrowing heart.

"The bathroom is behind you, dear," Mrs. Hyun said, "if you need to use it."

Sadamu rescued me just in time. "We must go pretty soon. I thought you wanted to talk about something."

Mrs. Hyun smiled. "It's not that important, really," she said politely. "What I had in mind was that there are many young girls like you on the island and I feel we must do something for them. They are in great danger, physically and spiritually. We'd like to open our home once a week and have them come to eat with us, talk with one another, and pray together so that God can heal them. We are all in the same boat, you know. We must help one another to live through this difficult time. Jesus said, 'When there are two or more gathered together in my name, I will be present.'" Mrs. Hyun looked at me serenely, waiting for my response.

It would be wonderful to hear the Bible again, I thought. But I didn't know if the manager would let us come. "I'll ask the manager," I said, wanting to leave as soon as we could.

"Good," Mrs. Hyun said in a pious tone. "God touches His people in a mysterious way. If your manager says no, we'll think of something else."

We thanked the Hyuns for the evening, said goodbye to the kids, and got up. The kids bowed at us bashfully as Sadamu shook their hands, saying, "See you soon, okay? Next time I come, I'll take you for a ride."

"Can we go to Washington?" Hoon asked.

"Omma, Hoon yi is being silly again!" Mia snapped, but Mrs. Hyun said, "Hush up, you!" and wished us a safe return.

As we drove down the path leading to the main road, millions of stars blinked at me. I wished Mrs. Hyun hadn't been so nice. What would the kids think of me? "I hope I didn't embarrass you too much, Sadamu," I said.

"Don't be silly!" Sadamu chuckled softly. "I hope you liked them, the Hyuns and their kids."

"Yes, they seem very nice. How did you become friendly with them?"

"I wrote an article about them. It's difficult for them, too, because everything's determined by the Japanese military—the price, the shipping regulations, even the quality of the pineapples they produce. But I've never heard them complaining or swearing at them. They take it as their fate."

The field looked somber and the earth seemed empty and dormant. Nothing stirred and no sound was audible for what seemed like forever. Suddenly an owl flew into the windshield with its wings wide open, shrieking, and I squeaked like a mouse. Sadamu stepped on the brake and parked the jeep. He looked at me closely to see if I was okay, his nose almost touching mine. In the dim moonlight, Sadamu's face looked bleached and his eyes wider. His warm breath mingled with my own. My heart raced. I wished he were my lover.

I shivered as I remembered Ayako's love affair with Moon Ho, which claimed her life as well as his. I was as much afraid of my own thoughts as the thick layers of darkness surrounding us.

"Are you all right?" Sadamu asked, his eyes glowing in the dark.

"Yes, I'm okay."

"Good," he said, taking a deep breath. "I don't like to hear a woman scream in the dark. It scares me," he said, then drove again. The road seemed endless. Neither of us said anything for a long time.

After a while, the headlights revealed the bridge, the pond where the pelicans had been, and the somber silhouettes of palm trees, and I knew we were getting closer to the House. The lights glittered in the distance as I imagined being held in his arms. I could hear my heart beating faster and faster.

When the House of Serenity appeared, I wanted to tell him not to stop but to keep going toward the sea. A crescent moon hung over the jungle as if urging me to join the night's calm festivity.

"Well, it was a fine evening," Sadamu said, as he stopped the car in front of the House. "It wasn't long enough for me. I don't know about you."

"Is it over?" I asked.

"Who said it was?" He pulled the jeep back onto the road with a screeching noise and headed toward the shore.

I laughed. I liked the boyish expression on his face and I liked myself laughing. All at once, everything surrounding me seemed to be dancing and laughing—the moon, the salty wind, and the palm trees.

Five minutes later we reached the reef overlooking the waves rising and falling in the immense pool of water. Sadamu parked the car in front of the reef, came over to my side, and helped me to step down. The ocean breeze caressed my throat and sneaked into my blouse. For a moment, every fiber in my body tickled with vitality. There was something magical about being under a crescent moon, walking next to a man I liked to be with, and listening to the waves. I almost leaped into his arms, pretending that I was too young and foolish to know the proper demeanor for a woman and confess my aching heart to him.

"I love watching the sea at night, don't you?" I said, excitedly.

"What is there to see when it's so dark?" he asked.

"Look at the waves breaking into millions of bubbles against those rocks! And the murmur! It's music, Sadamu! Can't you feel the wind caressing your face, whispering in a soft voice? Listen!" I stopped walking, with my hand behind my ear.

Sadamu imitated me and listened. Then we laughed, looking at one another. Sadamu took my hand and we ran to a huge rock and sat. Far away, some tiny lights blinked like stars. No doubt they were battleships exchanging messages and codes, but from a distance they looked beautiful and romantic.

For a while we said nothing. Then I felt Sadamu's shoulder pressing mine. I leaned toward him. My heart pounded again. Afraid of my own emotions, I asked, "When do you think the war will end?"

"Not too soon," he said, straightening a little, but not completely. "It will take at least three more years for Japan to realize they can't win. I heard in the news the other day that Japanese soldiers are dying at the rate of two hundred daily, but youths are coming of age at the rate of a thousand a day. There are still too many generals, admirals, and officers willing to sacrifice their troops for the emperor, like merciless cattle owners slaughtering their livestock."

"Is the emperor healthy?" I asked.

Sadamu laughed. "He is too healthy, Soon-ah. You know why? He has been taking Korean ginseng since Japan occupied Korea. He might live to be a hundred and fifty!"

"A hundred fifty!"

"But remember, the Americans are destroying Japanese ships so fast that no one can predict what'll happen the next day. Since last January they've sunk nearly 1.5 million tons of military supplies heading to the Solomon Islands. That means the soldiers have to live without rice, clothes, weapons, and medical supplies. Now they're trying to hide merchant ships in desolate islands during the day and move them only at night, but the American pilots always seem to find them and destroy them. I think it's crazy to send six thousand soldiers from Palau to Guadalcanal when so many soldiers have already died there. They'll all die, not from enemy bullets but from starvation and diseases like malaria, dysentery, and beriberi!"

"You sound anti-Japanese," I said.

"My nationality doesn't mean anything to me, Soon-ah. When we die, our ID card is useless. Did you ever think about that? It doesn't matter whether you're Japanese or Korean or American or Chinese. Our decaying flesh is our only ID when we're dead. We all give off the same stench when we decay, attracting animals, vultures, and maggots."

As I listened, the faces of the soldiers I had served appeared in my mind, one by one—the evil ones as well as the naïve, young ones. They were now in Guadalcanal, smelling the decaying flesh! I shivered. I had no heart to curse them or laugh at their misfortunes. Hadn't the Allies already bombed Tokyo, destroying thousands of people? Death seemed much nearer to the Japanese than to us Koreans. Someday the war would be over and everything I had witnessed would be recorded in history books!

I asked, "Where do you want to live, Sadamu, when the war is over?"

"Hmmm!" he said then paused for a moment. "If I had a choice, I'd live in the Alps, milking cows and yodeling."

I laughed. "It's hard to picture you under a cow, milking and yodeling at the same time."

"No, really, it might be good," he said earnestly. "Switzerland is a peaceful place. No country can invade Switzerland, not even Japan. If I had enough money to buy some land there, I'd love to live in Switzerland writing novels in a chalet overlooking the ridges of the snow-covered mountains." Without warning, he wrapped his arm around my shoulder. "Someday, I want to live in the Alps and marry a pretty woman like you," he said, kissing my cheek.

I felt small and safe in his strong arms. My face seemed to

be on fire. A memory flickered in my head of Violetta in *La Traviata* which some Tokyo music school students had performed at our school last fall. The passionate love song Violetta sang for her lover Alfredo had been unforgettably beautiful.

I leaned my head gently on Sadamu's shoulder, feeling like Violetta on her deathbed telling Alfredo how much she loved him and how much he meant to her. I wanted to love this man like Violetta loved Alfredo!

Sadamu's cheek now touched mine, and I could hear his heart drumming. Then his face slowly moved, like in the opera, and his lips pressed mine. I remembered Violetta's words:

> *Alfredo, my sun, my love!*
> *In the stormy night I awaited thee!*
> *When the moon was bright and the wind calm*
> *I cocked my ears to hear thy footsteps.*
> *You'd never know the hidden anguish of my heart,*
> *Oh, Alfredo!*

But another voice pierced my ears sharper than a dagger. *You're only a whore!* The words repeated again and again until I was lightheaded. It was worse than a death sentence. *You can't love this man! He is the kind of man every good woman dreams of loving. Remember what happened to Moon Ho? Ayako shouldn't have loved him. Moon Ho was a good man like Sadamu!*

A sob escaped my throat.

"What's wrong?" Sadamu asked, letting go of me.

"Nothing," I said. I covered my face and tried to smother my sob but I couldn't. My shoulders heaved and I sniffled. How tragic that opera was! Now I glimpsed my future. Who'd love me even if I went back to Korea? What decent man would look into my eyes and say he loved me?

"I'm sorry if I upset you." Sadamu apologized, without knowing why I was crying.

"No . . . please don't say anything!" I said. A part of me still wanted to love him innocently and blindly but another part ordered me to get up and run without looking back.

"I want to go back," I announced.

"Why?"

"Don't ask me anything! Don't even try to understand me," I said hysterically. My voice sounded harsh.

Sadamu stood without a word. I glared at the ocean with hatred. I didn't know why I wanted to see this dark abyss in the first place. There was no beauty, nothing! It was dark.

$\mathcal{T}$he House of Serenity glittered in the distance. His gaze fixed on the windshield, Sadamu looked hurt and angry. I wanted to say something, but what? Tell him why I couldn't accept his affection? Tell him how much I was hurting because I couldn't love him? Nonsense. Even a thousand words wouldn't do any good. The wall between us was high and unyielding.

The jeep jerked to a stop in front of the House and I jumped out, saying, "Thank you for the evening." Sadamu didn't say anything. I heard the wheels screeching loudly behind me but I didn't turn around. We were both hurt and angry. *It's wartime, Sadamu! Let's hate each other to death!*

I walked haughtily into the House. The twanging sound of the kayagum seemed to be floating above the thick layers of cigarette smoke, and the roomful of officers each sat with a woman, touching them everywhere—inside their blouses and under their skirts—laughing and drinking.

Vile creatures! I thought. I pictured myself holding a gun in my hand. I felt powerful. I could kill them all, then I would laugh and laugh, looking at their corpses sprawled in a sea of blood. What a triumph it would be! That's what these men did everywhere they went; China, Burma, Philippines, Korea, Malaya, Indonesia, and all these Pacific Islands. Why couldn't I?

My fantasy disappeared when I noticed Auntie Myung in the corner looking at me, plucking her kayagum strings. Under the ceiling light filtering through the cigarette smoke, her fingers resembled an eagle's claws shredding a dead animal. I was uncomfortable as if my wickedness was revealed. I quickly nodded in her direction and walked upstairs.

My room was dark. I lay on my mat against the wall with my dress on. The crescent moon hanging above my window exuded a thin, frail light. The sky was full of tiny stars. Omma would be looking up at that sky, too, from the other side of the globe, I thought. The distance between us was unbearable. I wished I could tell her how devastated I felt. *Omma, I might never find a man who'll love me. I might not have my own kids either. My life as a woman has ended before it even began. What should I do, Omma? Don't cry. I can't stand it when you cry . . .*

I was crying too. Sadamu's face appeared in my mind's eye. His gentle touch, his scent, and his drumming heartbeat were alive again. I moved my hand to my lips to see if his kiss was still there. It was! I could feel it on my fingertips. Sadamu, what condemnation was this, not being able to accept your affection? I love you more than anyone in the world. I buried my head in the pillow and sobbed.

I heard a knock at the door and lifted my head. Then the rice-paper slid open quietly in the dark. "Are you asleep, Agha?"

"Come in, Auntie Myung." I called all older women "Auntie."

"Auntie? tss, tss, tss. . ." she clucked. "Why is it so hard for you to call me 'Omma'?" She turned the light switch on. The bright light blinded me.

I sat up, straightened my dress, and wiped my eyes.

"Are you not well?" she asked. "You looked pale when you walked in. Is everything all right?"

"Yes." I mumbled. I wasn't in the mood to tell her anything.

"Come on, don't lie. I know you were out with that correspondent. Was he a dog like the rest of them?"

"No," I said, anticipating her interrogation. She had to know everything.

"Why are you so upset then? Why are you crying?"

I sighed. How could I describe to her what was inside me?

"You can't talk about it, eh?" she said impatiently. "Listen to me, daughter, I've been in this business ever since I was twelve. I know everything about men. I can feel the pain in your heart. My father sold me to a tavern owner when I was twelve, and I've lived around men more than thirty years. Do you think that's not long enough to learn about them? Ask me anything, I can tell you! If I could've gathered all my tears, there'd have been another Han River in Korea!"

More than thirty years! My curiosity rose and I wanted to know about her. "Auntie, have you ever felt you weren't good enough to love a man?" I asked.

"Tss, tss, tss, the same old story!" she clucked knowingly. "Of course! I was a very foolish young girl then, unable to know my worth."

"Foolish?"

"Yes, very foolish. I wish I could go back and live that period of my life again." She somberly looked at the dadami floor as if her painful past was written on it. "I was nineteen, just out of kiseng training school. Back then, my fingers on kayagum strings flew faster than birds. One night after a performance the waiter brought me a note, saying a tall and handsome man asked him to give it to me. The note said, 'I would be honored if you would join me for a drink.' It was common for men to invite me to their tables to compliment my kayagum solo. But this man, a lawyer from Seoul, wanted more than just a conversation. He told me he had just lost his wife and came to Pyongyang to escape from his grief. I gathered that he had come to look for a new wife, too. Two weeks later, he proposed marriage.

"I couldn't accept his proposal. See how naïve I was? He was a lawyer and I a low-class woman, a woman with a history. What would be there for me other than a duty as a stepmother and the scornful looks of neighbors and relatives? I thought any man would fall in love with a woman who was pretty and talented. I was certain he would reject me someday, leaving me with nothing but wrinkles and spots on my face. I knew so many kisengs who had been divorced by their husbands and crawled back to the Kiseng House. It took courage for me to say no.

"The lawyer was so hurt and angry that he took my best friend with him, who wasn't as pretty or as talented as I was. You know something? They live happily together in Seoul. He's the father of my daughter who died of tuberculosis, you know."

I was stunned. She had never told me this. "Auntie! How sad!" I cried.

"Since then no man ever loved me enough to propose marriage, except bums. I learned my lesson, but it's too late. Anyway, why did you ask me this?"

I told her briefly about what had happened at the beach and why I felt I couldn't accept Sadamu's affection.

"Tss, tss, tss," she shook her head. "You are so cruel to yourself, just as I was when I was your age. Deep down, you want to cling to him. I know it because I can see it. You're terrified that he might reject you someday."

"Yes, Auntie," I said. "Sadamu is the kind of man any woman would dream of falling in love with. He's handsome, smart, and has a great sense of humor. But look at me. What am I?" I said bitterly.

She shook her head. "You're just like me, too proud to trust a man's love. But let me tell you something! That's cheap pride! Why decide for him? Why not let him decide for himself? If you have any feelings for him, don't try to protect him. That's a quick way to destroy a man's ego as well as a relationship."

"But why would he want a woman like me? He has a whole future waiting for him. If he has any feelings for me, it's because he feels pity for me. He probably thinks I'm too pitiful."

"What future are you talking about at a time like this, Daughter? Why try to analyze his feelings?" she asked gently. "We might all die tomorrow or the next day. The future isn't here yet and might never come. Why go against your own feelings, creating terror in your heart? A wise woman must never accept misery so willingly. That only shows her weakness!"

She was right, I thought. I hoped Sadamu wasn't too angry with me. What if I could never see him again? I wanted to run to him, dashing through the darkness, and apologize to him for my stupidity.

"What's your zodiac sign?" Auntie Myung asked.

"The tiger."

"A strong character! Sensitive and courageous. What is his?"

"I don't know. He told me he's twenty-two."

"Twenty-two. Let me see. . ." She opened her palm and counted her fingers, mumbling, Ox, Rat, Boar. . . . She nodded. "He must be a dog. Dogs are loyal and honest. You are a good match. Most dogs are faithful husbands and ardent lovers."

Ardent lover! He was. He kissed me tenderly. If I ever saw him again, I'd fall in his arms and let him kiss me again and again until he couldn't kiss me any more. But on second thought, how did I know how he really felt about me? He kissed me but that didn't mean that he really loved me. What if he only felt pity for me?

Clouds of self-doubt crept in again and I was miserable. Cheap or not, I couldn't jeopardize my sense of pride, which was already at stake. I disliked pity. I would rather die than look pitiful in Sadamu's eyes. Besides, he was Japanese.

As I retreated into stony silence, Auntie got up. "Remember, Daughter. Life is short. If you can't live today, you'll never fully live another day in your life."

I slept little. I kept tossing and turning, fighting with my own voice persistently telling me I was worthless and shouldn't love Sadamu. When a sliver of light hit the window facing the ocean, Auntie Myung appeared in my mind's eye. "Daughter, you are too cruel to yourself. Remember, a wise woman must never accept misery so willingly. Be gentle with yourself!"

Her voice gave me courage and I got up and faced the broad horizon. Light was spreading across the ocean, revealing the layers of a steam-like fog rising upward. A sense of conviction stirred me, and I knew I was no longer the woman with cheap pride. As I whispered to Sadamu how much I loved him, tears welled up in my eyes.

The next morning I sat at the breakfast table, watching a fly circling my bowl of gruel. Auntie Myung came and sat across the table and glanced at me through her all-knowing eyes. Like a doctor observing his patient, she was observing whether or not her wisdom had any effect on me. This annoyed me, and I brought up the Hyuns and their plan for a weekly gathering at their home.

"To listen to the Bible?" the girl next to me almost shrieked, frowning. She was known for her temper and Manager called her a mad snake. "They must be crazy, if not stupid. If I have time, I'll get some extra sleep or do my laundry. Everything stinks in my room, but I have no time to go out to the creek to wash," she said and left the table.

Another girl who was an opium user said the same thing. "If they'd give me some spending money, I'd go," she said, blinking and trying to keep her eyes open, "but to talk about my miserable life? No, thanks!"

We all had the same fear. We wanted to hide from Koreans, fearing they would remember us and spread rumors about us when we went back to Korea.

Finally Auntie Myung summed up what they said and concluded, "The pineapple farmers came here to make money but we are here for a different reason. There's not much to talk about, really. Besides, the manager will definitely say no since he's busy with the upcoming farewell party for the officers. The important messenger from Tokyo Imperial Palace is still here, as you know."

"What messenger?" I asked.

"*Aigo!* Why are you so forgetful at your age, Daughter?" Auntie Myung exclaimed. "Don't you remember the banquet we had out in the courtyard for him the other day?"

I remembered it. How could I forget the tragic show I watched in tears? It was a few days ago. Manager announced in the morning that a messenger from Tokyo had arrived and that we must attend a banquet at noon to welcome him. Flies were swarming about the food on the table as we sat on folding chairs under a white canopy, fanning vigorously. Next to us sat a few native women, shifting their eyes between food and the guards walking back and forth. On the opposite side was a raised platform where two soldiers busily moved about, nailing and setting up the native instruments—several drums and a long bugle.

Soon, a man in a white high-necked uniform with gold buttons appeared with the manager and sat in the front row. A native boy ran to him, bowed, and began fanning a palm-leaf fan.

The show began with a drum roll. Several Japanese men with painted faces, feathers on their heads and wearing loincloths gathered on the platform and danced a horrid dance, jerking their heads and twisting their bones. This wasn't the first time I'd watched such hideous performances, and I was sickened. The message was that the Japanese valued the native rituals and enjoyed interacting with them, but in reality they were showing their power and superiority. It seemed to me that the natives hated such displays of arrogance: they looked bored.

The dance stopped. One of the soldiers with a painted face stood on the podium and kowtowed toward the messenger.

"Your Highness, the native children prepared a program to show their gratitude for our majesty's generosity and to wish him longevity. They're immensely grateful that we, imperial Japan, liberated their country from the barbaric Westerners. Please, your Highness, applaud them heartily." He kowtowed again.

The messenger nodded stiffly and clapped. We all clapped.

Turning his back to the audience, the soldier waved his hand in the air, and a dozen little boys wearing plumes and breechcloths appeared on the platform.

The soldier counted the heads twice. "One is missing!" he said.

One of the boys on the platform pointed to the audience and shouted, "There he is!"

"Come forward, boy!" the soldier ordered, looking at a little boy sitting on his mother's lap.

The boy shook his head. His mother whispered something in his ear, pointing at the other children.

"No!" he yelled.

The soldier walked to him and picked him up. "Come! We're going to have fun. You must show that you're a brave Nippongo!" he said as he walked to the podium with the boy in his arms.

The boy turned his head toward his mother, kicking and hitting the soldier, and shouted, "No! I don't want to! Let me go!"

The soldier dropped the boy on the podium. "There! You must obey your teacher, you understand? If you don't behave, I'll punish you!"

The next words chilled my spine.

"I hate you! You killed my father! I hate you, I hate you."

The soldier turned around to look at the messenger. The messenger grabbed the fan, and fanned himself vigorously, muttering, "Damn flies!"

The soldier slapped the boy across his face.

The boy shrieked even harder, "I hate you! You killed my Daddy! I hate you! I hate you!"

I felt sweat on my palms as I watched the boy sinking to the platform. The soldier heaved as he struck the child repeatedly, his painted face frowning like a monster.

The mother of the boy ran to the man, grabbed the soldier's arm, and begged him in Japanese not to hurt her son. The soldier hit the mother with his fist. She fell back, crying loudly.

The messenger from Tokyo coughed loudly, fanning even more vigorously, and ordered the manager, "Let's hear some music!"

Auntie Myung rose, her eyes glistening with tears. She moved to the podium and began singing in a quivering voice.

> Omma, let's live on a sunny hill,
> Gathering wild flowers
> and watching birds nestle on a treetop.
> Omma, let's live on a sunny hill!
>
> Omma, let's live on a riverfront,
> counting our footprints on the golden sand
> and floating paper-boats on the river.
> Omma, let's live on a riverfront.

I cried quietly, remembering that "Omma" in this song

symbolized our country. Not having one's own country was the same tragedy as a child not having a father. All the Korean women cried.

By the time the song was over and Auntie Myung came back to her seat, the boy and his mother had disappeared, and the Japanese men with painted faces came to the platform again to dance another horrible dance.

☘

"This party the manager is preparing is very special," Auntie Myung said, lowering her voice a little. "I overheard from an officer that the messenger will award a prize to each departing officer. Guess what will be the prize?"

"Money, maybe?" I said.

"Money? To officers going to the *Death Valley?* See how naïve you are? Tss, tss, tss. Guess again! Think a little harder."

"I don't know. I give up."

"You shouldn't give up so soon," she said, almost angrily, "you must try again. It has something to do with why you're here and what you're doing . . ."

"Auntie, no! That isn't true."

Auntie Myung laughed. "Can you imagine going to that island, Daughter? I can't! This was Emperor's idea, of course, to boost the officers' spirit. No officer wants to go to Guadal-canal. I overheard them talking about "evaporating." This is a serious problem for the army. A very serious problem!" She looked about the table. Raising her voice a little, she said, "Girls, are you ready to die in the arms of an officer? Are you brave enough to meet thousands of ghosts?"

That finished the conversation about the Hyuns and the party. Everyone was quiet. It wasn't at all uncommon to be picked by high-ranking officers and moved to the front. I sensed that everyone at the table was contemplating hara-kiri—a commonly practiced method of killing oneself among

Japanese people. When a division or regiment lost a battle to the enemy, the commander of the division felt responsible for the loss of his troops and killed himself. In a recent battle near Yap Island, a captain refused to be saved when his ship was struck by an enemy torpedo and plunged a dagger deep into his heart on the deck while his crew members on lifeboats watched his final performance. I often thought about slashing my own flesh and spilling my own blood. Even if I had the courage to perform hara-kiri I disliked the thought that I'd bleed so much. My father had once said that when he saw a dead body he could tell what kind of life he or she lived. Given a choice, I would have wanted to die in a calm and clean environment. We had heard that some Korean girls who followed officers to the battlefront took their lives after the enemy killed the officers, because they didn't want to be captured by Americans. We never talked about them: we somehow felt betrayed by their undaunted action; not that we envied them, but our conviction to hang onto life was endangered.

As Guadalcanal often became the topic of our conversations, I withdrew from everyone, trying hard not to dwell on scary thoughts. Unexpectedly, a letter from Sadamu rescued me from my fear of dying.

Dear Soon-ah:

I have two things to tell you. First, my friend in Mindanao Island in the Phillipines wrote, telling me there's a Korean conscript whose description fits your brother's. This is very exciting news, don't you think? Enclosed is his address. Your letter might not get there because of the frequent Allied attacks in the Pacific, but it's worth trying.

Secondly, I feel terrible about the other night. I hope you don't hate me. It was such a beautiful night. I must have lost my mind momentarily. I was in a dream world, see what I mean? I couldn't help it. You looked disturbingly feminine and beautiful under the crescent moon. I've done enough penance, though. What can I say except I'm sorry? I understand how you feel about Japanese soldiers and promise I will be careful next time.

I'm under a lot of stress, Soon-ah. It seems October isn't a good month for all Japanese. Not only did the war situation worsen in the Solomon Islands, but I'm ordered by the military to report from Guadalcanal in two weeks. This was decided after a reporter of *The Pacific War News*, the military newspaper, suddenly died of malaria. The truth of the matter is that I'm scared of dying. I'm a coward according to the Japanese standard. The more I think about it, the more I'm certain that I'm not yet ready to sacrifice my life for the Emperor. Would the Emperor die for me? I don't particularly feel I'm less important than him. Why should I die for him when he wouldn't for me?

I hear Death calling us in a cunning voice. All those who were sent there months ago have died and all new arrivals will soon end up either in Heaven or Hell. They have no choice. The Emperor will call them his heroes, and Tokyo streets will be filled with marching bands and teary spectators, but alas! I don't want to be one of the proud ghosts hovering over the parade. So help me, God!

Let's get together again, soon. This purposeless life is killing me.

Yours,
Sadamu

I immediately wrote him a note.

Dear Sadamu,

I apologize for being rude the other night. To tell you the truth, I have been feeling so unworthy and so ugly since I came to Palau. If you could peek into my mind, you would see how much I'm hurting from this torture. Not knowing what I am and what is ahead of me causes me to despair. Why am I here, Sadamu? I feel so low and so pitiful that I envy animals.

I am glad you don't want to go to Guadalcanal. Your friendship is sunlight for me in this dungeon. Please arrange another outing for me to the Hyuns or elsewhere. Even Hell would be a delightful place if I could be with you.

Waiting,

Keiko

I went downstairs and dropped it in the mail deposit box with a slight tremor. I hoped Sadamu would come see me soon, but at the same time, I knew I would be torturing myself, looking at the front door whenever someone stepped in.

That night I sat alone on the back porch, looking at the dark sky. The moon was nowhere and the sky was empty of stars. But my head was full of thoughts. I imagined Sadamu sitting next to me and holding me as he did that night by the sea. His drumming heartbeat, the scent of the sea, and the whispering wind were all alive again.

The door slid open and Auntie Myung came out. "All alone, full of thoughts in her head," she said poetically as she sat down next to me. "What's going on with you and the correspondent?"

"You were right about him, Auntie. He wrote to me. I think he really likes me."

"See, what did I tell you? Always watch your own thoughts in your head: they can be dangerous. You must protect yourself from all enemies, including yourself. Beating your head and blaming yourself for everything isn't the way a decent woman treats herself. When a man cares for you and shows you a path that is inviting to you, go with him without hesitation. Don't do what I did to that lawyer."

A ship called *Midori* arrived and anchored about a hundred yards away from the reef. The small boats that had "House of Serenity" painted on the sides made several trips to the ship, moving tables, chairs, boxes of beverages, dishes, gramophones, and other items for the party. Three natives brought baskets of clams, fuzzy crabs, and fish with silvery scales, and each received a pat on the back and a coin from the manager. A Filipino boy, Marco, about seventeen or eighteen, was employed to help the old Korean cook and her mute son in the kitchen.

The manager circled around the house without stopping, checking with the cooks in the kitchen, ordering the comfort women to make origami flowers to decorate the tables, and taking boxes himself to the small boats. His excitement made me nervous: what if an officer picked me? Every time I thought about it, I felt chills on my back. I anxiously waited for Sadamu to come and tell me that there was nothing to worry about.

Two days before the party he came to me, not as a rescuer but as a refugee. I was still on my mat when the manager called me from downstairs. "Keiko, Sadamu is here!" I hurried down and met him in the entry way, but alas! I couldn't believe my eyes. He looked like a mouse rescued from a pan of oil. His dark hair clung to his forehead and his uniform was wet with sweat and blood.

"Sadamu!"

"Can we talk?"

I motioned, and he followed me upstairs in silence. As soon as he came in, he stumbled onto the floor.

"Are you all right?" I asked, wanting to cry.

He shook his head, tears forming in his eyes.

"Tell me what happened."

"Sergeant Asai . . . he is after me."

"Why? What have you done?"

"He's a beast."

"What happened?"

He looked at his uniform as if he'd been unaware of his appearance, then closed his eyes. I saw his hands trembling. He leaned against the wall.

"Can I bring you something? A cup of tea or a glass of water?"

"Water would be nice!"

I went downstairs to get a glass of water from the kitchen.

"Is he all right?" the manager asked me, holding a notebook in his hand. He was always recording something in his notebook, maybe who owed him how much and which soldier was with which comfort woman.

"He seems to be," I said.

"I hope he's not in serious trouble. I don't like trouble-makers," he mumbled.

Sadamu emptied the glass at once and lifted his eyes to the

ceiling. He still looked frightened. "Last night," he said, shifting his glance to me, "Sergeant Asai came to our room, grinning.

"He said, 'I want everyone at the jungle tomorrow morning at sunrise.' He turned to me, saying, 'You too, Izumi. This is an order!' I asked him why. 'Two Yankee pilots were caught last night by the patrolmen. There will be an execution.' He knows I hate watching executions, but he always insists I watch them anyway, hoping that I'll write a report on his excellent killing performance and send it to the *Kyoto Daily News*. Sergeant Asai is the kind of commander who looks for excuses to punish his men: he's especially cruel to Korean conscripts. He beats them mercilessly, knocking their teeth out and breaking their ribs for no reason at all. Every time we're on a mission, Sergeant Asai makes the Korean privates take the front line so that fewer Japanese soldiers will be injured. He orders only the Koreans to wash his stinking feet, shine his boots, and shave him, then beats them, blaming them for not doing their jobs properly.

"He disposes of his accumulated anger by beating his soldiers, just as he empties his bowels every day. I once tried to protect one of the Korean privates from a beating, reminding Sergeant Asai that beating a private without reason was a violation of military regulation. You know what he said to me? He said that I was a 'Chōsenjin-lover!' Can you believe it?" Sadamu shook his head.

I shook my head too.

"Sergeant Asai reminds me of Lucifer, the prince of darkness. If you show him you're hurt, he wants to hurt you even more; if you smile at him, he wants to make you cry. You're never right with him.

"Anyway, going back to the execution, the whole regiment was at a small area in the jungle which we call 'Death Chamber.' Surrounded by thick bushes and vines, no sunlight ever enters into that spot. The soldiers were chattering excessively, as if they were about to watch an exciting sword dance.

To them, the prisoners were no longer humans but mere fish on Sergeant Asai's cutting board. Their appetite for blood was obvious.

"The prisoners were blindfolded and their hands were tied behind them. One prisoner was about twenty-two with broad shoulders, and the other was slightly older, maybe twenty-five, and slender. They were kneeling quietly in the dirt.

"Sergeant Asai cleared his throat. 'Now, you are going to die, my American friends,' he said. 'I wish I could spare your life but I can't. You're our enemies. It's too much trouble for the military to keep you alive. If you have anything to say, say it now!' He looked at them both, obviously feeling very powerful.

"The prisoners shook their heads, both of them. I was surprised at how calm they were. Sergeant Asai ordered a soldier to give them a drink of water, showing his generosity, and the soldier brought two glasses of water. But the prisoners refused to drink.

"Sergeant Asai moved them about six feet apart, positioned himself next to the older pilot, and examined his sword, turning it this way and that. The pilot began praying. 'Our Father who art in heaven. Hallowed be Thy name. Thy kingdom come . . .' The Lord's Prayer—one of the first things our English teacher, a nun, taught us in high school. I started to remove my hat. The prayer abruptly ended as Sergeant Asai's saber rose into the air and landed on the pilot. The pilot's head, separated from his body, rolled on the ground and stopped. The blood rushed out, *sshhhh*.

"The soldiers applauded and cheered. Grinning proudly, the Sergeant waited until all of the blood rushed out of the pilot's body. Then he moved to the younger pilot. He asked the younger pilot to stretch his head. He did. With his eyes bulging, Sergeant Asai raised the saber above his head again.

"Then something happened! I heard a voice singing the American anthem: 'Oh say, can you see by the dawn's early light . . .' It was the pilot. He was still kneeling and blindfolded, but was singing! I couldn't believe it. I felt goosebumps on my arms.

"Sergeant Asai's raised arms began to shake. The saber quivered and seemed to escape his hands. It made a sweeping curve through the air and landed on the ground. Dirt flew in all directions. Sergeant Asai had told us a thousand times never to drop our saber, but that's what he did!

"As if he was totally unaware of the sergeant's mistake, the pilot continued his reverence. Sergeant Asai's facial muscles twitched and he was pale. Sweating profusely, he picked up his saber and lifted it again. I feared he would lose control of his arms, Soon-ah. The sword clumsily struck the pilot between the shoulder blades instead of his neck. The singing stopped.

"When I saw the pilot's body lurch forward like a timber and slowly become still, something snapped in me and I shouted, 'Wonderful, Sergeant Asai! What a beautiful performance! You're truly the Emperor's favorite. Bravo! He will praise you forever for your unforgettable performance.' I was crying and laughing at the same time.

"The Sergeant's eyes, as cold as a devil's, stared at me. To my horror, he began walking toward me, slowly but straight, with his sword still in his hand. I was afraid, now that he'd lost face before his troops, he'd certainly kill me. All his life he'd taken great pride in his own physical power, but just now he felt powerless. At that moment, I caught a glimpse of every Japanese soldier's fate, and fear left me.

"'I'll kill you, you Chōsenjin lover! You son of a bitch!' Sergeant Asai charged me, swinging his sword aimlessly. I ducked and he hit one of the Korean conscripts, then a tree trunk, then the ground. Dirt flew, blood spurted, screams erupted. I ran as fast as I could toward the main road. I heard the sergeant screaming like an injured animal, but luckily the leaves and vines were so thick Sergeant Asai couldn't see me. I was lucky, I guess." Sadamu inhaled a gulp of air and let it out.

"Did the pilot die?" I asked.

"I think so. Even if he wasn't dead then, he must be dead by now. He probably lost too much blood to stay alive. I hope he died quickly. If he didn't, oh God!" He touched his forehead and was quiet.

"He probably did die quickly, Sadamu," I said.

"There was something extraordinary about that pilot," Sadamu said, looking at me again. He seemed more composed.

"What do you mean?"

"He wasn't like any Japanese soldier I know. The Japanese soldiers can fight viciously as long as there's a commander ordering them, but they don't know how to make their own choices. That American pilot didn't need an order. He was freely living out the last moment of his life. It was powerful, watching him singing like that in front of his killer."

The sun reflected off the splintered mirror in the corner and lit Sadamu's face, and I knew the spirit of the fearless pilot was standing in the room. Why did he come? I didn't know. Maybe he wanted to thank Sadamu for standing up for him? Maybe he wanted to shake his hand?

The reflection moved toward the wall and lit the tiny cherry blossoms on the wallpaper before it disappeared.

His eyes fixed on the floor where an ink stain formed a cross, Sadamu was lost in thought. I figured he was still with that pilot, maybe saying goodbye and shaking hands. What made the pilot sing? I wondered. His devotion to his country and his fellow American citizens? Or was it his body's extravagant farewell to his departing soul?

The screeching noise of wheels under my window startled me and my thoughts vanished. Sadamu sat up, widening his eyes. "Soon-ah, the MPs!" he whispered. The front door rattled loudly.

I walked to the rice-papered door and opened it a crack. Two military policemen were standing at the front door. I froze. The manager looked up in my direction. I heard the MP saying,

"We're looking for Private Izumi, the sharp-looking private in Sergeant Asai's squadron."

"I haven't seen him today. Something wrong?" the manager asked calmly.

"He is sought by the Military Police. If you see him, tell him to come to the military police station immediately."

"All right!" the manager said casually.

As soon as the jeep moved away the manager rushed up to my room. "Izumi San, what happened? The Military Police are looking for you."

"Mr. Kim, it's a long story. Would you mind if I stayed here for a couple days? The MPs will not search this place. They don't want to disturb the high-ranking officers, you know."

"Izumi San, no! It will be a disaster if they discover that I'm hiding a troublemaker."

"Trust me, Mr. Kim, no MPs are going to search here! I'd never bring harm to you, Mr. Kim. But I need time to think. Here, take this! This is ten yen, my entire salary for the month." Sadamu handed the manager ten large bills.

"No, this isn't necessary. You should never expect me to take such things." The manager waved his hand vigorously, but his broad smile couldn't hide his appetite for money.

Sadamu quickly stuffed the money into Mr. Kim's shirt pocket. "I insist, Mr. Kim. You must help me! You're my friend!"

The manager scratched the side of his head. "All right, then. I'm risking my head for you, Sadamu. No other manager would do this for a man chased by the Military Police!"

"I know, I know!" Sadamu said, patting the manager's shoulder.

"Follow me."

The house was still quiet. Most girls slept until ten after they had night guests.

The manager climbed the steps to the third floor and

unlocked the door. Behind it was a large living room with many old pieces of Japanese furniture and a musty smell.

We walked in. The manager opened the closet door on the left, and I saw a ladder standing against the wall. Two rifles hung on the wall along with an officer's uniform and hat. On the floor were several dust-covered boxes stacked together. "The owner's nephew left these here," Mr. Kim said, touching one of the boxes with his foot. "I'll get rid of them if he doesn't show up soon."

We climbed the ladder to the attic. By the dim light of a dust-covered window, I could see boxes of all sizes scattered on the floor.

"You'll be safe here, Sadamu," the manager said. "Keiko will bring meals for you. When you leave, use the back door. Be careful!" He shook Sadamu's hand and left, ordering me to bring the comforters from the owners' bedroom for Sadamu.

We pushed the boxes into the corners and brought a pillow and a comforter from the owners' bedroom. We laid them on the floor.

"I must go," I said, not really wanting to.

"Soon-ah, please stay with me," Sadamu whispered.

Yes, Sadamu, I'll stay with you forever, my heart whispered, but my head shook sideways against my will. "I'll get in trouble if I stay here," I said.

"Mr. Kim doesn't mind if you stay," Sadamu said pleadingly. "I gave him ten yen."

The truth was that I wanted to be with Sadamu even if the manager came back and dragged me out of there, but I wasn't going to tell him that.

Sadamu put his hands on my shoulders. I was filled with the same excitement I felt the night at the shore. *What if I fell into his arms and kissed him? Or should I close my eyes and let him kiss me?* But Sadamu removed his hands from my shoulders and walked to the window. He wiped the window with his sleeve. More sunlight came in.

I felt dizzy, as though I had been thrown from the peak of a mountain to the depths of the sea. He might still think I disliked being touched by him. *Sadamu, can't you forget anything?* I wanted to say.

But it was too late. Sadamu was glued to the window as if he had forgotten all about me. A pathetic sigh slipped from my lips. I threw my gaze over Sadamu's shoulder and I saw the broad and calm expanse of blue. A group of American airplanes in the shape of a "v" were moving into the window frame then passed, leaving a rumbling noise in my ears.

"Soon-ah, let's run away together!" Sadamu unexpectantly exclaimed.

"Run away? How?" I shrieked.

"If we could get a boat, we could go to another island. There are more than two hundred islands out there. Some are uninhabited. We might survive if we hide on one of them," Sadamu said fluently, as if he had been practicing this speech.

My mind reeled. What would stop me from running away? Nothing! My fear of dying in Guadalcanal in the arms of an officer was tremendous.

The truth of the matter was even if I had no fear of going to Guadalcanal, I would have still wanted to run away with Sadamu, like a thread following a needle. But where? These Palau islands were surrounded by the vast sea full of Japanese and the Americans fighting mercilessly, bombing one another and sending columns of flames into the sky. Where could we go? How could we survive?

"We'll both die!" I exclaimed.

"We might," Sadamu said turning his back to me.

"You mean you don't care?"

"No!"

He didn't care! How thoughtful! When Death seemed so near that I could almost hear its powerful wings flapping, how could he ask me to run away without worrying about dying? How could he be as calm as Buddha lost in meditation when I was scared to death? I wanted to smack him or kick him or both.

As if he sensed my frustration, Sadamu turned around, his lips forming a placid smile. "You know how to boil crabs?" he asked.

Boil crabs? "Who cares about how to boil crabs at a time like this?" I said angrily, flashing my eyes at him.

Sadamu came and sat next to me. Through the corners of my eyes I saw him grinning serenely, as if he had just unearthed some long-buried ancient wisdom and couldn't wait to reveal it to me. "Once, I heard my mother instructing our servant how to cook crabs. It was a long time ago. She said to her, 'Don't ever put live crabs into boiling water, because they'll fight to the death. Put them in a pot, fill it with cold water, then raise the heat. They won't notice the gradual temperature change and will slowly die.'

"We're like crabs, Soon-ah. We've became accustomed to this hell on earth. We are slowly dying, little by little, without even noticing it. Look around! So many people we know have died or are dying. Now I suddenly feel that I must jump out of the boiling pot and crawl away before it's too late. This is my life, but someone else controls it. If Sergeant Asai finds me, he'll kill me. If I go to Guadalcanal Island, I'll die of malaria or dysentery. Wherever I go, death is waiting for me. So, why not try to do something about it?"

"But running away will certainly quicken our death, Sadamu. Is that what you want?" My voice quivered.

"Soon-ah!" Sadamu's voice was firm and strong. "This is no life! Are we pretending that someday, somehow, someone will rescue us from this hell? I'm tired of waiting. I want to go out there and live, even if it would be for only one day. It's time to show samurai spirit, not to draw blood, not to kill, not to gain more power, but to live honorably and earnestly."

I wasn't listening. Even if we escaped, who could guarantee that we wouldn't die of starvation? What kind of honorable life can you have when you know you can't survive?

I felt Sadamu's hand on my shoulder. He slipped his hands under my arms and pulled me to my feet. He gently wrapped his arms around me, and I felt his thigh muscles pressing against my body. His uniform buttons poked my breasts and I squirmed. His eyes searched mine, and I felt his warm lips covering my mouth. My heart raced rapidly again. I couldn't breathe or move. I wanted to faint in his arms and never wake up!

A tide swept over me, pushing me farther and farther from fear, time, and place. I was intoxicated. How wonderful it felt to be in his arms!

"Come!" Breathing heavily, Sadamu pulled me toward the comforter. I felt I was floating rather than walking. He unbuttoned my blouse, then he undressed himself. My face burned. He laid me on the comforter, carefully and gently. "Let this moment find us together! Don't be afraid," he whispered. His voice didn't seem like his own. I felt his warm hand on my breasts. A shock of electricity passed through me so strongly that I nearly jumped.

"Let it happen," Sadamu said again. "We only live once. Let me love you, Soon-ah. I want to take you with me to a new world filled with love and pleasure."

"But . . ."

"*Shhhh,* let it happen. Live first before you deny yourself. You deserve to be happy."

Sadamu's heart, pressing against my own, pounded louder

than any drumbeat. He kissed me hard, moaning. He touched me all over. A sense of adoration numbed me. As I felt him moving deeper and deeper, I clung to him desperately. Suddenly I was surrounded with silent music floating me like a feather on a calm river. Every nerve and fiber in my body sparked. This was something I'd never felt before. I was in a new world, full of hope. At last, I was free!

"I'm yours, Sadamu," I whispered in his ear when the stormy passion passed.

"Soon-ah!" he moaned and pulled me tightly. "I'll never let you receive another soldier as long as I live!"

It didn't feel right to be so happy. All this time my body had been used to serve Japanese soldiers and all I remembered was pain, intolerable pain, pain that made me hate men. God must not have created sex to punish women after all.

"Sadamu."

"Yes, Soon-ah."

"Doesn't it bother you that I have been with hundreds of men before you?"

He didn't say anything for what seemed like an eternity. Maybe he regretted it? Maybe he had forgotten I was a comfort woman?

"Soon-ah," Sadamu said, rising. His face resting on his palms, he looked at me through dark, sparkling eyes. "There are things that make us feel ashamed of ourselves and things that make us feel angry at others. When we wrong others or fail to do something, of course, we feel ashamed of ourselves. But if someone else has wronged you, you must never feel ashamed of yourself, only angry! That's important! Don't be confused about your feelings, Soon-ah. I'm angry that our country is using me and seven million other Japanese soldiers to demolish the world. I'm also ashamed my country-men are using thousands of young women like yourself as sex slaves, ruining their lives. What shames me the most, though, is that the Japanese worship Emperor Hirohito as if he were a god and do whatever he orders them to do. 'Invade China and take whatever we can use,' he ordered in 1936. Within months the soldiers took over all the major cities in China, killing innocent civilians and raping women on the street. When many soldiers contracted venereal diseases and died as the result of their barbarous behaviors, the emperor ordered again: 'Use Korean girls as comfort women. They are ignorant but clean because of Confucianism.' So hundreds of military officials combed Korean towns and villages, kidnapping girls. The Japanese mindlessly obeyed this puppeteer."

I remembered the two soldiers from the Imperial Palace walking into our classroom and urging us to help the Emperor, promising we would be nurses and entertainers. I could smell the dark underground shelter where I had hid. Omma had cried so much, begging and pleading with the soldiers not to take me. *Omma, why do we have to suffer so much? Only because our country was poor and powerless?*

"You have no reason to be ashamed of yourself, Soon-ah," Sadamu said sternly, yet warmly. "The Japanese injured you physically, mentally, and sexually. What's important is that you are free now."

Tears flowed from my eyes. It was an angry, painful cry. Sadamu patted my back as if I were a child needing his comfort.

"I love you, Sadamu!" I cried. "I want to live until the day I can tell the world what the Japanese have done to me. I hope I'll have courage to tell everything."

He kissed me again. "Yes, Soon-ah. You can do it. If you can see clearly why this has happened to you, you'll be able to separate the shame and guilt from the anger. Your mind can save you or kill you. You have a choice. Never let your own mind betray you. You're the woman I love, Soon-ah. Don't think of anything else."

I tasted tears on my lips. I was sobbing uncontrollably, but I felt I was worthy of love. Love wasn't something you deserved or didn't deserve, but a gift. My lover knew my value. I saw a gate opening before my eyes.

Renewed and exuberant, we plotted our escape. Sadamu brought boxes from the closet downstairs, and we inspected the contents. We found a tent and some camping equipment; a tin jug, an ax, a portable stove, canned goods, and an oil-burning lamp.

"Marco might be able to get us a boat," I said, remembering that Marco's father was a fisherman who had evacuated his family to Palau Island when poverty hit the Philippines.

Sadamu lifted his head. "Soon-ah, talk to him. Send him to me as soon as he's available."

"I'll see if he's free now." I got to my feet and headed to the door quietly.

"Be careful! Don't let Mr. Kim see you talking to him. We only have two days before Thursday," Sadamu said again.

Thursday! I remembered the party. All of the patrolmen would be busy worrying about the high-ranking officers at the party. They would circle around the *Midori*, determined not to let any Yankee come near the ship and spoil the party.

The manager was nowhere and Marco was alone in the restaurant, cleaning tables. It must have been long past the lunch hour. Most of the guests were with girls upstairs about this time of the day.

"Marco, the new guest on the third floor is wondering if you can bring his lunch now."

Marco looked at me, surprised. "The new guest?"

I blinked my eyes fast. "You know, the new guest from Tokyo?" I lied.

Immediately Marco went to the kitchen and I followed him.

"What are you talking about?" he whispered.

I quickly told him Sadamu was in trouble and needed a boat. "He wants to see you."

"If you can finish the tables for me, I'll go see him!"

"Sure. Take him a tray." I grabbed a bowl of rice and a plate of leftovers and set them on a tray.

Marco took the tray and disappeared behind the staircase like a gust of wind.

❋

On Thursday evening around six, the manager stopped me in the corridor. "Keiko, let Sadamu know that guests are arriving between seven and eight. Tell him to avoid those hours, know what I mean?"

"Yes, Mr. Kim. I'll make sure he locks the door, too, so that the natives can't steal things."

"Good idea. Don't be too late. I'll make sure someone looks for you."

"Don't worry."

At half past nine, Sadamu and I slipped out the back door and headed toward the reef. We waited to make sure everyone had left the House and all of the patrolmen were on duty.

The *Midori* glittered in the distance, concealing the mystery of the future. *Where would we be tomorrow?* I wondered as I walked next to Sadamu. *Would we still be alive?* The patrol boats, at least two dozen of them, cluttered the darkened water. Clouds covered the sky, barely revealing the obscure shape of a half moon above the thick and somber jungle. Sadamu's backpack, which we had found in the closet along with the rifles, rustled against his stiff uniform, making me nervous. Every noise beneath my feet annoyed me. Somewhere, wild animals were fighting, howling and shrieking.

After five minutes, my legs ached and I was out of breath. I had only a small bundle of clothes to carry, but the frightful thoughts in my head exhausted me. What if Marco wasn't able to get a boat and we had to go back? Sadamu had given him his gold watch in exchange for a boat. He had to get us a boat. We marched on, turning around several times, to make sure a patrolman wasn't following us.

The reef separating the land from the sea was quiet except for the wind whistling through the rocks. The cool ocean breeze soothed my anxiety. I breathed deeper as I followed Sadamu down the stiff reef toward the water as Marco had instructed him. The rocks were slippery. Half way down, my foot slipped on a moss-covered rock and, to my horror, I screamed. Luckily, Sadamu grabbed my arm in time to save me from cracking my head on a rock.

Reaching the water, we stood at the foot of a rock as tall as a tree and looked for Marco and his father. We saw no one. Nothing moved. As time passed, I became even more nervous. What if Marco just took Sadamu's gold watch and decided to forget about the boat?

Just then a long whistle startled me. Sadamu whistled back. Another whistle came, then another, competing with the wind.

I heard water splashing quietly and saw dark shadows approaching.

"Marco, is that you?" Sadamu said in a hushed tone.

"Yes, it's me!"

"This way, Marco!"

Two boats stopped in front of us. Marco and his father stood on the first boat and behind them was another boat with two shadows. I remembered Marco's father: he had brought the sea produce to the House.

"Everything you need is here," Marco whispered, handing Sadamu a bundle, "your fisherman's outfit and some food."

"Thank you, Marco." Sadamu quickly took off his uniform, wrapped it around a big rock and dropped it in the water. He put on the fisherman's outfit, tattered like a rag.

"Now tell us which way we must go," Sadamu said.

Marco's father stepped forward. "Go west," he said, raising his arm and pointing. "There are many, many islets in the Philippine Sea. If you are lucky enough, you might be able to go to

Mindanao Island. It's risky and it would take a long time but it's possible."

"Thank you for everything," Sadamu shook hands with each man. They stepped into the other boat and merged into the intense darkness, leaving the murmuring waves behind them.

Sadamu rowed quietly. Fear overwhelmed me when I saw the *Midori* on the far left. What if the Japanese guard on the ship noticed us and followed us, shooting? I closed my eyes and prayed: *Dear God, extend Your powerful hands over us and shield us from the Japanese. Order the ocean to be calm tonight, too, so we can find a safe place to hide.*

Auntie Myung's face emerged in my mind. 'Daughter, are you leaving me?' she seemed to say. I hadn't said anything to her because I feared she might accidentally reveal our plan, causing the MPs to arrest us. She'd be terribly hurt when she discovered I was gone. She'd think I had betrayed her trust and friendship, which I had. A pang of guilt hit me. But what could I do? If I had told her our plan, she might have stopped me, telling me I'd die in the sea. "Sorry, Auntie Myung," I whispered. "Forgive me. This is a matter of life and death. Please understand."

The boat glided quietly and softly toward the unknown, hauling my fear and anxiety. The wind was calm, as if God had heard my prayer.

Sadamu's shoulders rose and fell as he laboriously sliced the water with the oars. The reef, loaded with tall and round rocks, moved farther and farther away without a hint of sympathy. I had no way of knowing what would await us when the darkness lifted.

"Look at that star!" Sadamu said.

"Star? Where?"

"There! Look straight ahead. Can you see that tiny star glittering like a diamond?"

I could only see clouds moving in the opposite direction. "Are you sure it's a star?"

"Keep looking in that direction. You'll see it."

Then I saw it. Near the almost invisible horizon, I saw a tiny speck glittering. "How amazing!" I said, "that tiny star is the only star in the entire sky!"

"Let's call it the Star of Hope."

This moved me. What could be a more powerful sign than that star, shining so brightly before our eyes? "Sadamu, as long as I'm with you and see that star, I won't be afraid."

Sadamu stopped rowing and extended his arms to hold me. Feeling his strong arms tightly wrapped around me, I felt secure. Like that star surrounded by darkness, we could survive these Japanese devils, I thought.

With the first light the following morning, we spotted a grayish triangular landmass in the distance. We were elated. "We survived, Soon-ah! We made it!" Sadamu shouted, forgetting hours of strenuous rowing.

The landmass grew larger as we approached it. So far, we saw neither air attackers nor patrol ships. The ocean glittered in gold, blinding us.

The island was about the size of the foothill behind our house in Sariwon, which allowed us to see rice paddies spreading from horizon to horizon under our feet. But this island was covered with palm trees and tropical bushes with thick leaves. A thin sandstrip bordered the island, showing where the water ended and the land began. It seemed no human beings had lived here since Adam and Eve.

Sadamu carefully pulled the boat into the area where the trees were thickest and tied it to a palm tree covered with dagger-like leaves. Several colorful birds squealed loudly as they flew away. Two bright-eyed monkeys sat in another tree, chattering. They showed no signs of hysteria and looked naïve and innocent. We concluded there were no Japanese on this tiny islet. Finally, we took off our clothes and jumped into the water. The cool water soaked my skin and revived me from exhaustion. All the nerves and senses in my body ticked with vitality, and I breathed the sweet-smelling air as if I had never breathed anything before. I was choking with happiness. Hot liquid gathered in my eyes and streamed down my cheeks. I was finally free. I had never known the sky was that broad and the trees that majestic.

Sadamu kissed me. His lips tasted salty. We slowly sank to the ocean floor. The water was so blue that I felt my eyes would turn blue any minute, like those of a Westerner. We swam gracefully under water as if we had fins.

Sadamu looked hilarious in the water with arms outstretched, spitting bubbles. A playful mood overpowered me so I dove and tickled his foot. He grabbed my hand, pulled me up, and threw me in the air like a basketball. I made a huge splash as I came down.

Sadamu held me and kissed me again. We sank again, like two mating whales, weightless in the buoyant water, and kissed some more. He picked me up, carried me to the shallow water, and laid me down. My head was on the dry sand but my legs were still in the water. The gentle flow of the water tickled my feet and my ankles and I was dizzy with desire. We made love, listening to the chorus of waves, birds, and trees. We sat next to each other under a palm tree and ate grilled rice, bananas, and mangoes from the bundle Marco had given us. Lethargy overtook me as I lay on the sand. Sadamu lay next to me. The leaves swayed before my eyes, tattering the sky. Somewhere I heard birds crooning.

$\mathcal{R}$aucous bird noise awoke me. I vaguely remembered the *Midori*, glittering mysteriously in the distance as we escaped the House of Serenity. It seemed like a dream, but I remembered everything—the oars hitting the water, the dark sea, and the Star of Hope glowing faintly on the horizon. If it were only a dream, I didn't want to awaken. Auntie Myung's face appeared in my mind's eye again. "Soon-ah, I'm glad you escaped!" she seemed to say.

Escaped! I opened my eyes.

Sitting next to me, Sadamu was examining his rifle. "Sadamu, is this a dream?" I asked in a sleepy voice.

"No. Certainly not a dream. Should we explore the island? We must find a cave before dark," he said mechanically. What had happened to the romantic man in him? I wondered.

"Let's go, Soon-ah. Come!" Sadamu pulled me up and I

stood. With a small ax in one hand and a rifle in another, he looked like a hunter.

The jungle was so thick with overgrown vines, trees, and bushes that Sadamu had to clear our path with the ax. After a few minutes, everything was green. We could only see portions of the blue sky here and there. Several multicolored birds with handsome red and blue plumes sat in a huge tree and observed us, shifting their eyes and whispering to one another, *Go-go-go.* Other than the birds, everything I saw was green. Even the sunlight squeezing through the leaves and vines had a hint of green. I felt I was in an emerald castle. What a wondrous kingdom of vegetation this was!

We walked farther and farther. The ground was mostly mud. Soon the thin, liquid mud filled my canvas shoes and my feet sucked rhythmically. Insects bit my legs and I bent over to scratch them. Then I saw a huge spider covered with brown hair, the size of a chicken egg, sitting on a large leaf. It rose as if I had invaded its sacred territory.

"That's poisonous! Stay away, Soon-ah. One bite can finish you off!" Sadamu cried, and smashed it with his ax. This annoyed me. "Why did you have to kill it, Sadamu? I didn't ask you to kill it."

"What? Are you blaming me for saving your life?"

"How do you know it's poisonous?"

"We learned about them in the army before we left Japan."

We walked in silence until we reached a clearing. I felt a change of air movement and stopped walking. Two huge black vultures whirled in the air, drawing circles. Black vultures were a bad omen. Back home, we used to chase them away, throwing rocks and sticks at them.

"Don't move, Soon-ah!" Sadamu suddenly shouted.

"What is it?" I said.

He stood motionless, staring at a spot on the ground. "The Japanese have been here. Look at those decomposing bodies!"

My eyes followed Sadamu's gaze and I saw the dark mass

on the ground—a heap of rotting corpses. Now I recognized the smell: it was the same odor I had smelled on the hill in Babeldaop while digging graves in sweltering heat. I gagged.

Sadamu moved a few steps toward the corpses. I was terrified. "Don't leave me," I said.

"Don't worry, I won't leave you." Still, he moved closer to the corpses.

The corpses were all Westerners, some with yellow hair and some with brown, curly hair. All were covered with white worms that writhed and buzzed like bees.

Sadamu came back and spat on the ground. "They were American Marines. I don't know why they're on this island." He opened his palm, and I saw an oval-shaped piece of metal glaring at me. "This was lying on a rock next to the bodies. It's puzzling, isn't it? I saw some yellow flower petals on the bodies, too."

The metal piece had a name engraved on it: Ensign Charles Smith. No. 588907 Bend, Oregon. Sadamu put the metal piece into his pocket as if it were valuable.

"His family will never know he's rotting here," I said. My brother Wook came into my mind. Was he lying like these men, rotting somewhere in the Pacific? I hated my grisly thoughts, and I too spat. *Why were they here, anyway?* I wondered, trying hard not to think of Wook. *Maybe the Japanese torpedoed their ship, and they escaped to this island on a lifeboat, and the Japanese found them and murdered them?*

"Soon-ah," Sadamu said.

"Yes."

"Can you help me? I want to bury them."

I couldn't believe my ears. "Bury them? How? It would take us a whole month to bury all these decomposed bodies," I said and spat again. The thought of being near the decomposing bodies was bad enough, but bury them?

"Digging would be hard." Sadamu said, poking the dirt. "Underneath is mostly pressed coral and gravel. But we must cover them with something, maybe leaves and rocks. It's worth the labor, I think."

I didn't say anything. All I wanted to do was go back to the boat, bury my head, and try to get some sleep, stop wondering about Wook.

"If I were lying here," Sadamu said, "I'd be terribly sad, not only because I was losing my flesh here and there, but also because I was losing my dignity. I'd be immensely grateful if someone buried me."

I can't bury a dead body, not even for a thousand pieces of gold. So, be my guest, I wanted to say. But Sadamu moved to the corpses as if he thought I had agreed with him wholeheartedly. "Shall we?" he said.

How could I say no? Sadamu chopped at the hard dirt with his ax, and I gathered huge leaves and rocks to cover the bodies. To avoid the stench, I chewed on wild mint.

We worked until the moon peeked through coconut leaves and owls hooted on treetops. I often startled, thinking someone was standing behind me, and turned around, but only the dark silhouettes of the trees met my eyes. I even thought I heard footsteps and said so to Sadamu.

But he just said, "You have a wild imagination. Who would watch us? There's no one here," and kept digging.

We completely covered the bodies with dirt and leaves and rocks and came back to our boat, looking at our long shadows walking ahead of us.

Sitting next to Sadamu later that night, many thoughts crossed my mind. I was glad that we had rendered a small favor to those dead American men. Their families would be glad, no doubt. It would be wonderful if we met them. "We wanted to give them dignity," Sadamu would say, proudly. They might cry, thanking us for burying them. Now I felt much better about my hard labor.

It was a romantic night. With my head on my folded arms

resting on my knees, I watched the shadows of trees dancing elegantly on the ground, creating mysterious patterns.

"Soon-ah," Sadamu said, looking at the shadows.

"Yes."

"Do you believe in ghosts?"

"Yes, I do."

"Good! That's why I wanted to bury the corpses. It's important that we do kind things for the dead, I think. Although they are dead, they are in our midst. We can't see them, but they're with us. We must treat them well just as if they were alive. If not, they'll haunt us. Strange things happen, you know."

"Do you suppose there are Japanese ghosts on this island?" I asked.

"Maybe hundreds of them," he said.

"Then they must be fighting with the American ghosts since they're enemies."

"I don't think so, Soon-ah. When you're dead you see things differently, I think. They might have become friends by now, who knows. They might be apologizing to one another for killing so brutally. It's us, the living, who can't stand other living beings."

I couldn't sleep all night, worrying about ghosts. Luckily, morning came in a hurry and we found a cave on the other side of the jungle. When the sun was directly above our heads, we finished moving our modest household into the cave and ate lunch, the grilled rice and some bananas. We curled up together on a flat rock, listening to the water dripping from the ceiling and making a hollow musical sound against the mineral formations. This was the beginning of our life together in this cave, I thought and smiled. Somewhere in the distance, I heard bats squealing and water gurgling.

Later, Sadamu cut the limbs of a tree and made two torches and we walked deeper into the cave. Bats flew angrily over our heads, flapping their wings. In one place we found a spacious dome where many stalactites hung like stiff pant-legs in all different lengths and we stood there for a few seconds, admiring the art work and the music performed by dripping water.

After five minutes Sadamu disappeared under the ground, yelling "Ouch!" The echo imitated his voice, *Ouch! ouch! ouch!*

Frightened, I yelled, "Sadamu, Sadamu!" Again, an eerie echo imitated me, *Sadamu! Sadamu! Sadamu!*

"Are you all right?" I shouted again, looking down where he had disappeared.

I heard his voice reply, "Here!"

I lowered my torch light and saw Sadamu getting up, shaking the dirt from his pants. The pit was about the size of a small room about four feet deep.

"Jump!" he said. "I'll catch you."

"How can we get out?" I said. I was afraid it might be a snake pit.

"Looks like some Japanese lived here," he said, pointing at the wall in front of him.

I jumped down. Sadamu caught me and we looked at the wall together. In the torch light, the letters were quite legible:

> For the Emperor, I die.
> For my ancestors, I offer my blood.
> Glory was my single aim
> Come death in your graceful attire
> and gather me in your restful bosom.

"Such devotion," Sadamu said to himself. He bent over and looked closely at the pile of dirt and debris next to his feet.

"What is it?"

"I don't know. They look like bones to me," he said, kicking the pile. Dust rose and a skull rolled out.

I screamed.

"Look! He was a Japanese soldier. See the uniform!"

A hat still rested in the dirt with a dulled metal badge. Next to him was a rusted dagger, telling how this soldier had killed himself.

My legs began shaking. I almost saw the skeleton rising and shouting, throwing his arms into the air, "Banzai! Banzai! Banzai!"

"Let's get out of here!" I whispered.

"He was a lieutenant. He must have been a little older than me when he died," Sadamu said, ignoring my plea.

"I want to go, Sadamu," I said louder, feeling my hair rise. I had seen too many dead bodies already and I couldn't stand seeing another.

Sadamu didn't notice how frightened I was. "But how did he bury himself before he committed hara-kiri?" he asked himself. "That doesn't make sense, does it? Maybe someone helped him die? Maybe someone killed him? I doubt it, though."

My knees felt weak at the same time the dirt jumped to my face. The next moment, I was lying on the ground next to the skeleton, our heads almost touching. I heard Sadamu calling me, "Soon-ah, Soon-ah!"

A rumbling noise woke me. I was alone in the cave. I could hear bats flapping around. I sat up, wondering where Sadamu had gone. I vaguely remembered fainting and being carried by Sadamu. *Did he go back to that skeleton?* The thought that there might be many more skeletons in this cave drained life out of me. It could take Sadamu days to inspect all of the skeletons, and I might have to go with him because I didn't want to be left alone.

"Quick, Soon-ah! It's a patrol boat." Sadamu rushed in, grabbed me, and almost dragged me to a huge column. A drop of water splashed on my head, chilling my bones.

"What is it?" I asked, feeling like a child.

"I said it's a patrol boat. If they come in here I'll shoot them! Prepare, Soon-ah!" he said, loading his rifle. His rigid expression told me he was serious.

The noise of the motorboat crescendoed and decrescendoed as the boat circled the island for what seemed like an eternity. After a while, we could hear nothing, but we were too afraid to move. When it was completely dark and the moon hung above the mouth of the cave, we crawled out and walked to the beach to see if our boat was still tied to the palm tree. We were relieved to see it under the branches and leaves, just as we had left it.

Early next morning when the sky was barely lit with a faint gray light, we went out, chopped branches, and gathered large rocks. We stacked the rocks at the opening of the cave and camouflaged it with the branches. Sure enough, the patrol boat came back in mid-morning. This time we heard the motorboat coughing and choking just offshore. I fixed my gaze on the mouth of the cave where a thin light pierced through the rocks, afraid to move. Soon I heard voices as the sound of bayonets clearing the vines approached us, *shhhhk, shhhhk, shhhhk.*

"Damn! We're wasting time, Shigeo. They can't be hiding on this island. Let's move on to another," a man said, then spat.

"Bakayaro!" another man said. "It's Sergeant Asai we're dealing with. We better search this island before we move on to another."

"But it's ridiculous! It'd take a month to search all of these islands. By now that son of bitch might be lying deep in the ocean with that comfort woman. What's so special about that fucking correspondent anyway!"

"Shut up and keep moving. Don't give me any trouble, you hear?"

"You're such an asshole, Shigeo! We don't know when we'll die! Why waste time on one man?"

"Just do what you're told. All you think about is going to the Comfort House, but don't be such an idiot. Sergeant Asai knows where you are when you're not in the barracks."

"So? He's the one who taught me what to do with women.

By the way, he was right about those Korean girls: they're delicious. They do anything we tell them to. Of course a schoolboy wouldn't understand what I'm talking about."

"You stupid idiot! You might never go back home but you're not even worried about it."

"Go back home? What for? So we'll turn into ashes? Didn't you know half of Tokyo turned into rubble last April? Wake up, schoolboy!"

"I am going back even if I turn into ashes. I belong there, next to my ancestors. A samurai must know where to die and be buried. Just shut up and follow me!"

Through the crack between the rocks at the opening, I saw a soldier appear. He was a short man. He stopped in front of the cave and spat again, *Tssst!* His bayonet flashed against the sun and blinded my eyes: everything looked black for two seconds. When I regained my sight, I saw him unbuttoning his pants and urinating. The stream of his urine made a multicolored arc under the brilliant sunlight. I covered my eyes.

"That swine!" Sadamu hissed, "I'll castrate him!"

A laugh bubbled up and I quickly clamped my hand over my mouth. Sadamu's eyes glowed in the dark, full of malicious delight. I thought I'd die, trying to smother my laughter.

"Let's go!" the soldier shouted, buttoning his trousers. He moved away along with the rustling noise. One of them hummed a popular Japanese song called "My Destiny," and the other shouted to shut up. The voices tapered, then merged with the sound of waves.

I took a deep breath as I realized we were alone.

Sadamu reached for me, pulled me into his arms, and kissed me. "Thank God, you're with me," Sadamu whispered.

"I'm safe as long as we are together, Sadamu," I said, choking with tears of gladness.

"Are you afraid, Soon-ah?"

"No, not anymore. I was."

"Good! Doesn't it feel like we are left alone in this wide

world? Think about Adam and Eve. Maybe they were like us, all alone in the Garden of Eden. If we don't worry about dying, life in this cave might be wonderful. Listen to this!" He then stood on a rock and talked aloud, just the way an actor did on a stage: 'Two young lovers are trapped in a cave surrounded by trees and bushes. All they hear is the sound of waves at the ocean and their own heartbeats.' Doesn't it sound romantic? Let's say I'm the ruler of this kingdom and you are my queen, what do you think?" Sadamu said.

"No, not a ruler." I shook my head. "You remind me of Emperor Hirohito. I don't like rulers! I don't want to be your queen."

"Okay. What are we then?" he said, his excitement diminishing.

"Two moles afraid of dying."

※

For two days we stayed in the cave for fear the soldiers would return. We survived strictly on grilled rice and the water dripping from the ceiling. When the rice ran out on the third day, Sadamu slipped out of the cave early one morning and picked wild berries and fruits and hurried back to the cave.

The soldiers didn't come back the next day or the next. Sadamu engraved our names and the approximate date of our arrival—the 25th of Tenth Month, 1942—on a white stalagmite column and drew a huge heart around it. Under the heart he wrote, "Sadamu loves Soon-ah. We fear no death."

The berries and fruits didn't last long and we were hungry again. Our stomachs growled noisily, taking turns. On the fourth day Sadamu chopped down a bamboo tree and made a snorkel and a fishing pole. With a snorkel in his mouth, he jumped into the water and caught abalones, mussels, and sea cucumbers clinging to rocks in deep water. There's nothing tastier than abalones and mussels hand-delivered by the fisherman himself.

The sea was so clear we could see crabs leisurely striding sideways on the ocean floor, catching snails and poking clams. They, too, became Sadamu's prey. Occasionally a school of colorful fish glided through seaweed and corals, but Sadamu couldn't catch them—either they were too quick or Sadamu not quick enough.

While Sadamu was busy at sea, I taught myself how to weave baskets with bamboo sticks and palm leaves. I finally mastered the skill one day and filled my baskets with leftover abalones and mussels, and laid it on a flat rock to dry. This was for the days we would be trapped in the cave again.

To our bewilderment, the basket disappeared the next day. At first we thought the monkeys had stolen our food and searched everywhere for the empty basket. Soon, we ruled out this suspicion. If they were monkeys or other animals, they wouldn't take the entire basket, and even if one of them was clever enough to take the whole thing, we would still find some signs of their clumsiness—a broken piece of basket here or a half eaten abalone there, but nothing! Our thieves could be humans!

Two days later we met our thief face to face. That afternoon, Sadamu was at sea and I was at the waterfall washing clothes. Occasionally, red frogs jumped up from the surrounding brushwood, startling me. When I finished washing, I spread the wet clothes on a flat rock to dry. I swam in the icy cold water. Soon I was cold, so I lay on another rock roasting under the sun and listening to the sound of cicadas.

A swishing noise of branches made me spring up. "Sadamu?" I said. No response. "Sadamu, are you there?" I shouted, looking into the brushwood, expecting him to jump up, laughing. Instead, his voice came through the leaves and vines, twenty yards away. "Yes, Soon-ah, I'm here."

Strange, I thought. "Would you please come here?" I shouted.

A man in a green uniform jumped out of the bush. He had

a monstrous face without eyes or nose, only a couple of holes oozing yellow fluid. I screamed. Limping, he ran into a thicket.

Sadamu ran after him. Bushes moved wildly in the jungle. Birds rose, fluttering their wings and chattering angrily. The cicadas stopped droning.

I quickly grabbed my wet clothes, and sat on a rock behind a tree trunk, shivering. How long had it been since they had disappeared? Ten minutes? An hour? The bushes moved again, and Sadamu appeared, alone. *Did he kill him?* I wondered.

"What happened?" I asked him, peeking from behind the tree.

"I don't know," he said, avoiding my eyes. He came over and sat on a rock facing me. Pulling a branch in front of him, he broke off a leaf and shredded it.

"Who was that man?" I asked.

"He was one of the American marines who were shot. We would have buried him, too, if the rain hadn't wakened him."

"What are you talking about?"

"He told me he doesn't remember anything but waking up in the rain. He couldn't talk very well, so I had a hard time understanding him. Can you imagine being alive alone on an island like this?"

"Why didn't you ask him to come stay with us?"

"I did, but he shook his head and said that we don't need to smell his rotting flesh. He thinks he'll die any minute. It was sad, watching him disappear into the mess of foliage, limping."

"If you had insisted, maybe he would have come. You never know."

"No, I don't think so, Soon-ah. The worst thing I could do was say that his judgment wasn't worthwhile. I respect his feelings."

That night, I was full of thoughts: what would it be like having such a scary face? A face is everything to a person because a face reveals so much: thoughts, agony, happiness, good health, and bad health. Was he a handsome man before he was shot? Did he have a wife? How would his wife feel when he returned home looking like a mass of dough? Weaving through a web of thoughts I drifted to sleep.

I was walking homeward with a bundle in my hand. I saw Omma dashing out of the gate, calling, "Soon-ah!" I ran to her, shouting "Omma, Omma!" The distance between us shrank and we stood face to face, ready to embrace one another. But she turned her head. "Oh, you aren't Soon-ah! I'm sorry. I thought you were my daughter."

"Omma, it's me. Look at me! I'm home!"

But she shook her head, sadly.

"Omma, I was taken as a gift of the Emperor, remember? But I came back!" I noticed that she had changed. Her face was like crepe paper, full of wrinkles. I read her agony, sorrow, and anger hidden between her wrinkles.

"No! You aren't my daughter," she said angrily. "Soon-ah didn't have those scars and bumps on her face. She was a pretty girl with big dark eyes and clean skin, as clean as an eggshell . . ." Then she lifted her head toward the hill where I often picked dandelions to make tea.

I was frightened. Was I dead and Omma couldn't recognize my rotting flesh? Wasn't I clean anymore and she could sense it? "Omma, I'm your daughter! I waited so long to come to you!" I cried, but Omma turned and briskly walked away.

A crow awoke me with a loud call. A sigh left my lips. I was glad it was only a dream, but at the same time I had a strange feeling: a crow was a sign of bad news.

We saw the man again once, sitting motionless on a large rock facing the vast sea. He looked as if he had turned into a statue, except for his long curly hair waving in the wind.

The next morning we found his lifeless body floating near where he had been sitting. Sadamu wanted to bury him next to his buddies but I told him to leave him in the water. I thought he'd be happier in the ocean.

※

Winter had come. Berries and fruit dwindled in the jungle but the foliage was still thick and green. Sadamu and I calculated the marks on the columns and decided that the New Year was around the corner. We celebrated by talking excessively of the food we ate on New Year's Day such as mochi, the sweet rice-cake, and thin bean paste soup, which both Koreans and Japanese ate on holidays. Occasionally we saw obscure objects appear and disappear on the horizon, sometimes battleships and other times dark clouds. One time, we counted forty-eight Japanese air attackers flying south.

One morning a thundering noise awoke us. Sadamu climbed a tall nipa tree on the shore and looked out. "They're fighting! I think they are shooting torpedoes!" he shouted.

I could vaguely see two dark objects spitting smoke at the horizon where the sun blinded my eyes. It was too far to tell which ship was American, which Japanese. The shooting went on for about half an hour before a yellow pillar leaped from the ship on the left. Immediately, black smoke surrounded it, and we knew it was a fatal blow. The ship on the left tilted, gradually sinking, leaving black clouds behind it. The other ship circled around the sinking vessel, shooting fiercely, before disappearing.

A few hours later, the roaring turbulence from the sunken ship reached the shore. Sadamu and I watched blotches of black oil making artful designs on the sand and the debris cluttering the ocean. Darkened splinters, floating bodies, boxes, and many other objects brought us a glimpse of the calamity.

My eyes caught a dark wooden barrel floating about twenty yards away from the beach and I told Sadamu about it.

"That's a wine barrel!" Sadamu said, jumping into the water to get it.

"Whew! It's heavy!" Sadamu said, pulling the barrel onto the sand. He lifted the rope-handle attached to the top. "My God!" he muttered.

I looked in. Crumpled in a fetal position was an oriental man in an American soldier's uniform. He was motionless, his mouth half open, hardly breathing. His face was the color of dead chicken in a poultry.

Sadamu shook him, "Wake up!" The soldier squirmed a little but didn't awaken. Sadamu gently slapped him on the cheek. "Wake up!" The soldier only mumbled some unintelligible words. Sadamu pulled him out of the barrel and ordered me: "Soon-ah, get some water!"

I ran to the cave and brought Sadamu's tin cup filled with water. Sadamu poured water into the soldier's mouth.

The soldier gradually opened his eyes and looked at Sadamu and me. His blank eyes looked scary.

"Where am I?" he said in Japanese.

"You're on a rock island near Palau," Sadamu answered. I noticed blood dripping from one of the soldier's boots, staining the sand.

Sadamu set him against the trunk of a palm tree and cut open his boots, removing them from his feet.

The soldier's eyes shifted nervously in all directions.

I went back to the cave and brought my cotton dress. I tore it with my teeth into several long strips.

Sadamu cleaned the wound carefully with sea water and let it dry. Then he applied aloe juice to the soldier's foot and wrapped it with a strip of my shredded dress.

The soldier endured his ordeal, moaning quietly. He ate hardly anything we gave him—dried abalone and mussels, berries, and mangos—but stared at the sea. Sadamu offered him coconut milk. He drank it. We left him alone to rest. When the early stars appeared, Sadamu welcomed him and asked him if he remembered anything.

He glanced at the shore cluttered with debris, asking, "Am I the only survivor?"

"Yes, you're the only one so far."

He bent his face and cried. Teardrops wet his parched lips and he licked them. A moment later he wiped his tears. "I am Robert Tanaka," he began in fluent Japanese. "I was a radio telegrapher for an American cruiser called the *Victor*. Near Sonsorol Island an enemy ship appeared from nowhere and followed us, shooting torpedoes. We zigzagged nearly a hundred miles, trying to escape its target range, but one of the torpedos hit the engine room. We lost all electrical power. Sirens wailed and the crews were falling on top of one another, trying to go back to their assigned positions. It was a disaster. Smoke was so intense I was unable to send out an SOS. Finally, the captain ordered us to abandon ship. We boarded four lifeboats. Then the *Victor* capsized. A dozen people, the last to leave the ship, jumped into the water and swam toward the lifeboats. The enemy fired at them. The water turned red below us. We rowed toward this island.

"I noticed a Japanese I-boat approaching us. Someone shouted 'Jump!' and we jumped into the water. I saw bullets breaking through the water and passing us, like fast-moving snakes. I dove deeper. One of the bullets struck my commanding officer in his white uniform. He sank like a rock into a mass of seaweed. I was so frightened my legs stiffened. I was going down, too. I thought I'd be the next target. But I never felt any bullet hitting me. My khaki uniform must have saved me.

"I held my breath so long I had a chest pain. I came up briefly to get a gulp of air. I saw the I-boat turning around and moving in the opposite direction. I stayed in the water for another few seconds, thinking my end had come, until I saw a barrel floating next to me. I thought it was Godsent. It was empty so I climbed inside. I suppose I fainted after that."

Robert looked at the barrel lying on the sand just the way my father looked at the tabernacle in his church.

Day by day, we learned a little more about Robert: he had been a medical student at the University of California in Los Angeles at the time of the Pearl Harbor attack. Three months after the invasion, U.S. Military Police moved his family to a Relocation Camp behind barbed wire at Tule Lake. Every student who had Japanese blood in his or her veins was the target of the white students' hostility. Many Asian students who weren't Japanese also had been beaten and shot on the campus. Soon every Japanese student received a draft notice in the mail. Robert and hundreds of other Japanese students protested to the military, but they were arrested and sent to the army training camp.

Robert was among six thousand Japanese-Americans who attended the Military Intelligence Specialist School and later were sent to intelligence units in the Pacific. Some volunteered to go to European combat units to show they too were American citizens.

"I love my country," Robert said solemnly, "but to my fellow Americans, I'll never be one of their own no matter how much I love my country or how hard I work to be a good American citizen. I know very little about Japan, but white Americans see my yellow skin and think I'm their enemy."

The foamy waves rose and fell, crashing against the rocks. In silence, we watched the waves carrying the wreckage to the island.

*R*obert was a quiet man. Every morning he dragged his injured foot to a large rock on the shore and watched the turquoise water swelling and falling, breaking into millions of white beads against the rocks. I thought he was praying. What else would he be doing, looking at the majestic ocean in the early sunlight, except talking to God?

Sometimes he whistled a tune. It was a beautiful melody. When he noticed me listening to him, he stopped and smiled at me uncomfortably. I asked him what song he was whistling, and he said, "It's called 'Swanee River'." I told him I liked it, but he just shrugged his shoulders, blushing.

He often sat on a rock next to Sadamu and watched him fish. Occasionally they got into a long conversation in English, but I couldn't understand what they were talking about. Here and there I could hear such names as: "MacArthur," "Nimitz,"

"Roosevelt," "Churchill," "Normandy," "Hitler," "Jews," "Chiang Kai-Shek," "Yamamoto" and "Tojo." I was as frustrated as a dog attending a scholarly conference, not understanding a word they spoke.

One day, I asked Robert to teach me English. "Sure," he said.

Immediately, Robert wrote some simple words in the sand such as: bird, tree, airplane, monkey, friend, dog, man, and woman, and told me what they meant in Japanese. Sometimes, he pointed at birds and trees or drew pictures on the sand, forcing me to remember what he had taught me. It was fun trying to guess what he was describing with his artistic skill which, in my opinion, wasn't outstanding.

Once he pretended he couldn't remember the word "snow" in Japanese, and he rolled in the sand, sprinkled it in the air, and put it on his tongue, saying "Cold! Very cold." Finally Sadamu, who normally remained silent, laughed from a tree branch. "Robert, you look like a puppy dumped in a snow pile." Then I understood what Robert was trying to say. By the time his foot had healed a month later, I was able to say a few sentences such as "How ah you, Roburt?" "I like ocean!" "Good fish, yes? "More abalon, please." I felt very intelligent.

One afternoon during a lesson, we saw an airplane spinning in the air, spitting a ball of fire. Within seconds, it had crashed in the jungle with a thundering noise, spreading fire. The earth shook loudly from the impact, and yellow and red flames licked the jungle with blazing tongues. When the flames died hours later, black smoke rose over the jungle for many days, mingling with mist.

Through the veil of smoke and mist, everything was revealed: blackened, half burned trees smoking like factory chimneys, featherless birds immobile under large rocks, the waterfall vomiting ink-black water, and the pond cluttered with burned leaves and ashes. We inspected the jungle and found the burned body of a Japanese pilot lying on the ground.

Surrounded by broken glass, metal pieces, and the panels of the plane, the pilot's eyes were still open and his jaws tightly clenched. The explosion blew away the dirt and formed a huge hole where he lay. The soot-covered rocks and trees glared at us horridly. It was a miracle that our boat was safe.

"Let's move to another island," Sadamu said. "The Japanese might be looking for their friend."

But Robert had a different idea. "The islands aren't safe. We don't know which islands are occupied by enemy. I might rather take a chance and head to the Philippines, hoping that we'll be rescued by an American ship."

Robert and Sadamu busied themselves in the jungle, cutting and hammering wood to install a roof on the boat. The sun in the Pacific was never merciful, and while traveling we would be easily roasted under the scorching heat and would eventually die.

Watching Sadamu and Robert working together, chatting and joking, sometimes in Japanese and other times in English, I was cynical about life's cruelty. They were both Japanese, yet enemies in the eyes of the world. Had they met earlier, armed and uniformed, they'd have killed one another without thinking twice about it. Now, hiding from the Japanese, they were trusting friends. No one knew what they would be tomorrow—friends or enemies.

Five days later we had a handsome boat with a roof on top, camouflaged with coconut and palm leaves.

We launched our new vessel and ourselves with it, desperately hoping to find an American ship. We had lost count of the days, because the water dripping in the cave had blurred the markings on the column and we didn't know what month it was. We only knew it was spring.

We took along two bamboo fishing poles, the wine barrel that saved Robert's life to store our food, and a white flag—my white blouse tied to another bamboo pole. Sadamu wore the dogtag we found next to the corpses as if it were a lucky charm: he believed somehow it would save our lives.

"How?" I asked him.

"It's obvious. When the Americans rescue us, I'll tell them how charitable we were toward the U.S. marines on that island. I'm sure they'll be charitable toward us too," he said, caressing the dogtag.

For several days we saw nothing at sea but some birds. Everywhere I looked, turquoise water stretched in all directions. We saw no signs of ships, American or Japanese, and no hint of civilization. Once a huge pelican flew over and paused on the wine-barrel, casting greedy eyes on our food but Sadamu shooed it away. Occasionally a large turtle, as large as a cushion, surfaced and followed us. In Korean folk tales, a turtle was a sacred creature bringing good fortune to people. I fed him every time I saw him. When he ate enough, he fell asleep, floating.

At night, we kept the North Star on the starboard and moved toward the west. When the sky was dark, we assumed the location of the North Star and moved anyway, since we had no compass to show us the direction. Sometimes the air-attackers swarmed in one area, spurting fire. We stopped rowing and watched the smoke-trailing airplanes descending like birds with very long gray tails. We couldn't see who was fighting who, but felt sorry for the dying.

It didn't rain. Sweating profusely, we drank only a mouthful of water and a small portion of dried fish or abalones each day to save our supply. On the sixth day at dawn, we saw a dark object on the horizon. We thought it was an island and rowed faster. But in the afternoon it turned into an enormous dark cloud carrying a heavy storm. The ocean roared loudly that night. Rain exploded on us like hail. Monumental waves rushed to us like a tribe of giant elephants, and the boat danced dangerously.

Eventually, the wind tore off our roof and threw it toward the dark clouds. Within minutes the wine-barrel rolled into the sea along with our food and sailed away as if it had a navigator. I held onto the jug of water with all my might begging God to save us.

The storm died the next day, and the sea regained its peaceful grandeur. We were hungry and exhausted, with only a jug of water to comfort us. Now, there was nothing to cover our heads. The burning sun bore down on us mercilessly as we clung to our dear lives.

Sadamu was eager to catch some fish, but the ocean stayed murky. He couldn't catch anything. Instead of fish, masses of seaweed floated everywhere and we ate it. It was tasteless and felt like rubber on our tongues, but we knew it was nutritious. When the water cleared, many tiny blue fish appeared around the boat. Sadamu caught several with his bamboo pole, and sometimes with his bare hands. We ate them raw. The next day he caught a long, large fish with sparkling white scales and we were elated. Robert thought the big fish was a white bass. I had never heard of that name before and wondered if it had a Korean name. The fish lasted for two days.

By the ninth day we were covered with painful blisters. I desperately wished we had a roof again but what good was wishing in the middle of the ocean? I wet all my clothes in the water and covered my head, arms, and legs with them but within minutes they became stiff like leather. Sadamu's blisters were much worse than mine or Robert's. When they popped, his skin turned red, like a monkey's rear end. I applied aloe to his reddened skin and covered it with my wet clothes. I felt fortunate I still had a few aloe leaves in the boat.

We often talked about food, real food. Robert was obsessed with the turkey dinners he had had with his family in California on holidays. Although his parents were originally from Japan, they ate like Americans.

Robert's turkey didn't arouse my appetite. There were no

turkeys in Korea and I had no idea how turkey tasted or looked. Was a turkey like a chicken? I asked. "No, much larger," Robert said. I tried to imagine a bird the size of a dog or a pig with chicken feathers and a red comb and asked Robert if my description sounded like a turkey. "No, it's not even close," he said, laughing. "A turkey is as tall as a toddler and cries 'Gobble, gobble.'" I was even more curious about this bird.

I craved kimchi and a bowl of steamed rice. My mother was an excellent kimchi maker. Even our neighbors and relatives praised her delicious kimchi. During the Full Moon celebration, my mother's kimchi ran out long before any of the other kimchi brought to the celebration.

Sadamu's favorite food was tempura udon, a noodle soup with fried shrimp on top. He talked longingly about a tiny udon booth near his campus site. "Their udon soup is the most delicious soup I remember. I wonder if the booth will still be there when I go back," he said.

Food-talk made me homesick. It seemed good things always happened around good food, and whenever I remembered the happy moments of my life, I always remembered what food we ate that day.

On one of those days when time stopped ticking, I recited a poem called "Friends" written by a famous poet in the Yi Dynasty. It was a desperate attempt to escape the boredom suffocating our spirits.

> How many friends do I have?
> The streams and rocks, the pines and bamboo;
> Moon rising over the mountain
> She too my friend.
> Beyond these five
> What more do I want?

Sadamu and Robert clapped. Sadamu suggested that since no rocks, pines, bamboo, and mountains were around us, we must revise the poem. We agreed. Instantly, he composed a new poem:

> How many friends do I have?
> The waves, the sun, and the growling stomachs.
> The fish jumping on the surface arouse my hunger
> Send us more fish, Mighty One in heaven,
> You are the only Friend who can keep us alive!

Laughing tortured our roasted skin but delighted our souls. Surrounded, as we were, by the immense sea day and night, banned from civilization, laughing was a luxury. But soon we looked at one another gloomily. If we weren't picked up by a boat soon, we would perish on the ocean. I watched the dull, foamy clouds with bitterness.

On the twelfth day we spotted another dark object on the horizon. Another storm? We were terrified. If it was another storm, we'd surely die this time. As it came closer, we trembled with a mixture of joy and fear. A ship! Sadamu began breathing loudly, anticipating the worst. No doubt he and Robert would be executed if it was a Japanese ship. They might send me to another brothel.

"It's a ship! It's a ship!" Robert was shouting.

"Soon-ah, lift the pole!" Sadamu ordered, but my legs were so shaky I couldn't move. Sadamu came over and lifted the pole himself. The ship made a loud noise, like a blasting horn, and I could see dark, miniature human forms on the deck waving at us. The water under us pushed the boat toward the ship. The sun was blinding and I couldn't see whether the passengers were American or Japanese.

A voice speaking English boomed, but I couldn't understand what they were saying. Robert shouted back to them, but a loud popping noise halted his words and water jumped on my face. All my energy rushed out of me and I saw bright light in my eyes: I fainted.

A hand forced my eyes open. Everything was blurry. Then a large blue eye peered into mine. Who was this? I wondered. I heard loud voices talking in English like squawking birds.

"Are you all right?" the man with blue eyes asked me in English. He reminded me of the French movie star, Maurice Chevalier.

"Yes," I answered.

Turning his head to the nurse behind him, he said, "She speaks English." His silvery hair made his face look gentle and kind. He said something again in English but I couldn't understand. I shrugged. I wished I could explain that I knew only a few words in English, mostly yes and no. I tried to sit up.

"No, don't move," the doctor warned me, showing his palm and waving it in my face. "You need to rest," he said. His blue eyes squinted as he smiled.

I wanted to know where Sadamu and Robert were. I gathered my courage and decided to test my English. "Where . . . is . . . my friends?" I asked.

"They're all right. They're resting. You'll see them at dinner." The doctor talked slowly enough that I could understand him. *At least my lessons with Robert were worthwhile,* I thought.

I was so tired I fell asleep again. I was still on our fishing boat, wrestling with waves. The endless waves rushed toward us then moved away. The wind jerked the boat, and the boat danced dangerously.

A hand tapped my arm. "Soon-ah," Sadamu said, standing next to me with a smile.

I grabbed his arm. "Sadamu!"

"Relax! We've made it! We're going to be all right!" he said, squeezing my hand.

"Sadamu, I love you. . . ." I whispered, wanting to be in his arms.

"Listen, Soon-ah. They're going to ask a lot of questions tomorrow morning. I don't know what they'll ask us, but be prepared. They won't consider us prisoners of war since we weren't fighting against them, so don't fret."

But I couldn't think about tomorrow: all I wanted to dwell on was that Sadamu was next to me and that we were alive. I drifted to sleep again, feeling Sadamu's warm hand in mine.

A knock on the door awoke me. I was in a box-like room with a circular window that disclosed a majestic view of the ocean. "Yes," I said, sitting up and straightening my dress and hair.

A young sailor with a boyish face came in and jabbered something unintelligible. He spoke so fast that I couldn't understand a word.

"Excuse me?" I said.

"Come!" he said, motioning me to follow him. "Food! Eat! Cafeteria!" I understood him this time. Suddenly I was very hungry.

We walked down the long, narrow corridor, to a huge room filled with men in sailors' uniforms eating and smoking. The sailor took me to the table where Sadamu and Robert were sitting and talking.

"We made it!" Sadamu said excitedly as soon as he saw me, getting up and pulling out the chair next to his.

I sat, but I couldn't share his excitement. Soon our destiny would be decided, once again, by others. Where would we be tomorrow?

Sadamu reached under the table and grabbed my hand. His hand was warm, and I fought my tears.

"This ship is going to Hawaii," Sadamu said, trying to cheer me up.

"Hawaii?" I asked, without any particular emotion other than that I'd lose him soon.

"That's right!" Robert confirmed.

We had a hearty breakfast with eggs, pink salty meat, some soury yellow drink, and grilled bread. I was the only woman in the entire room, and it made me nervous. And I wasn't comfortable using a fork and knife; I didn't know which one went in which hand. Unlike chopsticks, they were heavy and slippery, and I kept dropping them on the wooden floor, making a monstrous noise each time. I noticed heads turning toward me.

Sadamu saw what was happening and tried to come to my rescue, only to make the situation worse. He reached for my plate and cut the meat for me, ordering, "Just use your fork now!"

I glanced at the next table through the corner of my eyes to make sure no one saw what Sadamu had done. Sure enough, a large sailor was looking at me, smiling. I looked away. Until the young sailor reappeared, I only stared at my plate.

We followed him to a conference room that contained a long table in the middle and an American flagpole in the corner. As we entered, I noticed three officers and a young Japanese man sitting on one side of the table, looking at us solemnly. Behind them stood a camera man, flashing lights in our direction.

We looked at our interrogators: on the right was a middle-aged officer wearing thick gold-framed glasses; next to him was a scrawny brown-haired man with small, dull eyes; the third man was a young officer with pimples; and at the end was a Japanese man.

The middle-aged man showed much authority. He looked at us grandly through his glasses, then said to Robert, "I'm glad to see you, Ensign Tanaka." Unlike his remote expression, his voice was friendly. "I understand you had quite a journey."

"Yes, sir. I was on the brink of death, sir. I can't describe how happy I am to be here, alive and well."

"I am happy for you, too. I have been there myself. Once I floated on a lifeboat alone for two days, without water and food. Get plenty of rest, Ensign. Tell the cook what you like to eat. I'll make sure he cooks your favorite dishes!"

"Thank you, sir!" Robert nodded.

Then the officer turned to Sadamu, his expression changing. His brown eyes blinked suspiciously before he began, "Tell us about yourself, Mr. Izumi. I assume you're a Japanese soldier."

"Not any more, sir," Sadamu said defensively. "You might find it hard to believe, but I ran away from my regiment a long time ago. I couldn't tolerate their brutality, sir!"

"Is that so?" the middle-aged officer said dryly. The other officers glanced at one another.

"My commander was a trained executioner. All together he executed at least two dozen men in a small clearing in the jungle: some were conscripts and some were deserters. The last two were American pilots."

The middle-aged officer narrowed his eyebrows. "American pilots? Tell us more about them."

Sadamu told them how Sergeant Asai beheaded them one by one, and added, "I never liked watching the killing, sir. It is a violation of the Geneva Disarmament Codes. But Sergeant Asai loved to demonstrate his killing skill in front of his troops and prisoners. We had no choice but watch him." Sadamu's voice dropped and he looked guilty.

"Go on, please!"

"I don't know what more to tell you, sir. It isn't a pleasant thing to talk about. All I can say is that the pilots were brave, both of them."

"How old were these pilots? What did they look like? What were their last words? Tell us everything you remember."

"One of them was my age, sir, twenty-two or three, a healthy looking fellow, and the other was slightly older and slender."

"What were their names?"

"I don't know, sir."

"Come on, you must remember something about them!"

"I remember the younger pilot better than the other, sir. He was particularly calm, even after his buddy was beheaded. He showed no sign of fear. I remember him so vividly, because he began singing as Sergeant Asai approached him with his sword."

"Singing? Singing what?"

"The American anthem, sir. Sergeant Asai stood next to him, ready to strike, but the pilot sang as if an act of reverence to his country was more important than anything he could think of."

The middle-aged officer sat erect, his eyes fixed on the far end of the room where the flagpole stood. All of the officers looked at the flag, silently.

What is the meaning of a nation's flag to a dying soldier, I wondered. I never remembered seeing a Korean flag but had bowed a billion times toward the Japanese flag without emotion. But once I had heard my parents arguing about our flag, the Korean flag, and had thought there could be some symbolic meaning behind bowing to a flag. It was after a Korean minister had been killed by Japanese policemen for refusing to display the symbols of the Japanese gods in his Presbyterian church.

That day Father was wearing mourner's garb and digging in our closet looking for something. Omma was pleading with him to stop. Father kept on digging and pulled out a yellowed cloth folded into a square of origami paper. Omma looked terrified. "Yubo, are you out of your mind? They'll kill you if they see you carrying our flag."

"How can we bury Reverend Hong without our flag? To him, our country was more important than his life. God will protect us!"

"Leave that flag where it belongs! If God could protect anyone, Reverend Hong would still be alive." Without a word, Father tucked the flag under his mourner's garb and disappeared.

✵

The interrogation ended unexpectedly. I wasn't too sure at what point the middle-aged officer picked up the phone, ordering the guards to come and arrest Sadamu. It could have been some time after Sadamu thrust the dogtag on the table, announcing that it belonged to one of the nine decomposed bodies we had buried in the jungle. Or was it when he told them about the disfigured man: that he had been alive but later was found floating in the water? There was nothing Robert or I could do but mutely watch the whole scene as the guards walked in, handcuffed Sadamu, and took him out of the room.

I don't know how I found my way to the deck. By now, the sun was in the middle of the sky and the wind was roaming mischievously, tickling my ears and lifting my skirt. I found a bench facing the sea and sat down. The waves danced joyously, glittering in the sun. Birds glided in the lofty sky, and white clouds sailed through an even loftier heaven. Everything seemed free and joyful except me.

Neither Sadamu nor I had imagined the dogtag would give

him problems. We had thought it would at least save our lives. How naïve we had been about Americans! I closed my eyes and prayed: *Heavenly Father, take away ten years of my life and save Sadamu from these American men. I don't mind dying early if You'd save him. You know how much I love him. Be compassionate. Be merciful, Lord!*

"There you are!" Robert appeared from nowhere and sat next to me. "I was looking for you."

"Looking for me?"

"Yes." His expression told me he had something important to tell me. "It's about Sadamu."

"What is it?"

He reached into his trouser pocket and took out a white paper. "Sadamu wrote this a year and a half ago for the *Kyoto Daily News* when he first joined the army. A telegrapher in the radio room brought a copy to me after he took it to Intelligence. Read it!"

I took the paper covered with Japanese letters, almost trembling. I felt as if Sadamu had died and I was touching his shroud.

> As our ship *Nagato* glided toward the horizon, dividing the vast sea, a flock of Zero fighters roared above our heads and the enemy ships spouted smoke and flames at the shore. The Yankee soldiers lay lifeless on the beach while their belongings cluttered the surface of the sea. It's evident that the God of Victory is showering His favors on us because we are making a gigantic step toward the brotherhood of mankind. Soon all Asian countries will be liberated from Western barbarians and the cries of our brothers will be replaced with their laughter. As the sons of Imperial Majesty we have a mission to accomplish. Toward our Imperial Majesty, all tongues must utter praises and all heads must be bent. Banzai!"

I gave the letter back to Robert. "I can't believe he wrote such garbage," I said. I was more worried about him now. He was once the Emperor's dog, wagging its tail, but now was a Japanese mouse trapped in a sturdy American cage.

Robert reached into his pocket, took out a cigarette, lit it, and puffed. I saw wrinkles between his eyebrows deepening but no sign of contempt or disgust for Sadamu's article. He stared at the rail in front of him intensely as smoke curled out of his nose and then sucked into his lungs again. When the cigarette burned down, he rose, dropping it on the deck and stepping on it. "I'll come and get you when I hear more about Sadamu. Don't go away."

Since I had no place to go other than to my tiny, box-like room, where the smell of tar seeped through the floor, I stared at the ocean all afternoon. I imagined I was pulled into the water and drifted to the far end of the ocean. Everything was vague and still on the ocean floor except a certain movement of waves that floated me weightlessly and carefree. I lost all sense of purpose, fear, or anxiety, and became calm. Then, without any warning, a current pushed me up to the surface, and I awoke again to the reality that Sadamu was in trouble and I didn't know where I would be the next day. Then I let myself become like a stone at reef listening to the whistle of the wind and the murmur of the ocean. A sense of well-being came over me. I realized that the more I resisted the cruelty of life, the harder it became to cope, but when I let go of my fear and floated with the current, I was at peace. This was what the Asian philosophers called "detachment."

By the time Robert returned, I felt so deeply peaceful that I asked him brightly, "Robert, did you bring me good news?"

"In fact, I did," he said, his lips curling into a smile. "The guard said we can see Sadamu for ten minutes. Is this good enough news for you?"

"Of course it is!"

The room where Sadamu was confined was a cubicle with

a cot in the middle, surrounded by barren walls. The smell of tar was stronger here than my room. As soon as he saw us, the guard walked out of the room, saying, "Ten minutes!"

Despite the fact that Robert was with me, I ran to Sadamu and embraced him. "Sadamu, you don't know how much I'm missing you. I can't stand being without you," I said with a quivering voice.

Sadamu held me tightly. I heard his loud breathing. But he straightened himself almost immediately, glancing at Robert who was looking at the wall. "Soon-ah," he said in a soft voice, "try not to think of me. I don't know what will happen to me. I worry about you. We must think more realistically now that. . ."

"How can I not think of you?" I cut him short. "I have been worrying about you all day, but you don't seem to care!" I was surprised that my voice sounded angry.

"Let's not make it more difficult than it is now, Soon-ah. I want you to understand my fear and anxiety, too. I'm in danger of losing my life."

Hurt and embarrassed, I turned around and left.

I came back to my room feeling as empty as a flower pot in winter. I sprawled on my bed and buried my head in the pillow. Sadamu's face, pale and intense, appeared before my eyes. I turned my head to face the wall. On the gray panel, many grooves ran parallel, one end touching the wooden floor and the other the white ceiling. I counted them, all twenty-four grooves. Again, Sadamu's face jumped out. This time he was smiling faintly, looking sad. *I'm so afraid, Soon-ah*, he seemed to say. *I'm afraid of losing you. Sometimes I'm on the verge of breaking, foreseeing myself trapped in a prison. How can I live without you? I don't know. If I made you angry, that's because I wanted to protect you. You're my jewel, but I'm too afraid to lose you or break you, so I better not touch you.*

So, it's better not to see one another and be "realistic"! I said sharply. *I didn't know people can love one another "realistically."*

Sadamu laughed hollowly. *The word "realistic" doesn't*

belong to lovers. I don't know what I was thinking when I said that. All I can say is that I love you and want you more than any man ever wanted a woman . . .

Still, I couldn't shake the cold expression on his face that shredded my heart.

The next day I fasted, mostly because I didn't want to face Robert in the cafeteria. By avoiding him, I also avoided Sadamu in my head: I was determined not to think of him, but many times I found myself worrying about him.

Robert found me again on the deck late that afternoon. "Do you want to hear something exciting?" he said.

"Of course," I said unenthusiastically.

"Sadamu's wish has come true!"

"What are you talking about?"

Robert sat next to me. "Last night after you left, Sadamu and I had a long discussion. I told him he should at least try to write a letter to General MacArthur, asking him to use him instead of sending him to a prison, and he agreed."

"That's crazy! How can you expect an important man like General MacArthur to pay attention to an enemy prisoner?"

"You never know, Soon-ah. If he thinks Sadamu is useful, I'm sure he'll use him. You know as well as I do that the Japanese prisoners will kill Sadamu if they find out that he's a deserter from the Imperial army. He doesn't have much choice. Anyway, I was running all day like a mailman, trying to find the right man who'd deliver the message to General MacArthur."

"Well? Did you find him?" I asked sarcastically.

"I did, but everyone thought I was crazy," he chuckled. "Captain Hummel was the worst. He thought the letter was a joke. He said, 'A Jap is begging Doug to save his life? How funny! Doug couldn't even save his own men from Bataan and Corrigidor. How can he save a Jap? Let's find out!' He dialed some numbers and said, 'Admiral Halsey, please.' When he came to the phone, Captain Hummel said, 'Admiral, are you ready for a joke? I have a letter addressed to General

MacArthur written by a Jap. A Jap, yes! . . . No, not a love letter, sir, ha, ha, ha. This Jap wants to die for America! A Japanese samurai wants to be in the American history books, sir.'

"But a few seconds later, he threw the receiver down, muttering, 'He's so unpredictable, that Bull. You know what he said? "There's always room for an enemy asking to help, Captain. Treat him like a guest until I see him." I don't get it.' I left the office quickly before he could let his steam out on me. Soon-ah, I really think something grand will happen to Sadamu. They might train him to become an OSS agent," Robert said proudly.

"What's an OSS agent?"

"Americans working with guerrillas in enemy-occupied territory. Many OSS agents are working in Europe and Asia, collecting information and interrupting the enemy network. In other words, OSS agents are spies."

Sadamu a spy? He will be spying against his own countrymen. If captured, the Japanese will probably torture him to prolong his agony, like they did to Korean activists. Father told me the Japanese inserted pipes into their noses and ears and forced water into their heads and lungs until they lost consciousness. In some cases, they drilled pipes into their anuses to blow them up with water.

"I can't believe you, Robert," I cried.

"What?"

"How can you let Sadamu offer his life to Yankees like bait? He'll die!"

"Stop talking like that, Soon-ah. He's a big boy and wants to do something meaningful with his life. Besides, what choice does he have other than going to a prison, where he'll probably die also? I don't think he'll die. In fact, we'll all die sooner or later. Who has the privilege of not dying?"

"Tell him to go ahead, then. I don't care!" I got up and headed for my room.

I spent my time alone looking at the ocean through the

small window. Although it was the same ocean I had been seeing for months now, it seemed different that night—the way the waves curled on the top, making laces, dropping to the surface, laying a foamy carpet all over, dancing and crawling with silent music. The signs were everywhere that Sadamu was about to leave me for good. I buried my face on the bedspread and wept.

I must have fallen asleep, because I suddenly woke up, sensing someone at the door. It was dark. *Who could it be,* I wondered. *Robert? But why would he come to my room at this hour?*

I tiptoed to the door and pressed my ear against it. "Who's there?"

"It's me. Sadamu!"

I opened the door in a hurry. "Sadamu! How can you . . . ?" He covered my mouth with his big hand, pulled me back into the room, and closed the door. "*Shhhh!*" he hissed. He cocked his ears toward the corridor. I looked at him mutely, trying to detect footsteps in the corridor, but heard nothing.

"How did you escape?" I whispered, feeling safe in his arms.

"I didn't escape."

"Then? Did the guard let you go free?"

"No, I don't think so."

"What? Tell me how you got here," I begged.

"Robert is such a loyal friend, Soon-ah. He's taking my place tonight."

"What about the guard?"

He chuckled soundlessly. "Robert brought a bottle of whiskey to my jail cell and we drank it, including the guard. By the way he looked at me and blinked, I knew he was plotting something. I did what I thought he wanted me to do. Robert doesn't drink and neither do I. Guess who drank all of the whiskey in the bottle? Robert and I merely motioned as if we were drinking, passing the bottle around, and tilting it into our mouths. Soon Robert began singing "Yankee Doodle" and I acted as if I too were drunk, humming the melody. The guard joined us at the top of his voice, and Robert and me tapped the floor in accompaniment. Oh, my God, that guy has a terrible voice! Even a pig giving birth would sound better than him." He stopped and laughed, looking into my eyes.

I laughed too, glad that his sense of humor had returned.

"By the time we sang the second verse, the guard's pitches started to go down and his head was about to hit the floor."

"Are you not going to get in trouble, Sadamu?"

"No, the guard was snoring when I left. I must be careful not to wake him when I go back. Robert said not to worry. 'As drunk as he is, only a bomb explosion will wake him up,' he said."

Sadamu gathered me in his arms and laid me on the bed, and we rolled like playful animals, happy and sad at the same time, kissing again and again.

"Soon-ah, this is our last night together," Sadamu said, tightening his arms as if he'd never let go of me. I said nothing. What was there to say when your hours were numbered? The moment the ship arrived in Honolulu we'd be separated without any promise of a reunion.

Moonlight filtered through the mist-covered window and lit our faces as if God's final blessing had been bestowed. Somewhere a saxophone soared, tearing our hearts with a sharp and painful melody.

"I'm not going to say goodbye, Sadamu," I whispered.

$\mathcal{M}$y last day with Sadamu arrived just like any other day: the sun rose in the east and the ocean was calm and indifferent. All I could remember was Sadamu's frame diminishing before my eyes as he followed the naval policemen on the dock and the mournful sound of a ship beating in my eardrums. Standing against the rail on the ship, I called to him, "Sadamu!" trying to compete with the whistle of the ship. Once he turned and smiled as if he heard me. Then I lost him. The huge pool of people swallowed him. I stretched my neck, desperately trying to get another glimpse of him, but he vanished. I felt abandoned. I shifted my gaze to the boulevard in the distance where shops, stores, hotels, and tall buildings stood, suddenly realizing I wouldn't find a single face that would recognize me, even if I walked all day and all night. I clung to the rail and lifted my eyes to the sky, hoping to see something familiar. The expanse of blue met my eyes. The sky was the only thing that was familiar to me, belonging to no one, belonging to everyone. *Sadamu will be somewhere under that sky*, I comforted myself.

"Keiko Omura?" a man's baritone voice frightened me.

I fixed my gaze on the man, then on the man standing next to him, with an unfriendly expression. Their dirty black boots were stepping on my shadow, my other self. Those ugly boots! Mud was all over them and the soles could have many holes, I thought. *How dare they step on my shadow!*

"We are from the Department of Immigration," one of them said. "You must come with us."

"Would you please step back?" I asked sharply. "You're stepping on my shadow." The boots didn't budge. I shouted again and again. One of them grabbed my arm and forced me to walk with them. Only later, riding in the back seat of the black car with two other women, did I realize that I had shouted in Korean.

Through the window I could see red and pink blossoms sitting on bushes, and a handful of seagulls soaring toward heaven. The thought that Sadamu was gone without leaving a trace stabbed me like a knife. I should have asked him to leave me a lock of his hair or his handkerchief, but it was too late. Everything was too late. I covered my eyes and tried to remember him. I saw him, turning around and smiling.

I spent four days in the basement of a three-story building that had many dirty windows. I don't remember much of my jail cell except four other women in the same room, speaking some other language, and that the floor was bare concrete where several cockroaches, as large as my thumb, skittered around fearlessly all day long.

On the fifth day two Korean men came to see me. I didn't know how they found me but was glad to see people from my own country.

"Welcome to Hawaii, my dear sister!" the man with a

sprinkle of white hair on the side of his head said, lifting his straw hat, when he saw me at the doorway. He smiled broadly, wrinkling his sun-baked face. Next to him was a young man, about Sadamu's age, with copper skin.

I bowed at them. "Ahn-yong-ha seyo? How do you do?" I said.

The older man nodded. "We have a small community of Koreans growing pineapples not far from here and we can use some help. I've already asked the immigration officials, and they said it's up to you, sister. We'll give you a place to stay and a wage."

A wage? My ears perked up. I had never earned any money in my entire life, except the yellow tickets at the Comfort House. They had told me my salary was twenty yen, but they'd never paid me. "I can work, but . . ." I turned and looked at the immigration officer behind me.

The officer, a pale-skinned man with dark eyes, smiled and said, "You are free to go with them. If you decide to stay there after six months, come and see me."

It was a long journey by truck. By the time we passed many green fields dotted with grazing cattle, swamps sheltering pelicans and great egrets, and sandy beaches with sparkling water where women and naked children gathered seaweed, the sun was heading west and the sky was feverish with red clouds.

We came to a village where Asian children as dark as chestnuts followed the truck. The pineapple plants surrounding the village seemed to be squirming in the wind, like a herd of green lambs. The scene reminded me of Mr. Hyun's pineapple plantation in Palau. The barracks was in need of repairs: the side panel had holes and the roof was a mass of brown leaves. Next to the building on the right lay a chicken coop with nesting hens, and next to the chicken coop was a large garden with green vegetables withering in the evening sun.

Several Korean women in cotton floral dresses stood aside

talking among themselves, giggling and laughing. I disliked their secretive glances at me and looked away.

"Welcome!" one woman came and greeted me. "We were talking about you. You are so light-skinned and pretty that when the men return from the field, they won't leave you alone. You know how men are," she said, turning to the other women who laughed again in agreement.

I laughed too. "I'm not pretty," I said.

"Don't be bashful," she said, pulling me. "Come! I'll show you where your room is."

The moment we stepped inside the barracks, I held my breath. It smelled as if a herd of horses lived there instead of humans.

My room was a little box-like space with a straw mat on the floor and a cupboard-box in the corner. "Now get some rest," the woman said. "You had a long journey today. I'll come and get you when dinner's ready." She left, throwing a friendly smile at me.

In the corridor several shirtless children stared at me curiously. Behind them stood two women with expressionless faces.

Besides the intolerable smell, the roof must have been leaking too: the ceiling was full of black spots. The jailhouse wasn't as bad as this, I thought. Still, I lay on the mat to rest. I was dead tired. Within seconds, an unfamiliar noise struck my eardrum, "Szzz . . ." and I sat erect. To my horror, a brown snake with red stripes, as long as my belt, was leisurely climbing the wall. I screamed.

Three shirtless boys rushed into the room, grabbed it with bare hands, and took it with them. I heard one of them shouting, "I got it first, it's mine!" and another saying "Shut up!"

When the sun disappeared from the window, the same woman came and announced that a Korean meal was prepared for their guest—me. About twenty Koreans sat around a long table in the courtyard and I joined them. Before we started eating, I was introduced to many people: Uncle this and Aunt that, Brother so-and-so and Sister so-and-so. I couldn't remember their names but I remember their huge appetites. After dinner, some men played Badook, a Korean chess game, and the children ran wildly, catching fireflies, and the women gossiped about men, giggling and chattering secretively.

When the moon rose from the mountain ahead of us, I excused myself and went back to my room. I was exhausted. I disliked the fact that the door had no lock and thought for a while on what to do. Should I push the cupboard box against the door or should I forget about it? I lay on my mat and told myself to relax.

Sadamu! My heart rushed to him again as soon as I closed my eyes. *Where are you now?* I whispered. *Come back, Sadamu. I miss you so much!*

I tried to remember everything about him—his scent, his voice, his laugh, his touch, his expression. . . . Then I remembered that our spirits were inseparable. *He is with me,* I told myself. He was. We were lying together on my mat holding one another. He whispered in my ear, *Soon-ah, we're together forever. I love you. You're everything I have.*

I wanted to say I loved him too and that he was everything to me, but I couldn't voice it, afraid that he might vanish. Clinging to him, I drifted to sleep.

A strange sensation woke me. I heard men's voices. I shivered. At the brothel, men's voices had made women scream or cry. I tried to wake up, but I couldn't. A hand squeezed my cheeks and poured some bitter liquid into my mouth. I choked and gagged. Still, I couldn't wake up. I screamed but no sound escaped my throat. My eyelids felt heavy and my facial muscles numb. I couldn't even move a finger. I thought I was bound with many invisible ropes.

A hand ripped my tunic.

"Go on! You idiot! Take her!" a man hissed.

"No, I can't do that. What if she wakes up?" another man said timidly.

"You stupid bastard! Why worry? If you don't make her yours someone else will take her. You know how much it costs to buy a woman from Korea, don't you?"

Get up, I ordered myself. *They're going to rape you. Run as fast as you can!* But I couldn't move.

I heard a different voice. "If you don't want her, I'll take her to Honolulu. As pretty as she is, I know I can get at least a thousand dollars for her."

My heart pounded rapidly. I squirmed, twisted, and tried to roll over. I lay like a cabbage at market.

"You vile things!" a woman's voice rang in my ears. My eyes began to focus and I saw everything: a young man with dark hair ready to jump on me, and two other men next to him, all with dark faces. My head was spinning rapidly: the whole room was dancing around me—the dark ceiling, the walls with holes, the faces, and the oil lamp.

"Get out! You can't do this to every woman who drifts into our village!"

The crowd quickly left the room, muttering something I couldn't understand.

"Are you all right, child?" the woman said in Korean, sitting next to my mat. I didn't remember seeing her before. She looked older than all the others I had met earlier. Finding my tongue again I yelled, "Send me . . . back to the jail. I, I . . . don't know why they brought me here!" My voice sounded muffled and my head was about to explode.

The woman clicked her tongue sympathetically. "Agha, I'm really sorry for what happened. If I had been here it would not have happened. I was gone all day to my son's house to take care of my grandchildren, *tss, tss, tss* . . . . You see, we have a great shortage of women here. Young people steal women from other villages, drug them, and rape them. We have brought thousands of picture-brides from Korea since the first group arrived here forty years ago, but we still need more women for our growing community. Young lads are marrying the native Hawaiians. It's terrible!" She shook her head.

It didn't quell my anger, nor did I feel sympathy for them. I had been mauled by my own trusted dog. I was disgusted and angry.

"Those you just saw are the troublemakers, but not all boys are like them. Some are quite decent. If you lived here with us a little longer you'd learn quickly that they are not all that bad."

"I want to go back," I said, feeling like a thousand needles were poking my head.

She got up. "I'll ask Mr. Kim to take you back to the jailhouse tomorrow!"

I cried until dawn. The fact that I had no place to go except the jailhouse, which I hated, brought me more tears. I missed Sadamu so intensely that I actually felt pain in my chest.

At the first sign of light, the old man came and I returned to Honolulu.

❦

We had limited activity at the detention center. Sometimes we were taken to a public beach by truck to pick up trash, remove debris, and clean benches, picnic tables, and chairs. Other times, we worked in a cornfield: we broke off the ears from the tall cornstalks and dropped them in a basket provided by the farmer. In the evenings, we gathered in a large room and watched war-documentary movies. By now I could understand and speak English well enough that I didn't have difficulty conversing with others. Besides the visual understanding of the war on the screen—the bomb explosions, burning ships, shooting or running soldiers—I became familiar with such names as Mussolini, Roosevelt, Churchill, Berlin, Sicily, Gestapo, Eisenhower, Mountbatten. But sometimes it was hard to distinguish whether they were the names of people or places.

I once asked my Mexican friend Maria, "Who's Kiev? Is he an American or a Russian?"

Maria was the kind of girl who felt no shame in teasing others. "He's a Russian," she said, her eyes full of amusement. "He drinks vodka and sleeps with Mrs. Sicily, his Italian mistress." Everyone laughed, but I didn't appreciate her sense of humor.

On another occasion I heard that the Allies had raided Milan and bombs fell on a convent, but I couldn't understand why they were bombing Italy where the Pope lived, so I asked her, "Why do the Americans bomb Italy? Don't they want to protect the Vatican?"

Maria hit my arm, laughing. "Soon-ah, the Pope is Hitler's secret agent. Didn't you know it? That's why he didn't help any Jews." I decided I'd never ask her another question as long as I lived.

In spite of her laughs and unlimited sense of humor, Maria wasn't always a happy person. Often she played the phonograph downstairs and sang with a voice that cried "Baby! Oh, Baby," swaying her long, dark hair and twisting her hips. I didn't know she had had a baby and asked her, "Did you lose a baby?"

"No," she said, laughing and crying at the same time. "I'm sad for my boyfriend, silly!" she said, but she never told me what happened to him, or why she called a grown man a "baby."

I was anxious to hear something about Korea on the news, but I never did. The only news was that the Allies were smashing the Japanese in the Pacific Islands while the Japanese desperately held onto them. "Of all the equipment America has piled up to fight the Japs," the narrator in the film said one day, "less than one-twentieth has been sent to the Pacific." I became hopeful of returning home. Someday soon!

Every Sunday a minister from a different religious organization visited the center—sometimes a Cuban preacher and other times a Chinese Buddhist monk—and conducted a worship ceremony. Since my father had been a Presbyterian minister, I had no desire to attend them.

One Sunday morning Maria woke me up. "Do you feel like going to a Catholic mass?"

"I never attended a Catholic mass in my life," I mumbled, awakening from my slumber.

"That's okay. Jesus forgives you for it," she said and smiled mischievously. The way she looked at me I sensed that she didn't want to go alone, and would take me even if I begged her not to.

"Listen, Soon-ah. I heard that Father Shimono is saying the mass. You might like him, because he looks just like you. He's a Japanese."

"I'm not a Japanese."

"It doesn't matter. You'll like him anyway: You two have the same half-moon eyes, the same tiny, round mouth, and the same beard. . . ." She burst into laughter.

I laughed too. "All right," I said, getting up. "I have to see the priest who looks like me, I guess."

The priest was a short Japanese-American who had a long, impressive grey beard touching his chest. As he began mumbling some Latin words and bowing to the altar table, I turned to Maria and whispered, "You're right, Maria. He does have a beard like mine."

Maria nearly choked to death, trying to smother her laughter. I too laughed, covering my mouth, imagining the long, bushy beard attached to my chin, sweeping my chest.

After the mass, I saw the priest walking in our direction and was worried. *Maybe he saw us laughing during the mass and was displeased? Is laughing sinful?*

But Father Shimono nodded and said a friendly "Hello" to both of us. "How would you ladies like to work in a refugee shelter and earn a dollar a week?" he asked.

"A dollar a week?" we chorused.

"Yes. We need two lively young ladies like yourselves to bring some sunshine into our Home. Besides a dollar a week, you'll get free meals and a room to share."

"Are you going to pay us a dollar a week just for being silly?" Maria asked.

"Basically, yes. You'll do some light housework and bathe old people occasionally. If you want the job, pack your belongings and meet me at the lobby."

The Shepherd's Home was a two-story building that had a broad view of the ocean in front and a dense forest in the back. Most of the residents there were old Japanese-Americans who were too old and weak to travel to Relocation Camp in California but not weak enough to stay in bed all day. Our job was to walk with them twice a day, play cards with them, and occasionally accompany them to nearby stores. Maria didn't speak Japanese, so for a change, I taught her and teased her when she made mistakes. I loved to say, "See? You laughed when I made a mistake! Now it's my turn!"

"Go ahead, Soon-ah! I won't stop you!" she said.

Most of the people at the stores were hostile toward Orientals, I discovered. When I earned my third dollar, I tried to buy a cotton dress at the souvenir shop that sold Hawaiian muumuus and odds and ends with "Hawaii" stamped on them.

The saleswoman with red fingernails was rude when I entered the shop. "Sorry, we don't have anything that would fit you," she said, even before I told her what I wanted.

How strange, I thought. Still, I pointed at the blue dress hanging on the wall behind her and said, "I think that dress will fit me. Can I try it on?"

"That's already sold!" she said without even looking. I knew she wasn't going to sell me anything.

When I returned to the Shepherd's Home, I told Maria what happened.

She insisted that we go back and argue with the woman.

Actually, I was curious to know what she would do when I went back with Maria.

Maria haughtily walked into the shop, but I stood outside, watching her through the window.

Maria pointed at the dress on the wall, jabbering, and the woman took it down with a long pole, her lips moving.

Maria lifted the dress in front of her and looked into the mirror, turning this way and that, admiring.

The woman was smiling, her lips still moving.

Maria turned and motioned to me to come in.

I went in.

"Try this one," Maria said, handing me the dress. "I think you'll look great in this!"

The saleswoman looked at Maria and me. She snatched the dress from Maria. "Sorry, I thought it was for you!"

"This is my friend," Maria said angrily. "Are you refusing to serve her?"

A short man appeared from behind the door. "What seems to be the problem, ladies?"

"Sir, your employee insulted my friend, and she deserves an apology."

"I'm terribly sorry, Madame, if we offended you," the manager said, without a hint of remorse. "If you want this dress, we'll sell it to you."

"I don't want that dress!" I said out loud.

"What?" Maria exclaimed.

I walked out of the shop as fast as I could.

Maria followed me, blurting, "Why not? He apologized, didn't he?"

"So?"

"I don't get it! You wanted that dress! Why did you change your mind?"

"Because I hate Hawaii, okay?" I said.

My dearest Soon-ah, Sadamu's letter began:

I'm sending this letter to the Immigration Office in Honolulu, hoping it will get to you somehow. I'm alone in my bunker, crouched down next to my radio, waiting for a message from my commander in Manila. We aren't supposed to write letters because things can leak to the enemy, but Bill Mason, another OSS member in my unit, is returning to Honolulu due to an injury he received. He promised to put it in the mailbox as soon as he arrives in Honolulu, so I don't need to worry.

My days are hectic with plots to foil the Japanese. To make a long story short, I am dearly loved by General MacArthur and Admiral Halsey but terribly hated by the Japanese. I am doing impossible tasks for the Americans because I can sneak into the Japanese domain much easier than any American can.

Yesterday I lectured all of the guards at Cabanatuan Prison through my radio, acting as if I were the temporary replacement for Colonel Sato, the director of the prison who's in Tokyo University Hospital having surgery. They believed me. The power of my words is simply unbelievable! My Filipino friends were wonderful too. They were hiding in the nearby bushes waiting for my signal. As I yelled at the guards, reminding them of samurai spirit, of the Emperor's expectations, and of the duty of every soldier to his ancestors, I signaled, and the Filipinos opened all the gates at once. Two-hundred-ninety-one prisoners walked out of the prison in broad daylight and escaped to the jungle. These are the men who were captured on Bataan and Corrigidor Islands when the Japanese invaded the Philippines a year ago: the ones who survived the Death March.

Can you imagine the shock of the Japanese when they discovered what had happened? Immediately the soldiers combed the area, shooting villagers, but the guerrillas took care of them, killing several. The Americans who escaped were fed and covered by the villagers. But alas! The news arrived that the Japanese murdered seventy-five of the remaining prisoners as revenge while the rest watched them die. Seventy-five! These young men were all beaten to death in the courtyard. Some were buried alive. Those murderers are my own people: I have the same blood running in my veins.

My partner and I are about to move to another island. We won't know the destination until five minutes before we take off. Sometimes I feel I am chained by two evils. Other times I feel I'm already dead and my spirit is wandering between the two continents. I no longer believe in Heaven. I try not to think, Soon-ah. The more I think about myself, God, and this killing mission, the more I worry about my redemption.

My beautiful Soon-ah, try to forget me as quickly as you can and promise me not to cry. As I write this letter, I see your face blooming with a smile. I'm dying to be with you, talk to you, and love you again. Sometimes I hear your voice calling me "Sadamu!" just the way you used to when you saw a snake or a lizard in the jungle, and I dash out to find you. I know what "letting go" means. The days we were together on that island were the most beautiful days of my life. I was a lucky guy. You were a white lily blooming in a desert: a miracle!

So long, my love. I'll try to write to you again when I have a chance but I can't promise.

Always, Sadamu

I read it at least five times before folding it and putting it in my skirt pocket. Then I walked to the beach. We had spent so much time at the beach when we had been hiding on that tiny island, fishing, digging clams, collecting seashells, or just staring at the water, that I knew I could find bits and pieces of memories there.

The sunlight was bright on the white sand and I squinted my eyes. In the haze of the shimmering sunlight, several moss-covered rock islands floated in the distance, luring me into joining them. The beach was nearly empty except for two Hawaiian women sitting motionless under a rainbow-colored beach umbrella and two men wearing straw hats fishing in the water, hollering at one another.

I passed the women, trying not to disturb their serene postures, and walked along the beach. The sand was soft under my canvas shoes. Once in a while a tiny crab, bite-size, peeked out from its foxhole and charged at me, spitting sand. Several times, I thought I heard Sadamu's voice calling me in the wind, "Soon-ah, come here!" and turned around to find him, although I knew it couldn't be him.

Finally I stopped walking and looked toward the horizon where a strip of gray cloud hung between the sky and the sea. I knew Sadamu was fighting over that horizon. *Sadamu, I wanted to shout at him, I'll be waiting for you, you hear? Don't ever talk to me about Death!*

Then I thought of Wook. My brother might be fighting somewhere out there, too. In fact, it's possible that he might be chased by Sadamu, without knowing who he was. Both Sadamu and Wook shared the same fate: Sadamu was fighting for Americans just as Wook was for Japanese. Such cruelty of life!

And what about you? a voice said. *You too are a victim, chained here in Hawaii. You don't know when you'll be released.* I had a sudden urge to break loose from all the invisible chains and ropes and swim toward the horizon to find Sadamu. Who could stop me?

I kicked my shoes off, grabbed two ends of my skirt and tied them around my waist, and walked into the water. It was cold and I shivered for a few seconds, but I jumped in with a loud splash. I aimed for the nearest tiny rock island and began to swim. I saw the dark mess of seaweed floating next to me and tried to avoid it. Once or twice, it tangled around my wrist and I quickly shook it off. I lost my balance and unwillingly drank a huge gulp of salty water.

After a while, a strange sensation overcame me. I thought I was seeing Sadamu standing in the water, shoulder deep, with a straw hat on his head and a bamboo pole in his hand. He used to stand for hours like that when we had been on the island, sometimes yanking his pole and saying, "Soon-ah, I think I got something! This guy is big," or merely shaking his head and muttering, "Shucks, I lost him!"

My heart ached with longing. How much I missed him!

The reflection of sunlight on the surface was so bright that I was about to become blind. I buried my head in the water again and kept swimming.

"*How can it be Sadamu when he's on Mindanao Island?*" a voice confronted me. "*We're inseparable,*" I replied. "*Our spirits are together.*" I swam more vigorously. I knew I was getting closer to the rock island.

I was out of breath, and I lifted my head to get some air. I saw Sadamu turning around and waving his arm at me, as if saying, "Soon-ah, hurry! A little faster!" *See?* I told myself. *We can hide together on that island again, maybe forever!* I swam faster and faster. The water was warm and buoyant, and through my water-filled eyes, the rock island looked more beautiful and exotic than minutes earlier. I was getting closer and closer to Sadamu and was glad. *Let's survive on berries, fruit, abalones, sea snails, just like before, Sadamu.*

I became very tired but I couldn't stop swimming. I kept finding myself going under. More water rushed into my mouth. I was angry at myself for not being careful. Then, the two ends of my skirt came untied, and it was more difficult to move my legs. *I must get to him, so he can help me. Only a little longer, and harder!* I ordered myself.

Something touched me. *Sadamu,* I thought. I lurched forward to grab him and fall into his arms, but instead I went under again, this time much deeper than earlier. Water rushed into my mouth, my nose, and my ears, and I struggled to breathe. I swallowed another huge gulp of water and choked helplessly. I saw the sun turning wildly, throwing diamond-like lights, and the horizon tilting and gradually sinking into the water.

I don't know what happened after that. All I remember is waking up in a room looking at a bright fluorescent ceiling light.

"Are you all right, Soon-ah?" a man's voice asked me. The voice was familiar, but I couldn't tell who it was. I turned my head toward the voice and found a man with a long, silvery beard standing next to a nurse with yellow hair. My head was bursting and my tongue stiff and heavy. Before I could gather my thoughts, the nurse exclaimed, "Thank God, she's coming back to life."

Coming back to life? Was I dead and resurrected like Jesus? I stared at her blankly. I was so tired and sleepy.

"Why did you do it, dear?" the nurse asked, accusingly.

Do what? I stared at her expressionlessly.

Father Shimono lowered his head and looked into my eyes and shook his head. "Poor child, you almost drowned," he said solemnly. "By the grace of God, two fishermen pulled you out of the water. Can you remember anything? Were you trying to kill yourself?"

Kill myself? What was he talking about?

"The men said they warned you not to go too deep, but you ignored them," the nurse said harshly. The way she looked at me, I knew she was scolding me for something I couldn't remember doing.

"I saw Sadamu," I said guiltily. My voice sounded like I was talking with my mouth full. "He was fishing in the water . . . He told me to swim with him to a rock island, so we can hide again . . ." My lips were heavy.

"Sadamu?" the nurse said and looked at Father Shimono. He shrugged.

"Who's this Sadamu you're talking about, dear?"

"Sadamu is . . ." I couldn't say he was my lover or boyfriend. Korean women never talked about men in public. "He was a Japanese soldier but now he's an OSS agent fighting for America in the Philippines."

This time, Father Shimono looked at the nurse before dropping his gaze to the floor.

The nurse blinked her eyes for two seconds. "Soon-ah, how can a Japanese soldier fight for America, dear? It doesn't make sense!"

Of course it doesn't make sense! I wanted to shout. *Nothing makes sense. I was dragged from home, loaded onto a truck, and was raped on a ship for no reason other than that I was born in Korea. My father was murdered in his own country by the Japanese, and my brother is fighting for Japan, and Sadamu is. . .*

I turned toward Father Shimono. "It's true, Father Shimono. Sadamu wrote a letter to General MacArthur last April after he was accused of murdering nine American marines. Admiral Halsey read the letter and told the Navy officers to treat him like a guest. They sent him to OSS in Washington. I received a letter from him today. He's now on Mindanao Island. He said General MacArthur, Admiral Halsey, and other Americans adore him because he's killed so many Japanese. He also tricked the Japanese into believing that he was the prison director who's having surgery in Tokyo. Oh, he helped American prisoners escape, too! Two hundred ninety-one of them. But later . . ."

"Soon-ah, please. Don't talk. You need rest," the nurse ordered me.

"You don't believe me! I'm telling the truth. You can read the letter if you want. I have it right here."

I searched for the letter but I was no longer wearing my skirt. Instead, a strange-looking thing that had freckles all over stared at me. I was embarrassed. "It's still in my skirt pocket. I put it there."

"We'll talk to you later, Soon-ah," Father Shimono said cautiously and headed to the door.

The nurse followed him.

That afternoon I was admitted to the mental ward and swallowed three white pills. I became dizzy and drifted to sleep. The evening of the next day, a young woman came into my room and asked me a bunch of questions: What made you jump into water? Did you hear any voices? Did you remember seeing something in the water? What did you see?

I told her everything: that Sadamu was standing in the

water, signaling me to swim to him so that we could hide together on the rock island, and that I was getting closer to him—I even touched him. If only I could have swam a little longer, we could have made it to the island.

The woman left and sent me a nurse. I was just about to eat my dinner when she stabbed me with a needle without explaining what she was doing. Again, I fell asleep for God knows how long.

Occasionally a doctor came in and checked my pulse, forced my eyes open, and scribbled something on his pad. When I protested, saying I'm not crazy and that what I said was true, the doctor increased the number of white pills, five instead of three. I couldn't keep my eyes open for more than five minutes at a time during the day and my mind was as fuzzy as goose feathers. I protested even harder, crying bitterly and hitting my pillow, but the doctor sent me the same nurse who stabbed me even harder. Soon my mind became as blank as a sheet of paper and my mouth felt like it was stuffed with sand. I watched endless, obscure forms in my eyes as they appeared and disappeared. I dreamed of ponds and ravines filled with molten steel. I heard steady noise, like a motor running next to me, and jumped when it got louder and pounded my head. Soon I shed hair like a dog in summer.

When I became as quiet as a tree and stared at walls all day, I was released and sent back to the Shepherd's Home. All day long, I sat on a stone bench overlooking the highway without a single thought flickering in my head. Often Maria sat next to me and jabbered on, trying to make me laugh, but when I only stared at her blankly, she left me alone.

Sometimes, I saw some Japanese-American soldiers and sailors driving up the hill, parking their cars, and walking up and going into the building. I knew they were all coming to see Father Shimono since he was the director of some young men's organization.

One morning a sailor with copper skin parked his jeep and

started walking in my direction, whistling a tune. I remembered the melody: Robert whistled that tune when he was alone at sea. I had asked him once what song he was whistling, and he had told me the name, but I couldn't remember it anymore. I liked the tune. As he came closer, he stopped walking and looked at me. My eyesight had been dim since the accident at the sea, and I couldn't tell who it was and stared back at him. The sailor rushed to me, saying "Soon-ah! Is that you?"

"Robert?" I asked in a tiny voice, not really believing it was him.

"Yes, it's me, Robert!"

"You look more slender and darker than I remember," I said.

Robert looked at me closely. "Soon-ah, what happened to you? You look so different. I almost didn't recognize you. You've lost so much weight, and . . . your hair . . . looks different."

I explained to him that I almost drowned and that I spent some time in a mental hospital.

"Shit!" he blurted. "Did they think you were crazy? Well, were you?" he asked.

"I don't know, Robert. I know I didn't try to kill myself, although that's why they put me in the hospital. I can't tell you what really happened because everything is vague now. I thought I saw Sadamu in the water and kept swimming. It's still unclear to me what really happened."

Robert hugged me. "I'm glad you're okay, Soon-ah. They shouldn't have put you in a mental hospital. That's where crazy people get crazier. Thank God, you're okay."

"How did you know I was here?"

Robert laughed. "I didn't come to see you, Soon-ah. This is a complete coincidence. I'm leaving for New Guinea tomorrow and I wanted to see Father Shimono before something happens to me."

"Nothing will happen to you, Robert, I know it."

"You never know." He looked at the highway ahead of us where cars and trucks busily passed by. "Soon-ah, someday the war will end but we'll have a hard time believing it," he said.

$\mathcal{T}$he war ended with Emperor Hirohito's surrender speech in Tokyo's Imperial Palace at noon on August 15, 1945, nine days after the Americans dropped the atomic bombs on Hiroshima and Nagasaki. Speaking as the "Voice of the Crane," Hirohito proclaimed over national Japanese radio:

> We have instructed the Japanese government to accept the Joint Declaration of the United States, Great Britain, Soviet Union and China.
>
> In conformity with the prospects handed down by our Imperial ancestors, we have always striven for the welfare of our subjects and for the happiness and welfare of all nations. This is precisely why we declared war against Great Britain and the United States. It was not our intention to infringe on the sovereignty of other nations or to carry out acts of aggression against their soil. . . . Our beloved! Let us

carry forward the glory of our national structure and
let us not lag behind the progress of the world.

How simple! I thought. After the destruction of millions of
lives and tons of material, the Imperial Majesty was now
squawking nonsense like a real crane, saying his sole purpose
in declaring war against Britain and the United States was for
the happiness and welfare of their people and all nations. The
stench of the decaying bodies was too strong to accept his
logic. Ships and airplanes lay still on the ocean floor with their
silent occupants. Millions of people had been conscripted or
abducted, used, and discarded all over Asia like a huge pile of
trash. Many parts of the verdant land of Japan including
Hiroshima and Nagasaki turned into smoldering plains. For
what? To hear this?

I was so angry I turned toward the Northeast where the
Emperor might have been and spat. I visualized my saliva
smacking his noble face and dripping onto his dazzling white
horse. Why was I here if Emperor Hirohito never "intended to
carry out acts of aggression and to infringe on the sovereignty
of other nations"? Why did my father die? Why was Sadamu in
the Philippines endangering his life? I wanted to live long
enough to see the destruction of the Japanese empire and
Emperor Hirohito, the way the Japanese had destroyed the Yi
Dynasty and murdered our King. I wanted someone, anyone,
to murder Empress Nagako in the same manner Queen Min
had been murdered.

In early September, I received a letter from the immigration
office: "The representatives of the Temporary Korean Provisional Government based in Chunking, China will conduct an
important meeting in the reception room at 1 p.m. on
September 25th, 1945. All Koreans residing in Honolulu must
attend the meeting. Afterwards, we will make a list of people
returning to Korea."

I went there early that morning. A roomful of men and women were gathered, talking excitedly in Korean. I sat on a bench in the middle row, listening to people's conversations. I could almost tell their occupations by looking at them: the dark-skinned and broad-shouldered men were laborers; the men with shaven heads and sullen expressions were the runaway soldiers rescued from the sea; the men in civilian clothes with oily skin and chubby cheeks were merchants who had been working for the Japanese military; a dozen pale women sitting together at the end of the room like malnourished hens were, no doubt, comfort women.

One woman sitting alone next to the window kept looking at me. When my eyes met hers, she quickly dropped her gaze. It took me a few minutes to realize it was Yun Hee, who had been at the House of Serenity before I had escaped Palau Island. I almost didn't recognize her because she was so thin and colorless. Memories of Auntie Myung flooded my mind, so I got up and walked over to her.

"Yun Hee!" I whispered as I sat next to her.

"Excuse me?" She glanced at me but turned her head to the open window where I could smell the ocean.

"Yun Hee, it's me, Soon-ah! We were on Palau Island at the same time."

"What are you talking about?" she said, with flashing eyes. "You are mistaken. I'm sorry. I've never been on Palau." She turned her head back to the ocean.

I was all the more certain it was Yun Hee. "I'm sorry. I thought you were someone I knew," I quickly said and went back to my seat. Soon, two Korean men and the director of the immigration office, whom I had met before, walked into the room. One of the Korean men, tall and handsome, took the podium.

"Dearly beloved brothers and sisters. My name is Lee, Dong Kiu, the Secretary of Mr. Syngman Rhee, president of the Temporary Korean Provincial Government. A historical moment has arrived: we are liberated from Japan at last! We are free, brothers and sisters. Thirty-five years of persecution have become history. This is a solemn moment of thanksgiving, renewal, and forgiveness.

"Today, Korea is bustling! In every city, on every street, and in every school and church, people are singing our own national anthem. Finally, they are greeting one another in our own language. Drums, gongs, and bugles are blasting. Church bells are tolling nonstop. The hateful red sun flags are ripped off and burned. Finally, brothers and sisters, our own flags with yin-yang and trigram patterns, a symbol of harmony and peace, are flying everywhere, covering the Korean sky. . . ." The speaker's voice suddenly quivered and everyone in the room began coughing, sniffling, and sobbing.

I too sobbed. How long had I waited for this day? I could almost see our village flooded with people waving our flags. Some would run to Shinto shrines and tear down Emperor Hirohito's portraits. Omma's weeping face zoomed into my mind and I missed my father. How much he had prayed for liberation and peace in our land! How exuberant he would be today if he were still alive. He would wear his best Korean outfit and greet people in front of the church, bowing and laughing.

"My brothers and sisters, new changes will take place in our country," Mr. Lee continued. "Korea will be administered by the U.S. military government. This was decided by the leaders of the United States, Great Britain, and China and was reaffirmed again at the Potsdam Conference last July. But on August 9th, the Soviet Union declared war against Japan and crossed the Tuman River and occupied Pyongyang, Hamhung, and other major cities in the North."

People fidgeted, turning to one another, "Why did Soviet Union occupy our country when it declared war against Japan?" "I don't get it! What's happening?"

Mr. Lee raised his hand in the air, halting all noises.

"There's no need to worry, brothers and sisters. We don't have the danger of losing our country to the Russians as we did to the Japanese. On September 2nd, General MacArthur signed the Japanese surrender document in Tokyo Bay. Six days later, the U.S. forces from Okinawa landed in Inchon, and General John Hodge accepted the surrender of all Japanese forces south of the 38th parallel in a formal celebration. We are forever grateful to the United States for helping us be liberated from Japan. We are entering into another historical era, brothers and sisters. Mr. Syngman Rhee, president of the Temporary Korean Provisional Government, reassures us that we will be in good hands and wants you to cooperate with the Americans when you return to Korea. We will make a list of the people returning after this meeting. Please answer all questions the U.S. military officials ask you to make this transition as smooth as possible."

I became worried, picturing our country divided in the middle. Were we finally free from one evil, only to worry about two?

Two American soldiers walked in and each sat behind a table in the back with a Korean at their side. Mr. Lee shook hands with the red-haired soldier and sat next to him. Standing in line, I heard two men behind me whispering in Korean:

"Why do Americans want to occupy our country?"

"Why not? What have they got to lose?"

"But we don't have anything left. Japanese stole everything from us. Why do they want a poor country like ours?"

"Who knows."

"Who's Syngman Rhee?"

"I never heard of him. I know who Kim Il-Sung is."

"He's a communist! I hope Syngman Rhee isn't a communist!"

"What do you know about communism?"

Finally, my turn came. The American soldier asked me my Korean name, home address, and date of birth in English and I told him before Mr. Lee translated for me in Korean. I was nervous that they would ask me some questions about why I was in Hawaii, but they didn't. They only seemed amazed that I was speaking English. Even in my ears, Mr. Lee's translations were inaccurate and hard to listen to with harsh consonants.

Up close, Mr. Lee seemed like a gentleman. He smiled and said in Korean, "Your English is beautiful, Miss. Much better than mine." He spoke with such dignity that I was almost uncomfortable.

"Thank you, sir." I bowed my head.

"Do you mind taking my place?" he asked, showing his white teeth. I remembered Sadamu: he too had such bright teeth.

"Your English is good, sir," I said.

"Really, your service would help our people to understand the situation better. No doubt, this gentleman would appreciate your help, too," he said, glancing at the American soldier. "If you don't mind, I can use a break."

Mr. Lee got up and moved toward the door. The soldier, a tall man, stood up, and extended a hand as large as a book toward me. "Nick Kamaroff. Nice meeting you."

I shook it, although I wasn't yet comfortable shaking hands with a man. I bowed my head politely to him and sat. His last name "Kamaroff" sounded like a Russian name, and I looked at him, for I'd heard about them a lot, but I'd never seen one.

As if he thought I were attracted to him, Mr. Kamaroff smiled, reddening his earlobes.

Many people questioned me, instead of asking Mr. Kamaroff.

"What's going to happen when the American Military Government takes over our country? Please ask this Yankee man," one man said.

When I translated to Mr. Kamaroff, he said coldly, "I can't answer that. I'm not authorized to comment on political issues. But I can tell you that we are going to make the transition smoothly and help you recover from Japan's colonialism."

"Are you going to control everything—grain, earnings, resources, manpower—like the Japanese did?"

"No. We'll be there to help you establish your new country. We'll not take advantage of you like the Japanese did but help you to grow financially."

"How long are you going to occupy our country?"

"I don't know. I'm not in a position to discuss that."

"What financial plans do you have to help us build our new country?"

"We don't have a definite plan yet. It's too early to discuss the details, but we'll work with Koreans."

When all of the questions were answered and the list of names was complete, the sun was peeking into the room from the western sky and I was tired. The soldier stood up and shook my hand. "Thank you very much, Miss. What is your name by the way?"

"Soon-ah Oh, sir."

"I hope I'll see you in Korea. I will be working for the Military Government in Seoul. So long!"

I bowed at him again and walked toward the door. Mr. Lee came in through the side door with a burning cigarette in his hand and nodded at me. "I hope I'll see you in our newly liberated country. We'll need many good English-speaking people like yourself. Don't hesitate to come and see me. Here, take my name card just in case." He reached into his trouser pocket and pulled out a white card and handed it to me.

I took his card, bowed at him quickly, and almost ran away from his presence: it wasn't polite for a young woman to accept a compliment from a man.

I found myself standing outside, trying to figure out my way to Shepherd's Home. I had taken a bus when I got there and I had to do the same in return. Then I saw Yun Hee walking toward me.

"Soon-ah, I do remember you," she said uncomfortably. "I

didn't want to talk to you when so many people were around us. I'm sure you understand."

"No problem," I said. I wasn't a bit surprised she didn't want to talk to me. We comfort women had a mutual understanding of our shameful past and unspoken words of compassion for one another. "Thank you for waiting for me, Yun Hee," I said as we walked toward a stone bench nearby. The cool breeze and the fragrant air delighted my lungs as we sat, but my mind was cloudy as I faced my old friend from Palau.

"I thought about you often, Yun Hee. What happened after I escaped? Did you go to Guadalcanal?"

"Of course! Soon-ah, we talked so much about you. You were so brave! The manager was furious. He yelled at us for not telling him about your escape. We didn't know. Even if we knew, did he think we'd have told him? Such an idiot!"

"How many were picked by the officers at the party?"

"All of us. The only ones who were left behind were the Japanese girls."

"You mean, Auntie Myung, too?"

"Of course."

"Where is she now?"

Yun Hee's expression changed and she looked at me angrily. "What do you mean, 'Where is she now?' Didn't you know most of the soldiers in Guadalcanal died, nearly thirty thousand of them? Do you think they'd evacuate comfort women to safety when they couldn't evacuate themselves?"

I couldn't believe her. If so, why was she still alive? But I couldn't ask her that.

Yun Hee suddenly drew a sigh, an angry sigh. "I know what you think, Soon-ah. I still can't believe I'm alive. We saw so many soldiers dying—screaming, rolling, jerking their bodies, and becoming still. When the squadron moved to the front line, they took us with them. A tent was set up next to theirs, and when the fighting stopped, our ordeal began. We received thirty to forty soldiers a day! They were animals,

Soon-ah, demanding oral sex and trying to reach orgasm several times. When they couldn't get what they wanted, they beat us often and slashed us with daggers for no reason at all. We were surrounded by devils dancing with swords. Our wounds became infected in the humid weather and attracted maggots. Oh, how much it rained! The entire island was a cesspool with the smell of swamps and rotting flesh. *Ugh,* the smell was nothing you could imagine, Soon-ah. It's like. . . ."

I covered my ears. "Please stop, Yun Hee. It's too much," I said.

Yun Hee drew another sigh. "I can't believe the way you react, Soon-ah. We went through hell: we were dying, but you don't care!"

"It's not that. It's very hard for me to picture . . ."

"How can you picture what it was like? You weren't there! It's easy for you to cover your ears and say, 'It's too much. Please stop!' Isn't it?" Yun Hee accused me, her eyes wide and blank, almost frightening to look at. "What I'm telling you is nothing compared to what we went through!"

"I'm sorry. I didn't mean to act like I didn't care. Actually I want to know what happened to everyone, including Auntie Myung."

"I'll skip the middle part so that I won't waste your time. Our last day on that island went like this: a shrapnel flew down on our tent like a firebird, and we were surrounded by flames. Everything was burning. Two girls died there as their skirts caught on fire. The soldiers ran in all directions, ordering and swearing in Japanese. Finally two soldiers yelled at us to follow them. We couldn't save anything from the fire and followed them with empty hands. We came into a huge cave, as large as the restaurant at the House of Serenity. It was crowded. We sat there like bean sprouts, our shoulders touching one another, until a soldier killed Kum-ah."

"Killed Kum-ah?"

"Remember her? The girl with a wart on her chin? She was

babbling nonsense, only because she was hungry. We were all hungry."

"What did she say?"

"That stupid girl forgot that the Japanese were everywhere and said loudly, 'I wish the Americans would bring us some ration cans.' Poor girl! A soldier immediately turned around and stabbed her with his bayonet. Her stomach growled loudly as she died with her eyes wide open."

"My God!"

"We had nothing to eat for several days, Soon-ah. It was terrible! There was a rumor that some soldiers ate dead Yankees' meat. I'm not lying. It's true. They also killed a horse that belonged to an officer and ate it. Later, the officer beheaded his own men for killing his horse. Human life was cheaper than a horse, much cheaper, because you can ride a horse but you can't ride a man. I saw soldiers catching bugs, bats, lizards, and snakes and eating them raw. Some girls I know ate worms and grassroots that grew in the mud. Several girls who didn't eat anything for many days lost their minds and ran wildly into the jungle barefoot, screaming, and the soldiers killed them all. Can't you see, Soon-ah, the hell we lived through?"

"It's a miracle you're here, Yun Hee. But what happened in the cave after Kum-ah died?" I asked, in an effort to shift our conversation. I was dying to know how Yun Hee survived when everyone died. And Auntie Myung. . . . How did she die?

"The cave!" Yun Hee paused for a moment as if collecting her memory. "An hour after Kum-ah was killed, two soldiers came over and barked, 'Follow us, Chōsenjin. We found another cave to hide in.' We came out of the cave, leaving Kum-ah behind. It was dark. We followed the soldiers. Soon, we came to a clearing dotted with rocks bleached by moonlight. We were out of breath. One girl asked a soldier if we could rest for a few minutes. 'Of course!" he said, searching for his cigarette. We scattered and sat on the rocks.

"The moon was round and bright. We sat in groups. 'I have a feeling that the war will end before next full moon,' a girl said. *Another dreamer,* I thought. Everyone dreamed the war would end soon, as long as I could remember, but it never did.

"'What are you going to do when the war ends? Go home and get married?' I snapped. I don't know why I was so angry. 'You think it's not a realistic dream?' she asked. 'I just remembered my Omma's birthday is the twenty-fifth next month. I wish I can be home for her birthday.'

"I heard some metallic noises and turned my head. The soldiers barked at us to stand. We got on our feet. Before we could gather what was happening, the guns spat: tan, tan, tan, tan, tan, tan, tan!

"'They're shooting at us!' a girl shrieked, falling forward like a tree. In panic, we all tried to run toward the bushes but stumbled helplessly on the ground. A burning sensation stabbed my side and I fell, as if an invisible hand grabbed me from the ground. A girl fell on top of me, then another. My energy rushed out of me and I thought I was dying. The noise of guns faded.

"Suddenly I woke up. Everything was quiet. I had no idea how long I had been lying there. I smelled blood. I wasn't sure if I was alive or dead. Sunlight was pouring down on me. I focused my eyes on an object. It looked like a hand covered with blood. I didn't know whose hand it was. It looked cold and slippery as if made of rubber. I wiggled my own fingers to make sure it wasn't mine. It twitched. It was mine, Soon-ah! A shock went through my entire body and I was wide awake. I pushed aside the dead bodies on top of me and sat.

"Everyone seemed to be sleeping with their mouth wide open. Blood was everywhere. I wanted to run away but had no energy. I was scared too. I shook them, hoping they'd wake up. 'Time to get up, girls!' I yelled, but no one seemed to be awakening. 'Come on! Don't play games!' Still, no one stirred. None of them yelled back at me, 'Shut up, Yun Hee! We're trying to sleep.'

"I remember screaming. I never knew my voice could be that scary next to a pile of corpses. I must have fainted again. Then I heard men talking in the distance: 'Shalla, shalla, whalla, whalla, okay, okay.' I didn't know who they were. I lay still, pretending I was dead. The voices got louder and I heard footsteps approaching. I still couldn't understand a word. I opened my eyes and saw Yankee soldiers with big noses standing around me. One man poked the corpses, then me. I screamed and he jumped."

"Was Auntie Myung with you?" I asked, fearing her response.

"Of course. She was in that pile of corpses," Yun Hee said with no emotion.

I covered my face. How I wished I hadn't asked her that. If only I hadn't noticed Yun Hee! But it was too late.

"You know, Soon-ah, when Auntie Myung was at the House of Serenity, she didn't have to receive soldiers, remember?" Yun Hee said.

"Yes. She was an artist. She only played her kayagum for important officers."

"But that wasn't the case in Guadalcanal. The officers didn't care about her music and forced her to sleep with them. She argued with the officer who picked her, but that officer, a dog, broke her kayagum to pieces and beat her, kicked her, slapped her until her teeth fell out and her face turned blue and purple. After that, she was a different woman, mumbling alone and laughing at trees. You wouldn't have recognized her even if you were there."

I don't remember saying good-bye to Yun Hee. I think I almost ran away from her, afraid that I too might die if I let her talk more. I don't even know whether she returned to Korea or remained in Honolulu. I never saw her again.

$\mathcal{F}$ather Shimono brought me stunning news one morning: Robert had been injured in New Guinea and was now recovering in the Naval Hospital on Sunset Boulevard.

"How badly is he injured, Father?" I asked.

"He lost a leg. He's coping with it quite well, though. But he's extremely fragile. He's not quite the same as before, if you know what I mean," he said.

I went to see him immediately.

The hospital bustled like a marketplace with patients in hospital gowns walking back and forth, visitors with armfuls of flowers coming and going, and doctors and nurses in white gowns busily moving about.

Robert was sitting up with his arms folded behind his head, forcing a smile through parched lips. Unlike the pink orchids blooming next to his bed, he looked withered: his eyes were hollow and his cheeks pale.

"How do you feel, Robert?" I asked, sitting on a wooden chair next to his bed.

"So-so," he said mechanically.

"Still in a lot of pain?"

He barely nodded.

"Is there anything I can do to make you feel better? Please tell me if there's anything," I said earnestly.

He rolled his eyes. "God!" he muttered, dropping one arm onto his comforter.

"What is it, Robert?" I asked, feeling uncomfortable.

"Why do people expect me to feel good and tell them everything is super-duper when I just lost a leg?!"

"I want you to feel better, Robert. I really do!"

"That's the thing I don't like about people," he said, lifting his now angry eyes to me. "I'm injured and lying here, grunting, moaning, squeezing tears, but everyone who walks in here says the same thing: 'Is there anything I can do for you?' meaning, how badly they feel for me. I hate it!" He looked out the window.

I didn't know what to say, or rather, I didn't know what *not* to say. I wanted to get up and walk out of the room, but I knew he was in pain. I wanted him to know I cared. "I think people mean well," I said. "Don't you want to know people care about you? What do you want people to say to you?" I noticed the sharp edges on my words, but I couldn't help it.

He turned back to me. "I'm in a terrible mood, Soon-ah, okay? My parents were just here. It's devastating when my own folks don't understand how I feel. You know, it's not easy lying here staring at walls all day, listening to other guys crying like babies, and worrying about your own future as an invalid. But my parents feel sorry for me and worry to death about me as if I'm incapable of anything. Thanks a lot!

"My father began lecturing me as soon as he walked in and

didn't stop until he left. I thought I would vomit. He told me not to dwell on my lost leg but be grateful for what I have. 'Son,' he said stiffly, 'having only one leg isn't the worst thing in the world, you understand? I'm sure you'll get used to it. The important thing is that you're alive; some men aren't that lucky, you know. You'll find something worthwhile you can do with one leg. It's a challenge for you.' I don't know why I didn't scream at him to get out.'"

"Robert, you don't really mean that," I said, feeling awkward. "He's your father. I'm sure he's hurting a lot because of your injury."

Robert didn't even blink as he stared at the ceiling. "Then there was my mother! While my father rambled on, she sat there sobbing, probably picturing me limping around with an artificial leg. She's probably worried about what to say to her gossip-loving Japanese friends. I'm sick of being her son. My parents were proud of me when I was whole and healthy. Now they pity themselves. I want to run away from them so that they don't have to feel sorry for me or for themselves. I can't look into their eyes because I know exactly how they feel about me." His gaze shifted between the window and the ceiling.

I could see he was angry—angry with himself, with the world, and with God. But how could he expect people to understand the depth of his agony? It was impossible for me to even imagine how it felt not having both legs.

"I'm sure it's difficult for parents to see their son lose a leg," I said. "They might not know how to deal with their own loss. How would you feel if you were them?"

"Don't you think I know how they feel? I do! They made a special trip from California to see me like this. Don't get me wrong, Soon-ah. I'm sure it's traumatic for them to see their son with one leg. I must be polite and pleasant to them, at least, since I owe them so much. But do *you* know what it's like lying here and looking at the stump where my leg used to be? No one knows and no one cares! To the doctors and nurses here, I'm their workload: they have a thousand men to look after daily and I'm one of them. Big deal! To my parents, I'm a burden. They wish I weren't injured!"

"Robert, you're so hard on yourself. Be kind to yourself. I don't like the way you talk."

"No one can understand how I feel. They each have two legs like everyone else, the way God created them. I'm the one missing a leg, the weird guy who wakes up at night trying to scratch a missing foot." He covered his face and was silent for a few seconds. "Everywhere I turn, men are crying, moaning, loathing, screaming, swearing, cursing. We've lost so much: friends, cousins, neighbors, squadron commanders, teachers, chaplains. . . . They all died. Every time I close my eyes I see the faces of my colleagues jumping like frogs in an explosion or floating like dead fish in bloody water. My dreams for the future and my passions for mountain climbing, surfing, and bicycling all vanished with my leg! Why am I alive anyway, when everyone else is dead?" Robert's face contorted as he burst into tears.

Tears were a strange phenomena. Robert's tears summoned mine, and I joined him. My heart ached for both my pain and Robert's. When my tears stopped, I said, "Robert, at least the war ended. No more men will die and be hurt anymore. That's something to be glad about, isn't it?"

He gradually stopped crying and stared at the ceiling again for a long while without a word. When he looked at me, his eyes glowed.

"No, I don't see it that way. It's the beginning of another war, a war even more difficult," he said angrily.

"What do you mean?"

Robert looked at the stump lying parallel to his right leg as if trying to remember how his left leg used to look. "At first I couldn't look at my amputated leg: I simply couldn't look at it. It looked so alien to me. But now every time I look at it, I think about the so-called liberation. Making Japan and Germany surrender to the Allies is the same thing as amputating a bad leg. It isn't the end of human suffering. My shattered bones and the fragments of the shrapnel that damaged the tissues and nerves in my leg are removed from my body, but the sensations of my legs are still alive in my brain. When I dream, I have both legs: I kick balls, I run, I swim. The moment I wake up, the war with myself begins—the war with my own ghost. I tell myself whatever I feel in my left leg is not real. *Forget everything about that leg, for Chrissake*, I say. But somewhere in my head, that leg still exists. It's the same thing with the world. Hitler committed suicide, Mussolini was murdered, and maybe Emperor Hirohito will be assassinated by one of his soldiers, but they are still alive in our brains, haunting us. The most difficult thing for me to deal with is that those who wronged me and all mankind are unable to apologize for what they did. Is that too much to ask? If they had any sensitivity for others, they wouldn't have begun the war in the first place. No matter who caused it, your pain is yours, no one else's."

"You can't force people to apologize, Robert. What's done is done. Even if they did apologize, it wouldn't do us any good. The best thing we can do for ourselves is let our painful memories fade away with time, so we'll have room for hope."

"Let our painful memory fade away, huh?" Robert retorted.

I stood up: I didn't want to watch him lament any more. "Robert, I'm going back to Korea in a few days. I hope I can see you again. I really do. As soon as I get there, I'll write to you, okay? I wish you a fast recovery." Smiling, I grabbed his hand and squeezed it. I was sad leaving him like this.

"Wait!" he ordered. "There's something I must tell you. I wanted to tell you the minute you walked in but I couldn't."

"What is it?"

"Didn't you just say, 'Let our painful memories fade away so we can be healed?' Sadamu is dead!"

"What?" I grabbed the bed rail. I felt dizzy.

Robert avoided my eyes. "A few days ago I met an OSS

agent named Bill who worked with Sadamu in Mindanao. He said they were good friends. He came to tell me what happened to Sadamu. Two Filipinos were responsible for his death, he said. At first I didn't believe him, but then he explained that some Filipinos worked for both Americans and Japanese. Sadamu was well loved by most of the Filipinos because he helped prisoners escape, blew up Japanese trucks and distributed food and clothes, and killed many Japanese. The Japanese were eager to capture him at any price. They bribed two Filipino convicts, promising them they would be pardoned and released immediately if they captured Sadamu, alive or dead. Within a week, Sadamu disappeared. Bill learned later that the convicts found Sadamu, told him that they were good friends of the guerrillas Sadamu trusted, and that they had just discovered the spot where some Japanese officers go for trout fishing. Sadamu left with them immediately. The guerrillas found him hanging from a tree."

I don't know how I stood there, listening to Robert without fainting. I was trying to remember the last time I'd seen Sadamu. He had been following the naval officers as I stood on the ship watching. I saw him turning, looking up, and smiling, without knowing that he was smiling at me for the last time. Or, maybe he knew: that was why his smile lasted for a few seconds so that it could be imprinted in my brain forever.

Robert opened his drawer and gave me the tiny notebook and the pen that Sadamu used to carry in his pocket. Finally tears blurred my vision: the notebook and the pen seemed to be flowing in my hands as I looked down at them. "Forget what I said, Robert," I blurted angrily. "I don't want my memories of Sadamu to fade away. Ever!"

When I boarded the Liberty, it was already crowded with soldiers, forced-laborers, and comfort women, all turning homeward like a flock of birds after a bitter winter. Some soldiers walked with canes, some had their arms in slings, and some had bandages on their heads. I overheard two soldiers talking to one another:

"Are we really going home? This isn't a dream, is it?"

"No, we are going home, Buddy! We're really going home!"

"I forgot what my wife looks like. It's been four years."

"Don't worry. You'll recognize her when you see her."

Some soldiers engaged in food talk: rice cakes, mung bean pancakes, and soybean-paste stews. "My mother is an excellent cook," a young soldier bragged longingly. "Her mung bean pancakes taste so scrumptious that for the Full Moon celebration, people had to order far in advance to get a taste of them."

"I've forgotten how mung bean pancakes taste," another soldier mumbled. "Since my head injury, I can't taste anything!"

People talked politics too:

"How are the Russians and Americans going to decide who rules where without getting into a fight?" someone asked. "This is not the first time the Russians have crossed the Manchurian border. We all know how they are. Remember how they raped women and stole gold watches from people on the street? Unless the Americans know how to handle them, there will be another war."

"I don't think they want another war," another man answered. "They'll somehow control our country without getting into a fight. They have to! Even the lions are tired of fighting. I believe the dividing line will be somewhere between Seoul and Pyongyang, so each side has a capital city."

"Is Haeju north of the 38th parallel or south?"

"North!"

"Is Sockcho north of the 38th parallel too?"

"I think it's south but I'm not sure. In any case, there will be political chaos when we go back. I read in the Honolulu newspaper that more than fifty political organizations mushroomed in Korea after Japan surrendered, all wanting to rule the country. Already several leaders have been assassinated by their rivals. There will be bloodshed as in India."

More than fifty political organizations all wanting to rule the country? Assassinations? I shivered. Why more violence after liberation? Where was this 38th parallel, anyway? I had never heard of such a line crossing the middle of our peninsula. Was Sariwon north of the dividing line or south? Sariwon was south of Pyongyang but north of Haeju. I would somehow find a way to move to the south. It will be painful to leave Father behind, but I knew it would be safer in the south.

The ship moved, whistling a hopeful tune. Everyone

looked lost in the anticipation of seeing the homes and countryside they had longed for so long. Somewhere, a man sang:

> Over the ocean and over the mountains,
> Ten thousand li away,
> There floats the tiny peninsula I long for.
> Mother, I'm coming to you now,
> Without glory, without gifts,
> Dragging my tattered body and soul.

From the open window, I saw a few patches of clouds roaming innocently in the sky. Soon I would be looking at the sky from the other side of the globe with Omma and Chin Soo. How much would she have changed? Would she have wrinkles on her face? Omma's joy would have been double if Wook and I had returned home together. I wondered where Wook was. Maybe on another homebound ship, anxious to be with Omma and Chin Soo, just like I was.

As long as I could remember, Korea had been under Japanese control. I knew nothing about being a Korean: our names were Japanese, we spoke Japanese, and we were forced to worship Japanese gods, ancestors, and emperors. I remembered my father telling us about the March First Movement in 1919. The declaration of freedom was proclaimed by thirty-three Korean activists and the Japanese cold-bloodedly fired on the demonstrators, killing more than ten thousand people. It was difficult to understand why the Japanese had been so cruel to us. Everything we knew—history, poetry, songs, children's rhymes, fairy tales—were Japanese or about Japan. We had only a few songs or rhymes of our own. We knew nothing about our own ancestors, only learned about the Japanese warriors, admirals, pirates, and bandits. No Korean poets or writers were allowed to express anything in Korean. When they did, the Japanese arrested them, tortured them, accused them of being "Thought Criminals," and sent them to a prison in Manchuria to die.

I remembered hearing about the great Kanto earthquake of 1923 in Japan, in which 130,000 people were killed. After the earthquake, the Japanese in surrounding areas murdered thousands of Korean immigrants, accusing them of making God angry. What caused the Japanese to hate Koreans so much?

And how long would it take for Koreans to develop their own identity as an independent people after years of being Japan's colony? We couldn't be proud of ourselves if we were still using Japanese soap and toothpaste, still wearing garments made by the Japanese, still singing songs composed by the Japanese. Liberation itself wouldn't grant us freedom, peace, and happiness, but it would demand that we know who we were and what goals we had. It would be like giving a pearl to a pig if we didn't appreciate our freedom. I realized that I was crossing an historical barrier. Even if Wook wasn't there, the three of us, Omma, Chin Soo, and me, should visit Father's grave site and cover his grave with our flag. I was eager to be home.

꽃

The last day on the ship, a pregnant woman went into labor. I had seen her climbing the steps to the ship, laboriously carrying her huge belly and wondered whether or not she was carrying a Japanese baby. It was none of my business, of course, but I kept thinking about the difficulties she might be facing if she gave birth to a Japanese child.

She lay on the floor, moaning helplessly. People shouted for a doctor, but no doctors were on board. An older woman got up and moved to her, rolling up her sleeves. "I know what to do. I've helped women giving birth before," she claimed. As the moans turned to screams, I too volunteered to help. I held the woman's hands, slippery with sweat. Another woman took out her chima, the Korean skirt, and covered the woman's bare lower half. After long hours of labor she gave birth to a little boy.

"Ah, such a strong cry!" a man muttered wiping his forehead.

"A loud cry for a tiny little fellow!" another said.

"Lucky woman. My wife couldn't bear a son!"

The new mother feebly looked up at me when I told her it was a boy. "Is he healthy?" she asked.

"Yes, he is beautiful!" I said. "He's a miracle baby, isn't he? Born on a homeward ship. You're so lucky!" I said.

"Thank you," she mumbled, closing her eyes. Tears formed in the corners of her eyes and dropped to the floor.

The older woman helped her back to her seat and deposited the baby in her arms. The young woman shyly lifted her tunic, exposing a swollen breast, and struggled to fit her purple nipple into the baby's tiny mouth. I returned to my own seat, exhausted.

"Whose baby is that?" a man grunted loudly in a northern accent. His voice made me shiver. "Is that a Japanese baby or a Korean?"

The noises of the crowd shifted to an angry mutter. People turned and whispered to one another, "A Japanese baby?" "Who wants a Japanese baby in our new country?"

Two soldiers, one with scars on his cheeks and another with thick eyebrows, moved toward the woman, grumbling something incomprehensible. By the sound of their voices, I knew they had been drinking.

The woman clung to her infant.

The man with scars leaned over and leered at the baby. "This is no doubt a Japanese seed!" he said.

"No! it's not," the woman shrieked in terror. "My husband is Korean. He's not here but he'll join me in Korea!"

A large woman behind her rose. "A Korean baby? Huh! What Korean man could father a child in the Japanese army compound? I know that woman! She only slept with the Japanese officers! Indeed, a Korean baby!" Making an ugly face, she sat.

The crowd gasped and talked loudly. I wanted to shout: *It wasn't her choice. Nothing was her choice! She was a sex slave!* But my tongue froze as I saw the man abruptly snatching the baby from the woman.

"Please don't hurt my child!" the woman cried.

"Let me see how evil it looks!" the man with thick eyebrows said angrily and began unwrapping the baby.

"Get rid of it! Don't let it touch our land. It's a bad omen," a voice yelled from behind.

"Give back the child to his mother!" the midwife shouted sternly, pushing herself to stand.

"Please don't harm my baby!" the mother pleaded again, but her voice was swallowed by the man's guttural voice. "Gentlemen! This is a Japanese baby. He has no business in our country. What shall we do with this demon?" He looked around as if he was certain that everyone hated the Japanese as much as he did.

The staircase to the deck suddenly opened and a booming voice rang in my ears, "Brothers, let's not be violent!" It was Mr. Lee, the man who had spoken at the meeting in Honolulu. "We all agree that the war has been long and the Japanese were cruel to us. But this ship is homeward bound! This is a journey all of us have longed for. We are only a couple hundred li from our peninsula loaded with golden mountains and silvery rivers. Your wives, children, parents, brothers, sisters, and friends are anxiously waiting for you. How can we be violent at such a moment? How can we be angry at the Japanese when we no longer have tyrants. It's time to forgive our foes. Only God can punish evil."

No one said anything. Everyone stared at Mr. Lee as if he were Moses. Nothing moved. The crowd parted as Mr. Lee made his way to the man holding the baby. "Sir, let's give the child back to his mother," he said calmly and took the baby and handed it to the woman. The man with the scar just stood there.

"Take good care of this child," Mr. Lee said gently to the mother. "Whether Japanese or Korean, God has given you a gift of life. You have a solemn duty to fulfill."

With tears streaming down her colorless cheeks and violently shaking hands, she took the child to her bosom.

Mr. Lee faced the crowd again. "This child has done nothing to evoke our anger, gentlemen! It's our privilege to witness the birth of a new life when our new country is about to be born. We are free now! But we must remember that we didn't earn our freedom. Someone else paid a price for this lofty gift, the gift of freedom. Because of this gift, the future of our country is in our hands. If we can't forgive and forget, our country will remain in the dark, and we'll never escape violence. Each and every one of us is responsible for reshaping our society and molding our dreams for the future. It is time to sheath our swords and embrace one another."

"Who gave you the right to preach to us?" the man who had snatched the baby earlier roared angrily as if awakened from his hypnosis. "What is your name, anyway?"

"I'm Lee Dong Kiu, Mr. Rhee Syngman's secretary. As the president of our Temporary Provincial Government, Mr. Rhee sent me to speak to you. He needs your support. He wants each and every one of you to spread his message to make this transition as painless as possible. Let us not repeat the evil war again. Liberation must serve people, not destroy them."

The man with thick eyebrows yelled, raising his arm in the air. "Syngman Rhee is a capitalist who was educated in the United States. Our new country will not survive under a capitalist. We support Mr. Cho Man Shik and the Chōsen Communist party. Communism is for people like us, laborers and working-class people. It's time for social reform!"

The crowd responded with loud applause.

"No, I'm against it!" another man declared. "Communism will ruin our country. Russians are communists. Look what they're doing in our country. They're just as bad as the Japanese!"

Still another rose. "Shut up! You don't know what you're talking about! Only communism will save our country and guarantee the stability of our society. I support Comrade Kim Il Sung. He's a true nationalist and patriot! He led the Liberation Army in the north region and fought the Japanese all his life."

"Gentlemen, why don't we discuss this privately?" Mr. Lee said in his calm voice. "Come to the deck and let's talk peacefully instead of yelling and shouting. Let us plan our future together without arguing."

A dozen men followed Mr. Lee and disappeared to the deck, talking fast. I was dizzy with fearful thoughts. The political organizations that had mushroomed overnight in Korea might consist of men like these.

That night, watching the moonlight creating obscure, mysterious beams on the ocean, I let my mind wander between the past and the future. Although my past had been painful, I decided that my future looked good. The first thing I wanted to do was go back to school and finish my diploma. Freedom is for privileged people, Mr. Lee had said. It's a gift.

Then I remembered Mr. Lee speaking to the crowd, pleading with them not to be violent, and reminding them that we didn't earn our own freedom. I could almost see him walking toward the rough-looking man, taking the baby, and dropping him into the mother's bosom, saying, "Take care of this life, Miss. Whether Japanese or Korean, God has given you a gift of life." It seemed he was asking *everyone* to love our country, which had suffered thirty-five years of slavery. Maybe he was asking me, a woman with a record, to be reborn again and learn what life is all about in spite of my past experience as a sex slave. Maybe he was telling me I could be reborn again in our newly liberated land and forget my past as a comfort woman.

❦

The ship arrived in Inchon the next day and I took a train home. The station in Sariwon bustled with people returning from all over Asia, shouting and crying. As I gathered my bag, I saw a young boy passing my window, looking up at each passenger. Chin Soo, my little brother! He was much taller and thinner than when I last saw him, but his features were the same.

I rushed to the door, yelling, "Chin Soo ya!"

Chin Soo moved a few steps toward me. "Noona?" he said. "Big sister?"

"Yes, it's me! You're so tall now!" I pulled him to me and held him in my arms.

He pulled away, shyly. "I don't recognize you, Noona! You're much older and skinnier than I remember."

"Of course, I'm much older. It's been three years since I last saw you."

"Omma is at market," he said, picking up my bag and walking beside me. "She's working for Mr. Shin until six every day, but she'll be home by the time we get there."

"Mr. Shin? You mean the clerk at Mr. Hirota's grocery store?"

"Yes, Noona, he became a rich man. That Mr. Shin! Mr. Hirota gave him everything he owned when he left for Japan."

"Why is Omma working for him? Isn't there anything else she could do?"

"No, nothing," Chin Soo said with an adult-like expression on his face. "She doesn't want to lose our house. Mr. Hirota bought our house from Omma when we had nothing to eat. Mr. Shin said if Omma worked for him long enough, she could buy it back from him."

We took a pedicab. Everywhere I looked, Kim Il Sung's portraits were posted with the slogans: "Comrade Kim is the Shining Star for Working People," one slogan said; "The Future of Chōsen is in Comrade Kim's hand," said another.

I tried to remember Kim Il Sung. I had seen his pictures posted on the streets as a "wanted man" by the Japanese police. Hehad been the leader of the guerrillas who had fought the Japanese in Manchuria and in the northern region. The Japanese had been eager to capture him and his army, but now he was looking at me with authority from his pictures. No doubt the Russians' advance into Korea had much to do with him, I thought.

"Noona, I have a uniform just like that," Chin Soo proudly announced, pointing at the soldiers wearing the uniforms bordered with red stripes. "I'm the leader of the Youth League at school."

"You're what?"

"I am the leader of the Youth League, the Little Red Army," he articulated each word. "We were the ones who hunted for the Japanese after liberation."

"What? What are you saying?"

"The Liberation Army told us to find them. I found eight Japanese altogether and reported to the Liberation Army. The District Leader gave me a medal after I reported where Lieutenant Hotsumi was hiding. Remember the policeman who killed Father, Noona? He was hiding in an abandoned shed, almost dead. The Liberation Army dragged him to the hill and hanged him."

"Chin Soo, I don't like to hear what you're saying. You're a child. You're too young for all that violence!"

"Too young? Are you joking?" he said, frowning. "Look what they did to our father! I'm not too young to feel for what they did to my own father. I'm his son. You know what else the Japanese did? They burned the ammunition depot and the grain store-house when they evacuated to Japan. They were afraid we might use the ammunition on them, but why burn the grain? That's why so many people were starving to death after the liberation."

The more I listened, the sicker I became. How could I explain to an eleven-year-old that violence was wrong even though our tyrants had been evil? How could he understand that we must break the cycle of hate somehow so that the seeds of peace could germinate in our midst?

"Chin Soo ya, Father wouldn't be happy to hear what you've just said. We should hate what the Japanese did but not the people. The Liberation Army shouldn't have used children like you to hunt for the Japanese. That's wrong, I think. You must know, Chin Soo, that people who want to do right things can also make mistakes. In any case, don't be involved with that Youth Group any more."

"Are you out of your mind, Noona? If I quit, they'll accuse me of being an anti-Communist! That's like a death sentence."

The pedicab stopped in front of our house, and I was glad. Chin Soo wouldn't understand why I was telling him to drop out of the Youth Group even if I talked to him all night. And I was eager to see Omma.

Our house was just the way I remembered. As I got out of the pedicab, I took a moment to look at the house I had longed for so long. In that house, I had been born and raised: in that courtyard, my father had died. Nothing seemed changed. The straw roof, the rice-papered shutters and doors, the persimmon tree loaded with tiny green fruits, its shadow sweeping the courtyard. . . . On the front step, I saw Omma's white boat-like rubber shoes telling me she was home.

I rushed into the courtyard, just as I had done millions of times when I was a child, shrieking, "Omma? I'm home!"

The rice-papered door slid open and my mother, thinner and older than I remembered, ran toward me barefoot. "Soon-ah? Is that you?"

"Yes, Omma! I'm home!"

Omma stopped and looked me over from head to toe, as if she was making sure that I was indeed her daughter. Her eyes filled. She slowly extended her arms toward me. "Welcome home!" she said, her voice cracking.

Clasping her frail body into my arms, I burst into tears. I sobbed uncontrollably. How long had I waited for this moment! When all my tears were drained out of me, I said, "Omma, let's move to the south."

Other Titles Available From Spinsters Ink

Spinsters Ink was founded in 1978 to produce vital books for diverse women's communities. In 1986 we merged with Aunt Lute Books to become Spinsters/Aunt Lute. In 1990, the Aunt Lute Foundation became an independent nonprofit publishing program. In 1992, Spinsters moved to Minnesota.

Spinsters Ink publishes novels and nonfiction works that deal with significant issues in women's lives from a feminist perspective: books that not only name these crucial issues, but—more importantly—encourage change and growth. We are committed to publishing works by women writing from the periphery: fat women, Jewish women, lesbians, old women, poor women, rural women, women examining classism, women of color, women with disabilities, women who are writing books that help make the best in our lives more possible.

Spinsters titles are available at your local booksellers or by mail order through Spinsters Ink. A free catalog is available upon request. Please include $2.00 for the first title ordered and 50¢ for every title thereafter. Visa and Mastercard accepted.

Spinsters Ink
32 E. First St., #330
Duluth, MN 55802-2002
USA

218-727-3222 (phone)   (fax) 218-727-3119
(e-mail) spinsters@aol.com
(website) http://www.lesbian.org/spinsters-ink

*T*herese Park is a native of Korea; she immigrated to the United States in 1966. A cellist with the Kansas City Symphony for the past thirty years, Ms. Park recently retired to take up writing full-time. *A Gift of the Emperor* is her first novel.